"No one's going [...]
out of town!"

"Cassie, what are you talking about [...]
asked, placing a placating hand on her shoulder.

"You know what I'm talking about. Jake Bradford
had me roughed up and threatened. I want you
to tell Jake that threatening me won't work. He's
the one who better get out of town. And while
you're at it, get you're hands off me," Cassie
demanded, shrugging his hand off her shoulder.

"Roughed you up—? Cassie, I can't believe Jake
would do any such thing."

"I know what I know, Trevor. Just kindly pass on
my message." She turned and walked away, her
shoulders straight and proud.

For a moment, Trevor just stood, watching in
stunned silence. The next moment, he'd caught
up with her, spun her around and trapped her in
a fierce embrace, possessing her lips with a
hungry passion that shocked Trevor almost as
much as Cassie....

ABOUT THE AUTHOR

Casey Roberts knows from her own life what romance is all about. Last year she married the man of her dreams, and for their honeymoon, the newlyweds toured California. But her real-life romance hasn't reduced Casey's interest in fictional lovers. After finishing *Homecoming*, Casey's first Superromance, she sat right back down and started on her second. We hope she writes many more.

Homecoming

CASEY ROBERTS

Harlequin Books

TORONTO • NEW YORK • LONDON
AMSTERDAM • PARIS • SYDNEY • HAMBURG
STOCKHOLM • ATHENS • TOKYO • MILAN

Published November 1990

ISBN 0-373-70429-1

To my daughter, Karen,
my cheering section and critic.
Without her, this book would
never have been written.

PROLOGUE

SWEET TANTALIZING SOUNDS of a country two-step drifted into the room where the small girl lay in the large four-poster bed. Her parents had told her not to interrupt the party, but she was wriggling under the warm covers with excitement and curiosity, trying to resist the temptation to creep down the stairs. Temptation won and she sat up, clutching the comforter for warmth against the cold night air. Listening carefully, she strained to understand the words of the music. She mustn't go. Mommy and Daddy said. But she would just sit on the steps. She wouldn't interrupt. She would be quiet. Mommy and Daddy would never know.

"Come on, Herby." Lugging a stuffed bear nearly half her size, she jumped to the floor. The thick rug was warm against her bare feet as she scurried across the floor, shivering when her feet hit the bare polished wood. She hurried to the hall runner, burying her feet in its deep pile and ran to the stairs. "Shh" she whispered to Herby, putting her finger against her lips.

She crept quietly down the circular staircase, dragging Herby behind her. Must be quiet now. Not a sound. Finally, the bottom. Her heart was beating madly and her eyes widened with delight as she gazed on the party in progress in the room across from the stairs.

Wide-open double doors revealed dancers moving to the sound of the "Virginia Reel." Tall handsome men in formal Western suits were taking small prancing steps, their backs straight and their heads held high, while brightly clothed women whirled around them, creating swirls of mesmerizing color.

Blue, gold, red and purple streamers covered the ceiling. The huge chandelier reflected their hues, casting colorful prisms throughout the room. Mirth filled the air.

With a toss of his head and a laugh, a tall dark man moved into the center of the circle, pulling a young blond woman with him. The child stared at the couple, awed by their beauty.

Laughing again, the man lifted the woman from the ground and whirled her around the circle. Her dress was white—pure gossamer white. Her fairness contrasted sharply with the man's dark complexion. Her white dress, so pure, made the other women's clothing appear brazen and tawdry.

They were dreamlike and magnificent, standing apart from the other dancers as though they were star performers and all the world their audience. The man twirled the woman faster and faster in an ever widening arc. Hypnotized by the color and beauty of the scene, the small girl sat silently, her eyes circles of wonder.

Suddenly she blinked in astonishment. The man and woman were fading, becoming ghostlike images. No, there they were. It was okay. But now they'd faded once more, and the girl blinked again, not trusting her eyes. The man and woman became momentarily clear, then faded again and again. The other dancers twirled around them, their brightly colored clothing also dissolving, merging into rainbowlike patterns, blending and swirling into a whirlpool of color that filled the room with garish hues. The tinkling laughter turned to harsh, derisive cackling.

The child's enchantment turned to fear, her wide eyes now full of terror instead of delight. Her heart pounded wildly in her little chest. She squeezed her eyes tightly shut as a small whimper escaped her throat.

"Cassie." The voice was gentle and melodious. Relieved, Cassie turned and saw the woman in white. The woman's face reflected amusement and affection.

"Mama," said Cassie. "Oh, Mama, I'm so afraid."

"What are you afraid of, Cassie?" A new voice, deep and resonant, sounded behind Mama as the tall dark man appeared out of nowhere.

The vision in white turned to the man and smiled. "Our baby was frightened by the party."

She smiled again and leaned toward Cassie. From somewhere in the distance, a low ringing sound began, frightening Cassie further, and she lunged at her mother, longing for her comforting embrace. But instead of coming to rest in her mother's warm soothing arms, Cassie went right through the vision in white.

She screamed.

"Papa, Papa!" She turned to the dark man.

"My baby, my poor baby," said her mother's melodious voice.

"Cassie, Cassie, don't be afraid." Papa reached out his arms. He smiled, revealing black rotting teeth.

Cassie screamed again. And again. And again. The ringing became louder.

Papa leaned closer, his arms beckoning. Terrified of this now strange man, Cassie pushed Herby between them and clutched the railing, frantically trying to scramble back up the stairs. Now she understood. This was her punishment. She wasn't supposed to be at the party.

"My poor baby," Mama repeated, and Cassie stopped to look back. She was fading again. Fading . . . fading . . . her dazzling white gown disintegrating, becoming torn and ragged.

"Mama. Papa," Cassie wailed. The ringing was now louder, insistent, demanding. It was calling her.

"Cassie, don't run away," Papa called. His face was melting. His elegant suit beginning to shred.

The ringing was deafening, assailing Cassie's ears. She clutched her head, riveted to the spot where she stood.

"Mama, Papa!" she shrieked. "What's happening to you?"

"OH, JEEZ, THE TELEPHONE," Cassie muttered aloud as she fumbled for the receiver. Ragged remnants of the dream clung to her consciousness. She wondered what time it was.

"Hello."

"Cassie." The voice on the other end choked back a sob. "It's your father, Cassie. He's been hurt in an accident. Come home."

"Aunt Julia? What's wrong with him?"

"Just come home, Cassie. Come home."

CHAPTER ONE

"MESQUITE, NEXT STOP."

At the bus driver's announcement Cassandra Cambridge shot upright in her seat. She was finally home after a circuitous trip ending in this dreary bus ride. Buses were not a mode of travel she preferred.

Home. Funny, it had been a long time since Cassie had thought of Mesquite as home—so long that she'd forgotten how cold it got in Wyoming in January. Her breath misted the dirty window by her seat, blocking whatever view she might have of the unlit road.

Cassie had managed to snag a pillow early in the trip, before a group of high-spirited college kids had boarded, overflowing the overhead racks with their duffel bags and ski boots. Now she set it aside as she eased her way into the aisle, and searched among the vacation gear for her buried travel bag.

The madcap students were on their fifteenth verse of "Ninety-nine Bottles of Beer," and the din of their singing, combined with the stench of cheap wine, beer and cigarette smoke threatened to overcome her. Their high good humor and boisterous antics merely accentuated the fear that was beginning to engulf her. When she finally pushed her way to the front, she realized that her eagerness to escape must have eclipsed her good sense, because the driver reminded her that Mesquite was still another ten minutes away. But then, how was she to remember how long it was between stops? She hadn't been home in twelve years. Rather than fighting her way back to her seat, she resigned herself to hanging on to a post. At last, she saw Simpson's Shell, the small gas station on the outskirts of Mesquite, appear on the horizon.

A minute later they were at the station, and at the first whoosh of air, Cassie bolted toward the door and, having successfully escaped, waited impatiently while the driver made his way out of his seat and down the stairs. He seemed annoyed to be making a stop just for her, and with several surly grunts tossed luggage out of the bus's baggage compartment as he searched for her bag.

"That's it," she said, spotting her brown-and-tan bag. She winced when it flew through the air to land with a thud a few feet from where she stood.

"Thank you," Cassie said without much enthusiasm as she watched the portly man reload the luggage. Her body felt battered from the grueling bus ride and her soul felt bruised from the fearful emotions she was experiencing. She wasn't up to dealing with a rude bus driver. The man grunted again, leaving Cassie to wonder if he knew how to speak, then lumbered back up the stairs, closed the door with another whoosh and drove out of the station.

Cassie suddenly realized she was all alone. A neon sign proclaiming the station's name was turned off, and the only light came from a lone fluorescent tube that hung in a window. The eerie blue light cast wavering shadows over the blacktop. The soft humming of the wind and an occasional snap from the light fixture were the only sounds to break the silence of the night. An unsettling shiver ran through her body, and she found herself uncertain if its source was the icy wind or the apprehension she felt standing alone in this isolated place. Aunt Julia had promised to pick her up. Where was she?

"Miss Cambridge?" Cassie gasped and whirled to face a tall, lanky man wearing a Stetson and a dark denim jacket.

"Oh, you startled me." The man stood so close that she had to tilt her head back to see his face, which was partly obscured by the shadow of his hat brim. Apparently realizing his proximity, the man stepped back, leaving behind the faint smell of musk.

"I'm sorry I scared you." His voice was husky— masculine and sexy.

Cassie smiled politely. "How did you know my name?"

His face broke into a wide, lazy smile. In the florescent lighting his even teeth appeared blue-white. Cassie still couldn't see his eyes, but the shadows cast on his face revealed high cheekbones and a strong angular jaw.

"I'm not starting out on a very good foot, am I? First I scare you to death. Then I fail to introduce myself." He removed his glove and thrust out his hand. "I'm Trevor Austin. Your aunt Julia sent me to pick you up. I'm sorry about your father."

"Thank you." She removed her glove also and took his hand in a firm handshake. His warm skin brought life back into her chilled fingers, and she felt curiously reluctant to withdraw them from his. His touch gave her a warm, friendly feeling. "It's nice to meet you," she said, a lump forming in her throat at this reminder of why she was here.

"Let me get your luggage." As he bent over, the light fixture snapped with a strong burst of light, illuminating his entire face. His gaze was still fixed on her, and in the sudden glare, his eyes glowed vividly. They were incredibly blue—like looking into a clear deep pool on a summer day. Cassie's breath caught in her throat and she pulled her eyes away. For a moment he had seemed almost like a legendary cowboy stepping out of the rugged past. Cassie was suddenly uncomfortable in his presence.

He picked up her suitcase and carry-on bag with one arm, then placed a guiding hand on her shoulder. "I'm parked this way." With gentle pressure he directed her toward a sloping drive leading to the street. A pickup truck was at the bottom.

His touch seemed warm even through her thick fur jacket. As they stepped outside the shelter of the station, the cruel Teton winds whipped viciously around her ears and collar. Cassie welcomed the sudden chill. It cleared her mind and gave a reason for the flush she could feel on her cheeks.

Stunned by her reaction to this man, Cassie discreetly shrugged off his hand. She studied him carefully while they walked to his car. Sure, he was good-looking. His shoulders were broad under his thick denim coat, and she was certain it hid a slim waist and flat stomach. But as the owner of an advertising agency, Cassie encountered handsome men daily and she was no longer impressed. In fact, extreme good looks tended to make her suspicious. In her experience, most handsome men were nothing but walking egos.

But he did have wonderful eyes. Looking into them had been like looking into the sun. They seemed to promise a spring day, cotton candy at a fair, all the delights of paradise.

She shook her head impatiently. Her purpose here was to see about her father. She had enough on her mind without becoming interested in a man. Besides, she'd left Denver in the middle of a major advertising campaign. Her partner might possibly have to handle things alone. But Cassie was the firm's creative genius, while her partner handled the business side. They were both worried about the ramifications of her sudden departure.

No, this was definitely not a time for romance. The more distance between Trevor Austin and herself the better.

"Here we are." Trevor opened the truck door. Apparently it had once been a red-and-white two-tone, but the paint was now faded and grimy, reducing the colors to pale rust and dingy gray. Cassie climbed inside and was immediately grateful she'd worn jeans. The upholstery was torn, with bits of foam emerging from the gaps. She sighed again. Wonderful. First a college party on wheels. Now a demolition-derby pickup. Her modes of transportation were declining at a disturbing rate. She wasn't even sure she'd make it to see her father.

She flicked absently at the foam pieces that clung to her legs, and as Trevor positioned himself in the driver's seat he smiled in amusement. "Not exactly a chariot, is it?"

"No, it isn't." His good humor brought a wan smile to her lips. "This truck has certainly seen better days. Will it make the drive?" Even this halfhearted attempt at humor made her feel guilty. Her father's life was in jeopardy. This was no time for amusement.

"You've got my word on it. I promised I'd get you safely to the hospital, and that's what I plan to do." He started the pickup and pulled onto the highway. "You must be very tired," he said sympathetically.

His husky voice was almost like a purr, and listening to it sent a warm shiver down Cassie's spine. "I am," she replied. "Also, I'm very worried about my father. How is he? I'm missing so many details." She rested her head against the seat as the truck rattled along the asphalt road. As she asked the questions, her earlier desolation returned. Her body ached from fatigue, but she needed to know what she most feared to ask. Was her father going to live? The question burned in her mind.

Memories of her father flooded her thoughts. She remembered him riding a stallion around the working arena, stopping to pick Cassie up and perch her on the saddle in front of him. "Hang on, Duchess," he'd always said as he nestled her small body into the safety of his strong arms. The words had become a joke, and each time they rode together they would say in unison, "Hang on, Duchess," while she climbed astride. As a small child she'd worshipped him like a god, never doubting that he'd be there for her. Now she realized that she still felt that way. Her whole sense of security was built around the safety net her father had always provided.

Now she was in danger of losing him. She couldn't imagine life without him and waited apprehensively for news of his condition. And the way Trevor had paused, as though carefully considering his answer, did nothing to ease her tension.

She couldn't wait any longer. "Well," she asked, "Will he be okay?"

Trevor cleared his throat before he spoke. "I won't try to kid you, Miss Cambridge. He's seriously injured. He's in intensive care. His car went off the hairpin turn on the way to your place."

"You mean Miller's Curve?" Cassie knew that turn well. It was hazardous even under the best driving conditions. But her father had been making that drive for years, knew that road like the back of his hand. Why had he suddenly misjudged the turn? "And?" Her voice sounded like a small, plaintive bleat.

"The car rolled two or three times, then slid fifty feet down the ravine. He wasn't found for a couple of hours and his long exposure to the cold didn't help any. Then there was the delay in getting him to the hospital."

"The delay?"

Trevor nodded. "Mesquite's only ambulance was at a three-car pileup on the road to Jackson and we had to take him to the hospital in this truck. I don't think the rough ride did him any good." Cassie studied him intently for any hidden meaning, but the shadow of his hat nearly obscured his face. The tone of his voice was infinitely kind. Clearly he was trying to spare her pain.

Cassie buried her hands in her face and stifled a moan. She had to control herself. Her father had taught her to face challenges and difficulties squarely and to forgo tears. Tears were to be avoided at all cost, especially in the presence of other people. "Is he conscious?"

"Intermittently," Trevor replied, and hope surged inside her.

"I'm going to have him moved to a hospital in Denver," she told Trevor. "We can get him out today by air ambulance." He needed better care than he could get in the little Mesquite hospital.

"Perhaps," Trevor agreed cautiously, and Cassie became aware that he was choosing his words carefully, wary of upsetting her. "But a specialist was flown in from Los Angeles last night," he went on. "You might want to talk to him first. The hospital is doing everything it can."

A specialist! The word was a live wire, snapping and popping through her mind. Papa's injuries would have to be very extensive for the hospital to summon an out-of-town specialist. Suddenly she didn't want to know any more. She leaned her head back, trying to revive the absolute certainty she had felt only moments before. The certainty that she could make her father live. If only because she willed it so.

A faint morning twilight hovered above the mountains. She glanced at her watch. It was nearly eight o'clock. She'd forgotten how late the sun rose in the Grand Tetons. The light hurt her eyes and she closed them, trying to find a moment of peace. It was going to be a long day.

She thought again of her father. She supposed it was only natural that they had become so close. Her mother was only a dim memory. As she'd been killed in a horseback riding accident when Cassie was three, her image would have vanished from Cassie's mind but for the many portraits that hung in the rooms and hallways of the Cambridge Stables house. She thought Papa must have loved her mother very much, for he had never remarried or removed any of the pictures.

He had poured all his love into Cassie, and she'd become his constant companion, riding the range with him and helping him handle the horses and oversee the endless chores that running a ranch entailed. She adored him in return and had broken-heartedly pleaded her case when he'd decided to send her to Montclair Boarding School after she'd turned fourteen. He was her mentor and friend as well as her parent, and she hadn't understood why he was sending her away. She'd vowed to return and now wondered why she never had. Still, their close relationship had continued, and just the thought of a life without him filled her with a devastating loneliness.

It seemed that only a few seconds had passed since she'd closed her eyes when she felt the movement of the truck slow, then come to a halt. She opened her eyes, surprised to find herself at the hospital already.

"I'll take care of your luggage, Miss Cambridge. Will you be going to the ranch or staying at a hotel in town?"

Cassie's mind felt fuzzy from the momentary catnap. Staying? She hadn't thought about that. "I don't know. I guess I'll stay at the Center Hotel. It's closer to the hospital."

"Fine. I'll register you and leave your bags there."

Finally grasping Trevor's meaning, Cassie demurred. "You really don't have to do that. I can take care of it later." His kindness was somehow overwhelming. His sexual attractiveness could be ignored, but his thoughtfulness was something else. After all, he didn't even know her.

"It's my pleasure, Miss Cambridge. Please don't worry about it. I know you're anxious to see your father." He tipped his hat with such gallantry that Cassie smiled for the first time since Julia's ominous phone call.

"Well, there is one more thing you can do for me, Mr. Austin."

"What's that?"

"You can call me Cassie."

He laughed lightly, his azure eyes crinkling at the corners. "That's a deal, Cassie, if you'll call me Trevor."

"You got it, Trevor," Cassie replied as she unbuckled her seat belt. "I hope to see you again," she added, instantly regretting her remark. There was a definite spark between them and the last thing she needed at this time was to see more of Trevor Austin.

"I'm sure you will." He riveted her with his compelling eyes. She turned away, feeling insanely afraid of becoming lost in them. He reached across her body and opened the door, causing his jacket and shirt sleeve to pull up. To Cassie's surprise he was wearing a Rolex watch. How on earth could a ranch hand afford a Rolex?

"Cassie," he said as she started to step down from the truck.

She turned back. "Yes?"

"I'm sure your father will be all right."

His words filled her with an unreasonable sense of gratitude. She nodded in acknowledgment, then turned and ran up the hospital steps. Reaching the top, she glanced back for a moment, just in time to see him get into a silver-blue Porsche parked at the curb. A cowboy with a Rolex watch and a Porsche. How intriguing. Then she stepped through the door and Trevor was already forgotten. Someone more important needed her.

"I THINK he needs to rest now." The nurse spoke softly as she placed a hand on Cassie's shoulders. Turning to face the woman, Cassie was immediately struck by her obvious youth, and thought that her father was much too ill to be in the hands of this child. Cassie turned her gaze back toward Papa's silent form and stood up. She leaned forward, placed a loving kiss on his forehead, then reluctantly backed out of the door, grateful for the repetitive beeps of the monitor, which proclaimed that life still ran through his veins.

When she'd first pulled back the curtain surrounding the hospital bed, Papa had been awake, but he'd soon slipped back into a pain-and-medicine-induced delirium, talking about things that didn't make sense. Cassie was very worried about him and, for some reason, vaguely suspicious of the accident that had placed him in this hospital.

She was anxious to locate the specialist Trevor had mentioned. She stopped to inquire at the nurses' station, learning that the doctor's name was Ferris and was most likely in the lounge. She hurried down the hall and found him there, writing notes on a chart. He stood as he saw her approach.

"I'm Cassie Cambridge, George's daughter. Will he live?" she asked, skipping the preliminaries.

The doctor introduced himself then looked at her intently for a moment, as though assessing her ability to withstand further shock. Apparently having decided she could handle the truth, he replied in a manner as direct as her question. "There are never any guarantees, Miss Cambridge. He has many broken bones—his pelvis and femur, along with other less dangerous fractures—and a minor concussion. He experienced some hypothermia, which though mild, is complicating matters. But he's a strong man and his chances look better than most." The doctor paused to cough before continuing. "His recovery is hampered, however, by his advanced alcoholism. He already has some liver damage and he's suffering badly from withdrawal along with the trauma of the accident.''

Cassie knew she was staring, but the physician's comments puzzled her. Who was he talking about? There must be some mix-up. ''Alcoholism? You must be mistaken, Doctor, my father's not an alcoholic. Do you have me confused with someone else?''

''You said George was your father. We are talking about George Cambridge, aren't we?''

''Yes, we are, but he is *not* an alcoholic,'' she stated emphatically.

The doctor placed a hand on her shoulder. ''Let's sit down, Miss Cambridge.'' He led her to the cracked vinyl couch where he'd previously been sitting and waited until she sat before continuing.

''It's understandable and reasonable to react in disbelief when we discover a loved one is an alcoholic, Miss Cambridge. I totally understand how you feel. But alcoholism is a disease, not a character flaw. Your father has a better than even chance to recover from the accident. But after that, he faces a long, hard road to recover from alcoholism. It is imperative that he have the support of his family and the first step in that support is acceptance.''

Cassie stiffened. Her body felt like a board, unyielding and unaccepting. She would never, ever accept such an idea. ''There is nothing to accept, Dr. Ferris. As I've told you, you're mistaken.''

''Accepting these things takes time.'' The doctor wore a sympathetic expression, but for some reason Cassie felt he was patronizing her. ''I understand you were traveling all night. We can talk later. We'll call you if there's any change in your father's condition. Why don't you go somewhere and rest?''

"Thank you for your concern but not right now."
She strained to control the edge of anger in her voice.
"I have things to do, but I'll be back later to discuss
this. I want to speak to my aunt first."

"I understand. The subject of alcoholism is
often—" But before he completed the sentence, Cassie stood and hastened away to find her aunt.

She spied Julia in the family waiting area. She was
talking with a tall, balding man. As they saw her approach, he tipped his hat at Julia then walked away
quickly. Cassie was grateful for the sudden departure.
She needed desperately to talk to Julia. Now.

TREVOR EASED HIS PORSCHE against the curb in front
of the hospital and had just turned off the ignition
when he saw Cassie hurry down the stairs and get into
Julia's yellow Volkswagen, alone. Her stride was brisk
and purposeful but her head was bent. Something
about her sad posture touched his heart.

He had been prepared not to like her. For nearly two
years he'd listened to Julia and George speak of her
virtues as if she deserved canonization. Their devotion
to her seemed unlimited. But where had she been all
this time? Did a woman who couldn't find time to visit
her family for twelve years deserve all that devotion?
She had the kind of family he only dreamed about and
her obvious lack of appreciation had disturbed him.

He'd pictured her as a spoiled child who put her own
needs above those of others and was surprised to find
instead a tousled, tired woman, obviously distraught
over her father's accident.

He'd expected her to be sleekly attractive, but
though her thick hair was combed back, rebellious
black curls insisted on breaking free to dance around

her face. And her eyes had startled him. They'd looked like large black smudges on her face.

When he'd first seen her frightened, pale face, Trevor had felt an unexpected urge to encircle her in his arms and smooth those dancing curls. He'd successfully squashed that urge, thinking she wouldn't want coddling, and when she'd resisted his offer regarding the hotel and luggage he knew he'd been right. Still, he had to admit that she was attractive and the way he was drawn toward her annoyed him.

He remained in his car and watched Cassie pull away from the curb, grateful she was out of his hair for a while. He'd registered her at the Center Hotel and taken her luggage up. Well, that was the end of his responsibility to her. At least for today.

He went into the hospital, pushed the button for the elevator and waited for its slow arrival, thrusting his hand in his coat pocket and jiggling the keys to George's truck. Perhaps he had misjudged Cassie. There might be more to her than he'd ever supposed. Julia and George would think so. As Trevor thought of Julia, he wondered why George had never married her. She was quite a woman. Strong, compassionate, full of life. But now it was too late, Julia had other—

His train of thought was broken by the sound of the opening door. He had to move fast. The elevator was slow to arrive, quick to leave.

He exited at the third floor and searched for Julia. He found her in the ICU sitting beside George's bed. The curtain was open and she sat close. They didn't notice his approach, and as he reached the door he could hear their muffled voices. He raised his hand to knock just as Julia handed George an envelope. George opened it and pulled out a thick packet of scribbled papers and gave it to Julia. Trevor lowered his hand, knowing somehow that he was intruding on a private moment.

He backed quietly away from the door and walked to the waiting area, then poured himself a cup of coffee and sat down to wait.

It was some time before Julia appeared. She walked toward him, her head bent over the papers in her hand, reading intently and wiping away a tear. Her shoulders sagged and fatigue etched her features. Trevor knew she hadn't slept since that midnight call and it was now nearly noon. When she glanced up and saw him, a sad smile spread across her face, and Trevor squelched a sudden impulse to take her in his arms and comfort her like a child. Julia did the comforting, not the other way around.

Trevor found her to be an interesting woman. She was the younger sister of George's late wife, Sara. But judging from the portraits of Sara that dotted the walls of the Cambridge house, there was little family resemblance. Sara had been fair, blonde and chilly looking. In contrast, Julia's features were somewhat exotic, as though she'd come from some foreign land. Black eyes sat over high sculptured cheekbones, their enormous size accentuated by the severe style of her heavy, straight ebony hair, which she twisted and pinned at the base of her neck. She couldn't be much over forty, Trevor thought, though today she looked much older. But other days she almost seemed to be a teenager, her natural vitality obscuring her physical age.

"It doesn't look good," she said, her normally animated voice, flat and expressionless. Taking a seat beside him, she leaned back with a sigh. "I don't know what to tell Cassie. She adores her father and she's convinced he's going to pull through. Now she thinks—'' Julia stopped, as though she had said too much, and glanced idly toward the window.

"Julia,'' Trevor said tentatively, not sure if he should express his opinion. But years of training in law had given him an unquenchable thirst for truth. "Why are you so worried about Cassie? If she didn't care enough to come home for twelve years...?'' He didn't finish because what he wanted to add was that she didn't deserve the consideration they were all giving her.

"It isn't her fault, Trevor. She wanted to come home at first...when George sent her off to boarding school. But George kept her away.''

"But George adores Cassie. Why would he keep her from returning home?'' Trevor asked in surprise.

"He didn't want her to know what was going on here. As far as Cassie knows, everything at Cambridge Farms is just as it was when she left. Every time she wanted to come home, he'd find some reason to fly to Denver. After a while she just got used to it. Cassie thinks the sun rises and sets on George, and he wanted to keep it that way. Don't you see?''

A sudden picture of a young Cassie, bereft from her father's unexpected banishment, flashed through Trevor's mind. He saw her tear-streaked child's face, struggling to understand why her adoring papa was sending her away. Then he had a second flash—a picture of a young boy, too proud to weep, experiencing the same unwanted separation. His heart filled with sympathy for both children. The young Cassie and the young Trevor.

Oh, the things a man's—or a woman's—pride would make him do. Yes, Trevor saw. He saw all too clearly. When understanding dawned, he wanted to ask Julia about the letter George had given her but decided against it. Julia had endured enough of his intrusions for one day.

TRUE TO HIS WORD, Trevor Austin had secured a room for Cassie at the hotel, and when she unlocked the door she discovered her luggage inside.

Cassie lost no time in shedding her rumpled clothes, and a moment later, she stood in a steaming shower to relax her tense, tired muscles and recalling what she had learned.

According to Julia, Dr. Ferris had been called in by the hospital, and Julia hadn't known he was coming until he'd already arrived. No, her aunt had said, she didn't believe George was an alcoholic but she thought the doctors knew what was best. She'd disagreed with Cassie about moving him to Denver, believing that he was too sick. So Cassie had conceded. She knew that Julia, like herself, only wanted what was best for her father.

But when Cassie had spoken to Julia about some disturbing words her father had spoken in his semi-conscious state, Julia had looked at her sadly and said, "He's not himself, honey. You misunderstood what he said."

"But Aunt Julia, what if there was an attempt on his life?" Cassie had protested.

Julia had been shocked and had forbidden any further discussion. That had hurt. Cassie had always been able to talk to Julia about anything and now she was cutting her off.

Papa's whispered words haunted her. He had babbled names. Hers, Aunt Julia's, her mother's and Jake Bradford's. Then a muffled word that had sounded like *murder*. He'd repeated the word over and over, but Cassie had never been certain she'd heard correctly. But now as she painstakingly reviewed the word, a suspicion was forming in her mind. It seemed as if her father was trying to tell her that Jake Bradford was responsible for his accident, had tried to murder him.

While seldom complaining directly, her father had told her between the lines of his letters of Jake's harassments. From childhood, Cassie had been aware of the enmity between them, and her early memories held a dim recollection of a time when Jake had stopped her father on the street, screaming obscenities and vague accusations, heedless of Cassie's presence.

Reluctantly, Cassie decided to go to the police. Dressing quickly and leaving her hotel room, she was soon walking along a grimy snow-bordered sidewalk toward the Mesquite police station. If Jake had arranged for her father's accident, then the car was the key, she decided. There had to be come clue, some evidence in the wreckage—evidence of impact or tampering. Something.

The station was an old renovated house and the hand-painted sign over the door was faded with time. The door creaked as she opened it, revealing an ancient counter but no one in sight. Wire baskets overflowing with papers cluttered the top of the counter all but hiding a small metal bell. Cassie struck the bell forcefully. One...two...three times. As she was about to strike a fourth blow, a short, round gentleman burst through an inside door. He was pulling his suspenders over his shoulders.

"Hold your horses, hold your horses," he blustered. "Can't a man even go to the bathroom?" He stopped short as he spotted Cassie and blushed beet red over his white mustache and beard. Even through her heavy burden of worry, Cassie could barely suppress a giggle. Why, the man looked almost like Santa Claus.

"I'm sorry, miss." He stammered. "I didn't know it was a miss...I mean...oh, forget it." Regaining his poise, he looked at her directly and continued. "After all, it's something we all do. What can I do for you? Captain J. T. Haggarty at your disposal." He beamed broadly and extended his hand over the cluttered counter.

Cassie smiled in response and returned his hand-shake. "I'm Cassie Cambridge and I've come to look at the report of my father's accident."

The kindly smile vanished, immediately replaced by a look of concern. "Oh. I'm sorry to hear about George, Miss Cambridge. How is he doing?"

"Resting comfortably," Cassie replied. This Captain Haggarty really was a dear old thing. "Thank you."

"It was a terrible accident. Terrible. I was first on the scene and pulled him out of the ravine myself. It wouldn't have happened, though, if he hadn't been drinking, but still it was terrible. I'm sorry."

Her warm feelings for the man diminishing rapidly, Cassie replied cooly, "Thank you. Now, the accident report, please?" His brow wrinkled, as though he were puzzled by her change in tone. Then, shrugging his shoulders, he reached into one of the myriad of baskets and by some miracle appeared to have found the right form.

"Fill out this request, please," he said in a brisk, businesslike voice. "When the paperwork is right, I'll make you a copy of the file."

As promised, as soon as she had completed the form he went to a battered cabinet and in no time withdrew a file. "Would you like a copy, miss?" She nodded and he proceeded to a rickety, old copy machine and soon provided a legible, if not crisp, reproduction. "You can review it over there." He gestured to an antique desk and a less than sturdy-looking chair.

To her surprise the accident report was comprehensive. She'd expected a few scribbled notes, but the file contained diagrams of skid marks, estimated speeds, both when leaving the road and at impact, estimated number of rolls, and explicit descriptions of her father's injuries.

Cassie's stomach lurched with sudden knowledge of her father's fragile hold on life. Nausea gripped her. She laid her head upon the shabby desk.

"Are you ill, miss?" She jumped in alarm as J. T. Haggarty touched her shoulder in a gesture of concern. She lifted her head weakly, forcing back tears that were trying to flood over her eyelashes. Her eyes burned.

"It's not easy," the old man said. "Especially when it's your own kin." He pulled a handkerchief from his pocket and handed it to her with gruff instructions to dry her tears. Although embarrassed that he was witnessing her grief, she took the handkerchief, anyway. "Would you like to see the car?" he asked, in a transparent attempt to divert her attention from the gory descriptions she had been reading.

"Yes, thank you," she replied softly and followed in the direction he indicated. The minute they entered the impound yard, as though realizing he'd made a mistake, the stocky man patted her reassuringly on the shoulder. The car was a mass of twisted, tormented metal, barely recognizable as a vehicle, and Cassie turned ashen at the sight. For a moment she paused, then walked resolutely to the crumpled mass. She ran her hand across the caved-in top and looked at Captain Haggarty, an unspoken question in her eyes.

"Your pa was thrown free before that happened, miss. That's how come he survived."

He wasn't such a bad old guy, after all, Cassie mused. He was surely trying to be helpful. With a sense of futility, she turned back to the mangled car and inspected it intently. It was useless, she thought. With all this damage, how could she find anything, especially when she wasn't sure what she hoped to find? A broken brake line, perhaps? A punctured tire? She might find both—and a hundred other broken parts—but she still wouldn't be able to tell what had actually caused the accident. The only thing which stood out in the whole tortuous heap was a streak of red primer on the left fender. The paint must have been scraped off by all the rocks the car encountered on its plunge down the ravine.

Just then, as though mocking her, the sun emerged from its day-long cloud cover and its rays glinted off tiny metallic specks in the red streak. The captain bent over and touched the spot. "This is the only strange thing. Looks like primer, but it isn't. It's metallic paint and a fairly fresh scrape. No one remembers seeing it there before the night of the accident. Your pa might have sideswiped someone before he drove home. In his condition no one can tell."

One more reference to her father's drinking. Cassie was weary of all these allusions but also too weary to fight. "Is there anything else…anything unusual about the condition of the car?"

"No." The captain looked down at her kindly. "It's about what you could expect of a car that tumbled down a ravine."

Crushed by a sense of failure, Cassie thanked Captain Haggarty and told him she had seen enough.

Feeling very heavy and tired, she walked the few short blocks to the hospital. All she wanted to do was see her father again. Hold his hand. Stroke his forehead. With leaden steps, she made her way up the hospital stairs into the rickety elevator, leaning against the wall as it made its slow ascent to the third floor.

The paging system was blaring as she stepped out of the elevator door. "Code Blue! Code Blue! Dr. Ferris to ICU, stat!!" The screeching words echoed in her head as she broke into a run.

CHAPTER TWO

"GEORGE CAMBRIDGE was a fine man. An asset to the community. A good and loving father. A fine neighbor..." The Minister's voice droned on, mouthing platitudes that denied everything Cassie had learned about her father in the past few days: *Drunk... Alcoholic... Appeared to be intoxicated.* She'd heard stories of brawls and charges of assault. How had he hidden this from her the past dozen years? How had she been so blind?

An icy wind blew around Cassie's neck, and she scrunched down into her coat and scarf, searching for warmth. Even the weather was melodramatic, mocking everything she had once believed. Papa had asked for a graveside service and here they stood, family and friends, huddled around an open grave. No pristine white snow graced this service, only an icy, drizzly rain and a gray, unfriendly sky. A multitude of umbrellas, fluttering in the wind, added to the melancholia of the gloomy afternoon.

Silence interrupted her thoughts as she realized the minister had finished his eulogy. The members of the funeral party were looking at her expectantly. As her father had requested, she took a rose from a bouquet in her hands and, walking to the grave's edge, dropped it on top of the coffin. A suppressed sob erupted and she closed her eyes, her heart aching. She didn't care

what he had done. He was her father and she loved
him. She bowed her head and said a small prayer for
his soul and while she spoke the words she had a sudden revelation:

She couldn't have been *that* blinded. Someone had
deliberately plotted to destroy her father's reputation
and, if she believed his dying words, possibly his life.
Only one person had motive for doing such a thing,
Jake Bradford.

She finished her prayer and stepped back, mouthing a silent farewell to Papa. Before, anger and grief
clashed within her in discordant battle, both emotions
caused by her father. Now the only emotion she felt
toward him was an infinite sadness. Her anger was all
turned outward, focused on Jake Bradford.

When she stepped back, other mourners moved forward, each taking a rose from her hand and each, in
turn, dropping it on the coffin. Finally only one was
left. Cassie offered it to Julia, who stared at it wood-
enly before taking it, then moved slowly toward the
grave, seemingly with great effort. She sluggishly raised
her hand and held the rose over the coffin for what
seemed to Cassie an eternity. Finally Julia dropped it,
and at the barely audible sound of its impact, her eyes
rolled back in her head and she began to sway.

Cassie rushed toward her aunt in alarm, but before
she could reach her, a large broad-shouldered man
dressed in a dark Western suit stepped forward. He
caught Julia just as her knees buckled and lifted her
easily into his arms. Cassie recognized him as the man
Julia had been talking with at the hospital.

"Aunt Julia!" Cassie quickly closed the distance
between them and took Julia's hand in hers, trying to
find her pulse. Julia's eyes fluttered, then opened, but

instead of looking at Cassie she directed her gaze toward the tall man who was holding her like a baby. A faint smile crossed Julia's face and then her eyes closed again.

Cassie shook her aunt's hand in an attempt to rouse her, feeling like a small, lost child. Her mind whirled and she attempted to assure herself that Julia had just fainted. But what if it were something serious? A small voice inside cried that it wasn't fair. They were just burying her father. There couldn't be anything wrong with her aunt, as well.

She brushed the voice aside and tilted back her head to look into the big man's eyes. He gazed at Julia with worry on his face. "Can you take her to the limousine?" she asked.

At her question, he lifted his head and scrutinized Cassie, his expression changing to sympathy. His eyes were gray, and small lines surrounded them. She felt as if she knew him. Where had she seen him before?

"Yes, I can." He appeared ill at ease. "We need to get her out of the rain. Someone should call a doctor."

"Is she all right, Pa?" a nasal voice interrupted. Even after all these years, Cassie recognized the offensive twang immediately. Marvin Bradford. Then this man must be...

"Jake Bradford." The man inclined his head forward in acknowledgment of her recognition. Stunned, Cassie simply stared at him a moment. Of course. She hadn't seen him in at least fifteen years and he had changed. But he was still tall, broad and imposing. Those gray eyes had been hard as steel the last time she'd seen him, hurling foul accusations at her father who'd been trying to hurry Cassie away from the ugly scene. But it was the same man, all right. Fury howled in Cassie's gut, reviving her earlier vow.

How dared he? What right had he to even be there, much less hold her beloved Julia in his arms?

"Mr. Bradford, kindly allow someone else to carry my aunt. Considering what's gone on between you and my father you should have stayed away from his funeral." Exerting control she hadn't known she possessed, Cassie spoke in a cool voice, a threat contained in its menacing softness.

"I'm not surprised you feel that way, Cassie. But I came to pay my respects." His calm reply merely fanned Cassie's rage. She took a huge breath before continuing.

"You didn't respect my father when he was alive and I have reason to believe you're responsible for his death. So what led you to think I would welcome you at his funeral?"

"I didn't expect a welcome. I thought I wouldn't be noticed. I'll carry Julia to the car. Then I'll leave quietly."

"I don't want your help, Mr. Bradford."

Jake looked at her levelly, then turned and began covering the ground in large strides, carrying Julia as easily as if she were a feather. Cassie ran after him, but with every step her high-heeled boots sank into the soft, snow-sodden ground, and soon there were several feet of space between them.

"Please. Leave us alone," Cassie asked him. "Why can't you leave us alone?"

"Ah, Cassie, my pa didn't kill your pa. He did it to himself," Marvin called from behind her. "He was drunk as a skunk that night. Luke here saw him stumble out of the Mesquite Lodge." Cassie saw him gesture to a third man as she spun to answer the challenge, catching her heel in the ground and losing her balance.

A steadying hand grasped her elbow as she started to fall, and a husky voice near her ear said, "Leave her alone, Marvin."

Trevor Austin supported her while she regained her footing, and she leaned against him momentarily, grateful for the support. As she did, she saw the few mourners remaining at the grave trying uneasily to avoid staring. She flushed, realizing she was creating a scene and fought to regain her composure.

"Are you all right?" Trevor asked. At her nod, he told her he'd be back, then turned and walked toward Jake.

Cassie saw them exchange a few murmured words, then Jake handed her aunt over to Trevor. Even from the distance, Cassie noticed the twinge of something that looked like regret flash in Jake's eyes as he surrendered custody of Julia's limp form. It seemed as though Jake were trying to take everything from her, and she interpreted his emotion as regret at having been foiled.

Cassie headed for the limousine as fast as her high heels and the soft ground would permit. Someone had opened the limousine door and Trevor placed Julia safely inside. The crowd parted to allow Cassie to enter, and she asked the doctor, who'd attended the services, if he'd meet them at the house.

Someone handed her a blanket, and she slid inside the car and wrapped it carefully around her aunt, who was now conscious.

"It's just nerves," Julia said to the fussing crowd. "I'm so embarrassed. Everyone must think I'm a fool."

"They think nothing of the kind," Trevor interjected. "They're just concerned, that's all. Sit back and relax. We're going to take you home."

He turned his attention to Cassie. "I'll ride with you and help you get her in the house."

She opened her mouth to refuse his offer. His help had been very welcome, but now she simply wanted to be with Aunt Julia. Sympathizers would soon be arriving at the house, and they both need a moment's respite.

"That would be nice, Trevor," Julia said, cutting off Cassie before she had a chance to speak. Cassie gave a nearly imperceptible shrug and occupied herself rearranging Julia's blanket.

The crowd moved away from the limousine, and the driver inched the car forward. Drops of rain clung to Julia's hair and face, and Cassie searched through her purse for a handkerchief. A smile flickered across her face when Trevor's hand emerged over the seat waving a large red kerchief.

Despite Julia's protests, Cassie wiped the raindrops from her face and hair, then encircled her small form in her arms. For once, Julia submitted without her usual assurances that she felt fine. How frail her aunt was. Her face, lined with grief, showed the toll the events of the past week had taken. Julia was a vital, energetic woman, but now she looked tired, weak and pale. Cassie was instantly anxious to get home and have the doctor examine her.

The ranch was nearly thirty miles from town, and Cassie was tense during the ride. Occasionally Trevor looked back to check Julia's condition, and Cassie avoided his eyes. But when she was sure he wasn't looking she stole a glance at his strong profile. A slight crook in the bridge of his nose added an element of interest to his otherwise classic good looks. Cassie curbed a desire to reach out and touch the crooked spot. His attractiveness disturbed her. It was so compelling and she didn't understand why, at the worst time in her life, he seemed to intrude upon her thoughts. She already had enough to think about.

As they got closer to the ranch, Cassie noticed Julia was growing increasingly agitated, glancing apprehensively at Cassie. "What's wrong?" Cassie asked.

Julia sighed. "The ranch isn't quite the same, Cassie. I've been meaning to tell you, but..." Her voice trailed off as though continuing was painful.

"Are you feeling dizzy again?"

"No. Oh, honey." Julia gazed out the window and in a faraway voice, continued. "I've been putting this off but I can't any longer. The ranch needs a lot of work. Money has been tight and your father... well...some things have been let go."

"It couldn't be that bad, Aunt Julia." Cassie tightened her loving embrace. "We can face it together."

"I hope so." Julia replied, sinking into Cassie's hug.

They both relaxed, and Cassie was still holding Julia close when she felt the car slow and turn. Home. She was finally home. The deep-set seats did not allow full vision from the windows, so she leaned forward to get a better view. When she did, she knew there was some mistake. "You must have the wrong place, driver." The gate hung absurdly on its hinges, barely latched. Her father would never let a gate fall into such disrepair.

"Nope, this is it." The driver pointed to the identifying sign—Cambridge Stables—swinging cockeyed from its mountings, its peeling white paint revealing rusted spots. Cassie involuntarily groaned from her deep sense of loss.

Julia took her hand and squeezed it. "I just couldn't find the words." Cassie nodded, unable to speak over the lump in her throat. In a few short days she had lost almost everything. Her father was dead, all her illusions of him shattered. Julia could be seriously ill. And now her childhood home stood before her, reduced to squalor.

Trevor had climbed out and opened the gate, and now the car moved up the drive. Blemished roofs, rotting corral fences and an unkempt drive all assailed her eyes. She wondered what new unpleasantness would face her when they entered the house. Julia squeezed her hand again and as Cassie turned to face her aunt, a gladness filled her. At least she had Julia. She reached inside herself, finding a reservoir of strength. She could, she would, be strong. Julia needed her now, and all they had left was each other.

The driver parked and Trevor jumped out to open Julia's door. He helped her out, then lifted her lightly in his arms. "Put me down," Julia said good-naturedly. "I'm not an invalid. I can walk."

Trevor shook his head with a smile. "I promise I won't drop you if you promise to stop wiggling. There'll be plenty of time to walk later."

Julia submitted with a laugh. "Might as well take advantage of it, I suppose. I've never had so much attention in my life."

With a sharp pang of regret, Cassie realized that her aunt's light remark was the truth. Julia had always taken care of them, and Cassie wasn't sure that she and her father had given much in return.

She was grateful to Trevor for his kindness, for the tender way he carried Julia up the stairs and held her while Cassie pulled back the bed covers. They left the room as the doctor, who had followed in another car, began his examination.

Trevor followed Cassie down the stairs and when they reached the bottom she allowed him to pass, then sat on the bottom step. She felt apprehensive sitting there, as though doom were only a few steps away. Seeing her sit, Trevor paused and stood about in awkward silence for a little while, holding his hat in his hand. Apparently noticing her uneasiness, he finally said, "She'll be all right, Cassie. She's a strong woman."

"Yes, that she is," Cassie replied and wondered why his simple, empty, words—words anyone could have said—made her feel so much better. "Thanks for your help back there."

"It wasn't any trouble."

They fell silent again, but Cassie felt a need to talk, to talk to someone, anyone, about any subject, to get her mind off the heart-wrenching events of the past few days. "I hear you're new to Mesquite, Trevor. How long have you been here?" she said at last and, getting up, walked over, and relieved him of his hat.

"About a year and a half," he replied.

"Do you like it here?" Cassie placed his hat on the coatrack and turned to study him. It was the first time she had seen him without a hat, and she liked what she saw. His hair was a deep russet color that shone in the light of the dusty chandelier. It was tidily combed ex-

cept for one defiant lock that hung over his forehead.
She resisted an impulse to brush it back.

"I like it here very much. Clean air, no traffic and
plenty of hunting. What else could a man want?" He
leaned indolently against the banister and smiled,
showing his genuine pleasure in what was apparently a
new life-style. Again, Cassie admired his even white
teeth.

"I take it you're from a big city, then."

He told her he was from San Francisco, and his
aquamarine eyes sparkled as he spoke about the many
benefits of living in the mountains. His manner was
laid-back and unassuming, with only the smallest hint
of cynicism. He seemed to have a way of making people feel at ease.

"What do you do for a living?" she asked, wondering about his Rolex and his Porsche.

"I work for some local ranchers." His gaze suddenly shifted and he seemed fascinated with the intricate crystals of the chandelier. "That's an interesting
piece."

"Yes. My mother bought it in Europe. I'm told she
traveled there often before she died. There's a similar,
much larger one in the ballroom." His interest surprised Cassie. She hadn't met many men who expressed admiration for crystal.

Just then the doctor came bounding down the stairs,
proclaiming Julia healthy, although overstressed. For
some crazy reason Cassie felt as though Trevor's earlier words had made it true.

"What happened," the doctor explained to ease
Cassie's worry, "was that stress caused her blood ves-
sels to relax. The blood left her brain and she fainted.
It's a common reaction to grief. Just keep her quiet for

the next few days." He snapped his bag shut, then with a chuckle added, "If it's ever possible to get Julia to stay quiet."

The doorbell rang and Trevor told Cassie he would see who was there as Cassie conferred with the doctor. Three neighbor women stood outside with casserole dishes in their hands and Trevor let them in. Without being requested, he led the women to the kitchen while Cassie showed the doctor out. She was surprised that Trevor seemed to know his way about the house.

She didn't have much time to think about it because soon the doorbell was ringing incessantly with people bringing food and kind words. Cassie thought wakes were barbaric and although the three women who'd arrived first took care of providing refreshments and laying out food for the sympathizers, Cassie tired quickly of listening to consoling words. Many of the neighbors had known her as a child, but some were new and didn't know her at all. Both situations were difficult because she either listened to comments about how much she'd changed in twelve years or about how much they admired her father. Considering the news she'd received about her father over the past few days, she doubted the sincerity of the latter compliments.

She would have preferred enduring her grief in private and was secretly glad when Julia entered the room, even though she approached her with a loving scolding about getting out of bed.

"I'm fine, Cass, and I couldn't rest, knowing I was leaving you here alone. Go upstairs and freshen up." Julia had obviously renewed her makeup because she now looked more like her usual self, and thinking she could use a little repair herself, Cassie agreed.

As she approached the stairs, she changed her mind. Fresh air would probably do more good than freshening up. She fetched a coat and stepped outside. The air was crisp and cold against her face. She pulled up her collar and stuck her hands in her pockets. The breeze was uncomfortable, so she strolled into the small enclosed courtyard located to one side of the front porch.

The Wyoming sky never had ceased to delight her, and as she looked up at the star-filled sky, she tried to remember the names of the constellations. There was the Milky Way and the Big Dipper. She looked for the Little Dipper but couldn't find it and turned slowly, searching.

"Amazing, isn't it?" Trevor sat on a redwood table, elbows on his knees, feet on a bench. "Makes me wish I'd paid more attention during astronomy class."

Recovering from her initial surprise at seeing him there, Cassie smiled. "I was thinking the same thing. When you live in the city, you never see these stars, much less think about them." She walked over and sat beside him on the table. "It's been so long since I've been here that I'd forgotten how much I love this place. I'm going to miss it when I return to Denver."

"You're going back?"

Cassie wasn't sure if she imagined it but she sensed a note of disappointment in his voice. Looking at him, she also felt a prick of loss, as though she would be leaving something important behind.

"Of course I am," she answered lightly, covering up her own sudden feelings of reluctance. "I have a business to run."

A lazy grin crossed Trevor's face. "I suppose now that I'm a man of semileisure, I forget that others have to work for a living."

"More's the pity," Cassie replied, some of the heaviness lifting from her heart.

"What were you looking at so intently?"

"I was trying to find the Little Dipper. Do you know where it is?"

"Ah, now that's a pursuit I can identify with." Trevor looked toward the speckled sky. Twilight was receding, but the sky still carried a slight bluish tinge, making the stars look like diamonds on blue velvet. He pointed. "There."

"Where?" Cassie couldn't tell in which direction he was pointing. Reaching around her shoulder, he took her wrist in his hand and, lifting her arm skyward, pointed in the direction of the constellation. His fingers were icy cold against her now exposed wrist and the sudden touch was surprisingly erotic. Her somewhat chilled body filled with delicious warmth and the fragrance of his cologne was decidedly heady. She relaxed slightly against his body, suddenly losing interest in the constellations.

"Do you see it?" His breath brushed her cheek as he spoke.

"No," she lied, not wanting to retreat from the warmth of his body.

His hand moved to her fingers, forcing her body even closer to his. Gently forming her fingers into a copy of his own pointed hand, he moved her arm across her body. "See? Right there."

Cassie lowered her gaze and turned her head to face him. The light of a quarter-moon made his blue eyes sparkle like the stars. Their gaze locked and she could see longing written on his face. A longing that stirred something deep inside her.

The porch light came on, bathing the courtyard in subdued lighting, and now she could see his face clearly. The color of his eyes had deepened to a rich midnight blue, and they contained unconcealed desire. She inhaled deeply.

The front door opened, and the hum of conversation intruded on their silent interlude. Guests were leaving and soon she'd have to go back inside.

"They'll be looking for me." It was hard to speak. Her voice sounded throaty even to her own ears. "I should go inside."

"And put an end to our stargazing? Let them leave. Everyone will think you're lying down." But even as he spoke, Trevor released his hold on Cassie's hand.

"Aunt Julia may be worried. She's been through enough today. Believe me, I'd rather stay here." Cassie laughed. The last thing she wanted to do was go back inside to that grim-faced crowd.

"And I'd rather you stayed, but I suppose you're right." He pulled his arm away from her shoulder, causing her to feel a tinge of regret. He spoke in a purring whisper, and she nearly yielded to the temptation to sink back into his arms.

With a force of will, she slipped off the table and stood. "Say goodbye before you leave, okay?"

"Yes," he answered in a thick voice.

"THERE YOU ARE," a cheery voice said as Cassie entered the house. The voice belonged to one of the three women who'd first arrived at the house. Cassie remembered her name was Mrs. Willis. "Where have you been all this time?"

"Just getting some air." She tingled with the thought of what she'd really been doing and smiled at her harmless deception.

"I've been looking for you. Your aunt Julia went back up to rest. The guests are leaving and I need your help." There was a faint tone of reproach in the woman's comments, which Cassie ignored. Instead she began murmuring appropriate social courtesies to the departing guests. Soon the house was cleared of sympathizers except for Mrs. Willis and her husband.

"Where's Trevor?" Mrs. Willis looked around fretfully. "It seems like I'm losing everyone tonight." Cassie didn't miss the thinly veiled reference to her earlier absence and while she knew she should be appreciative of the woman's help during the evening, her bullying ways grated. Cassie searched for a polite response.

"Oh, there you are," Mrs. Willis squealed before Cassie could answer. Trevor had just walked into the hallway, and Mrs. Willis rushed toward him with a take-charge air. "Now, Mr. Willis is pulling the car around and I'm going to finish up in the kitchen. Don't you dare move or you'll miss your ride home." She wagged a bossy finger at him then rushed to the kitchen.

Trevor stood beneath the chandelier with a bemused, indulgent expression on his face. Cassie's barely suppressed laughter erupted as soon as she was sure Mrs. Willis was out of earshot. Trevor responded with a sheepish grin.

"Quite a whirling dervish, isn't she? I feel totally chastened." His grin widened and he gazed at Cassie fondly. His gaze made her feel warm.

"I hope it isn't a long ride home." Cassie giggled again at the thought of Trevor being subjected to continuous admonishments for the duration of the trip.

Trevor's smile subsided. He walked to the coatrack and got his hat. "Where's my raincoat?"

Cassie walked to the closet, still curious about Trevor's sudden change in mood. She retrieved his coat and handed it to him. "Did I say something wrong?"

She felt rewarded when his smile returned. "Not at all. I'm just tired and—well, frankly, it's been a long day."

Cassie understood and started to tell him so when Mrs. Willis rushed back into the hall, carrying several empty bowls and containers. Cassie wondered if the woman ever moved at a normal pace. "Now, Trevor, there are still some bowls in the kitchen. I wonder if you'd be kind enough to carry them out for me. Cassie can show you where the kitchen is." She then whirled out the door, which Trevor opened for her. The car was waiting close to the house.

Suppressing an urge to remind the overwhelming woman that this was, after all, her home, Cassie followed Trevor to the kitchen. "You've been here before," she commented when she realized, for the second time, that he knew his way about the house.

"A number of times," he replied. "I'd come to know your father quite well before . . ." He allowed his voice to trail off, obviously trying to avoid the painful subject. "And your aunt is one of my favorite people."

"Yes. One of mine, too. How did you come to know my father?" She was no longer making polite conversation. She now found herself vitally interested in what this man did, thought and cared about.

"He asked me to review some paperwork for him. Oh, there they are." Trevor pointed to the bowls that sat on the tiled kitchen counter and left Cassie's side to collect them. Disappointed that he'd interrupted his answer, she thought it strange that Trevor was taking his newly assigned duty so seriously that he couldn't continue the conversation.

Gathering the bowls in his arms, Trevor moved toward the kitchen door. "Miz Willis is awaiting me," he quipped. "I must not tarry."

Laughing lightly, Cassie followed him, wishing he didn't have to leave. When they reached the door, they stood for a sweetly awkward moment just looking at each other. Finally Trevor broke the silence.

"Good night, then, pretty lady. The Willises are waiting. Miz Willis is undoubtedly fuming over my delinquent ways." He placed a hand on the doorknob, then stopped and turned. For a brief moment time became suspended. A spark ignited between them and a nearly visible current flowed from one to the other. Mesmerized, Cassie gazed at him fondly, then realized she was staring like a gawky teenager. She tore her eyes away.

Trevor smiled enigmatically. "Good night, again," he said softly, then turned and ran to the car. Cassie stood at the door, watching his departing figure. She could still feel electricity surging through her body and she floated dreamily to the stairs.

Suddenly she was swept away by a flood of guilt. Shame burned her face. For over an hour, on the day of his funeral, she had completely forgotten her father.

"YOU MEAN JAKE BRADFORD owns everything else?"
Cassie was incredulous. Harry Teitelbaum, her father's
attorney, peered at her over his reading glasses. He had
just informed her that her father had left her everything and, in the same breath, had told her that nothing was left. All that remained of their vast land
holdings was five acres.

"It's a disaster, Miss Cambridge," Harry said with
a nod, solemnly gazing at her with that expression of
pity she had grown to hate. "Your father was terribly
in debt. Your only hope is to sell out."

Sorting through the canceled checks, papers and
unpaid bills that Julia, who'd been keeping the Cambridge books for the last several years, had brought to
Cassie for the meeting, she found something important missing. "How much is the mortgage payment? I
can't seem to find any records on it."

"Well, that's the thing, Miss Cambridge. There is no
payment. Actually you don't even own Cambridge
Stables. Or what's left of it, that is. You own part of a
trust. By the terms of the trust you may live here.
However, the remaining partners may call in their percentage of the trust at any time. All that's required is a
thirty-day notice."

"You mean I could be asked to pay back two
hundred and three thousand dollars just like that?"
The thought was appalling.

"That's right," Harry answered. "The trust is called
Evergreen Enterprises. It was executed without my
knowledge and I would have advised against it. The
other partners are anonymous. We're trying to locate
them, but it's a blind trust and so far my staff has been
unsuccessful. My advice to you is to sell your percentage. It will get you out from under a tremendous debt

load. Also, it will force the other partners to surface. This is not the smartest thing your father ever did,'' he concluded.

If Cassie had ever heard an understatement, that was it. "No, it isn't," she replied with a bitter laugh. "But how can I sell the ranch? It's been in the family for four generations. It was built by my great-great-grandparents. Selling it would be almost like selling a part of myself."

Cassie instantly regretted her outburst. The look of pity on Harry's face intensified. He told her he thought she had little choice.

Cassie reluctantly agreed, thanked him, and showed him to the door. *It's a fine mess you've left me in,* she thought, as though speaking directly to her father, but the anger she had felt at the funeral had not returned. Thinking of him only brought memories of piggyback rides on his broad shoulders; unruly black hair; a hearty fun-loving laugh; large, strong hands that could fix anything, even a little girl's broken heart. Her memories belied all the pictures left behind, pictures of a desperate, drunken, self-destructive man. They didn't mesh. Where was the truth?

She wandered aimlessly down the wide hall leading toward the great room at the far end. She noticed jagged glass edges on several of the gaslight fixtures strategically placed on the walls for use during power failures. Their wicks peeped obscenely through the broken glass and reminded her how much Cambridge had deteriorated. She stepped into the great room. It seemed so empty, so desolate without her father, and it echoed the presence of all the ranch hands and their families who had once used this room as a recreation center. A huge flagstone fireplace covered one wall, its cavernous mouth empty. Above the mantel hung a portrait of her mother. Cassie stared at the painting of the fair-skinned blond woman she could barely remember. Only a faint recollection of a flowery fragrance remained in her mind, and she realized how little she knew about this lovely woman who'd given birth to her.

Her name was Sara, and Cassie wondered what she would have thought about the decline of Cambridge Stables. Surely it would have broken her heart, and Cassie was glad her mother wasn't here to see it. Cambridge Stables of Mesquite Valley, Wyoming, had been a cultural center during her mother's lifetime. People came from every western state to attend the Cambridge parties, to admire and purchase their horses, to breed their mares with a champion Cambridge stallion. Well, those days were over.

She felt physically drained. Julia, still worn out from the burden she'd been carrying, was taking an afternoon nap. Cassie decided to do the same.

As she started up the stairs she noticed one of the ballroom doors ajar. She stepped over, intending to close it, but instead pushed the door open and walked inside. As far as she knew this room hadn't been used since her mother's death and was now a place for storing discarded furniture, saddles requiring repair and miscellaneous cartons. It was an enormous room built in the center of the house; the second story wrapped around it so that its height was a full two stories. A balcony that served as a hallway between the two bedroom wings ran across the far wall. An enormous chandelier hung from the ceiling, the crystals opaque with years of dust.

Wainscoting ran beneath subtly flowered wallpaper. A skylight was the only source of daylight, and in its gloomy illumination the faded wallpaper appeared forbidding and decayed. Dust motes floated in the air, highlighted by the stream of sun peering through the skylight. The room gave Cassie the creeps. She'd always hated it without knowing why, supposing that her dislike stemmed from never seeing the room at its best. In its present condition it was like a mausoleum. A faint shudder ran through her as she stepped back outside and closed the door.

She continued her aimless trek upstairs and lay on the bed, but sleep didn't come. Instead, images of her first inspection of the ranch flooded her mind. Twelve years of neglect had taken its toll, and judging from the condition of the grounds and buildings, they had been years of total neglect. Nothing else could explain the state of massive disrepair. Shutters were torn from the windows. Shingles were loose on the roof. The barns and corrals were near collapse. Cassie had been shocked by the sight, feeling as though the foundation of her life had been torn from beneath her.

Julia, with her usual industriousness, had kept the inside as spotless as possible. Floors were polished, windows washed, furniture dusted. But the house was too big for one person to clean, and her efforts could not hide the holes in the walls, broken light fixtures and other small signs of neglect. When Cassie had asked her aunt where all the staff was—the household help, the wranglers—Julia had merely shrugged and replied, "Gone." Cassie had not pressed her.

The greatest shock, though, came when she toured the barns to view the livestock. Stock? What stock? She passed stall after empty stall, finally coming upon four puny brood mares. Mares? No! They were nags! What kind of colts would these scruffy excuses for quarter horses ever throw?

These thoughts passed through her head over and over again. So much work, so much money to ever make Cambridge Ranch whole again. It looked like the ranch of her parents, her grandparents, her great and great-great-grandparents was gone. She would have to take Harry Teitelbaum's advice. Sell. All the king's horses and all the king's men, she thought as she drifted into a restless sleep....

"Mama, Papa. What's happening to you?"

Cassie awoke with a start. Her nightmare, again. She thought it curious that the nightmare had resurfaced, after all these years, just before her father's death. She hadn't been troubled by that ugly dream since her early teens.

Then she heard the noises just outside her window. Talking, accompanied by the crunch of feet and hooves on gravel. Groggy from the nightmare, she reluctantly pulled herself from the bed, walked over to the window and drew aside the curtain.

Was she still dreaming? There in the unloading area stood a stallion. A magnificent black quarter horse. All sleek, powerful muscle and quivering vitality. His long, flowing mane and tail glistened in the afternoon sun. Cassie was an accomplished horsewoman, able to spot quality in a horse, and the stallion's perfection took her breath away.

Two men approached the horse, one holding a halter, the other poised to block any escape. But with very unstallionlike behavior the breathtaking animal merely lowered his head obediently into the halter. The two men looked at each other in surprise. Then one shrugged and they both smiled. One man held the lead rope while the other started walking to the house.

Cassie ran down the stairs. Had Papa ordered a stud for those sorry mares? Surely not. But if he had, she would just tell them to take him back. Cassie opened the door just as the man was beginning to rap. Startled, he nearly fell across the threshold.

He stared at Cassie for a minute, then regained his composure, removed his well-worn hat and asked if she was Miss Cambridge. When she replied she was, he said, "Well, ma'am, I'm Nate from the Tripe Bar in Cheyenne—"

"If you brought that stud to breed my mares, you'll just have to take him back. My father died last week and there is no money to pay for him," she blurted. She didn't want to see that stallion again. She'd kill to own a horse like that and the decision was already made. She was going to sell Cambridge Stables.

"In Wyoming," he continued as though she hadn't spoken. "We're returning your stallion. Expect to get a lot of nice babies from that fella."

Cassie's mouth fell open in astonishment. "Do you mean he's mine?"

"Why, yes, ma'am." The wrangler looked at her curiously. "Didn't you know? And lucky you are at that. Not just good-lookin' but he's got a nice disposition."

"No," Cassie replied, dumbfounded. "No, I'm sorry. I didn't know. I haven't been back here in years. As I said, my father died...." It was hard to go on. Talking about it still distressed her. It made everything too real.

"I'm sorry too, ma'am. About your father, I mean. Too bad. George was a good old guy. A fair man, too."

He paused for a moment, fondling his hat uncomfortably, and then said, "Where do you want me to put him? The stallion, I mean."

"Oh. I'm not sure. I'll walk with you to the barn and look for his stall. If there isn't one, I'll just fix one up."

"Believe me, ma'am, there's a stall for him. This guy was George's pride and joy."

And there was a stall. Chauncey, said the nameplate. "Chauncey," Cassie murmured. "Is that your name?"

The wrangler nodded at her question and replied, "That's it ma'am. Chauncey. Nice name. Nice horse." He handed Cassie an envelope. "Stud fee," he explained, then repeated his condolences and left.

Cassie stood in front of the stall for a long, long time just looking at the beautiful animal. He was a champion, of that she was certain. His conformation was perfect. Tall, broad chested, round flanks and straight, strong legs. He nestled her occasionally, and whinnied softly when she stroked his head.

Cassie didn't doubt he would bring a good price when she sold the Stables but cringed at the thought of parting with this magnificent creature. The training of her early years told her that such an animal came along all too seldom. If his ability to work calves proved to be half as good as his looks, he would go clear to the top of the quarter-horse circles. An idea nudged at the edge of her mind, but she dismissed it. The decision was already made. Cambridge Stables had to be sold.

The surly rumble in her stomach reminded Cassie she was hungry. She quickly fetched hay for the stall and covered Chauncey with a blanket then walked back to the house, still battling out the two ideas in her head. Only then did she remember the envelope she had stuffed in the pocket of her jeans. She pulled it out and opened it.

Ten thousand dollars! She stared in wonder at the check. A check made out to Cambridge Stables. "Chauncey," she said aloud, "I think you're a gift from heaven."

CHAPTER THREE

"Now LET ME get this straight." Al Collins, Cassie's long-time partner and business associate, leaned back in his chair and adjusted his glasses. "You want to sell your half of the advertising agency to me so you can return to Wyoming and save your father's bankrupt ranch. Is that right?"

Cassie laughed in response. Al's dry way of stating things never failed to amuse her. That was one of the reasons she liked him and why their partnership worked so well. While working together at another advertising agency, they'd been lovers briefly, but even though they'd quickly realized their relationship had no future, they'd been bright enough to recognize each other's talents. Thus, C&C Agency was formed.

Al had since married and now had a son. Cassie was a friend of the family and surrogate aunt. All in all, it worked very well and in a few short years they built one of the most successful agencies in Denver.

Now she wanted to dissolve it and Al was justifiably shocked. "What do you expect me to do, Cassie? I'm just the financial whiz around here. You're the creative liaison. I'm not going to keep our clients happy by paying bills and scrutinizing balance sheets. They expect your unique ability to know what they want."

"Yes, and I love you, too, Al. But believe me, you can function without me now. Janet has a real flair for copy and ideas and Lorna is a dynamite artist. You can deal with the clients. I know you'll survive."

Al leaned forward and put his elbows on his desk, burying his face in his hand. Running his fingers through his fine brown hair, he looked up and sighed. With a jolt, Cassie realized she'd been comparing his comfortable good looks with Trevor Austin's compelling masculinity. The shallowness of those comparisons appalled her, and she forced her attention back to matters at hand. "Yeah," Al was saying, "I'll survive. But in all seriousness, Cassie, I'm not sure this is a good move for you. Have you thought—?"

Cassie raised her hand, to stop him. "Yes, Al, I've thought. I've thought and I've thought and I've thought. Please don't give me any more to think about."

Grimacing, Al nodded. "Okay, Cassie. I'll think about it and call you tonight. You always have been a bullheaded little witch."

"Like I said, I love you, too." She rose, walked around his desk and planted a noisy kiss on his forehead. "I'll wait for your call."

Al smiled at her. Then suddenly his face became serious. "It was pretty bad up there, huh?"

"Oh, Al. I never dreamed that those things were happening. Papa never told me, never even hinted at it, even made up stories to hide the way things were. It's incredible that Jake Bradford, of all people, owns almost all the property that once belonged to Cambridge Stables." Cassie's heart began to pound as she talked about Jake. Even mentioning his name sent rage coursing through her veins. "That man is sleazy. He started from nothing. When I left Mesquite, all he owned was a tiny boarding stable. Now he's one of the biggest ranchers in the Southwest."

Al listened sympathetically as Cassie continued telling him about the events of the past two weeks. When she'd covered all the details of the financial situation, she then filled him in on Chauncey's sudden appearance.

"Until he showed up I'd decided that my only option was to sell. But with a horse like that, Al, I know I can pull Cambridge Stables out of this slump. I researched his bloodlines and they're impeccable. With a little training, that stallion will be a champion. His stud fees alone would cover expenses, and with a few good futurity purses the Evergreen trust could be bought out."

"Whoa, Cassie. What on earth is a futurity?"

Cassie smiled. Two weeks in ranch country and she was a horsewoman all over again. "A futurity is a competition during which trained cutting horses keep calves from a herd. They used to be held as training for true working horses. Nowadays they're big-time competition with big-time purses."

Al appeared to be seriously reflecting on the information he'd just learned. "So you think you can turn a profit from this mess you're in?"

"You bet I do." Cassie's reply was emphatic. She knew good horses and was certain that, barring major disaster, by summer's end the Cambridge Stables balance sheet would show black.

They talked for a while about the financial prospects, with Al making an occasional note. Cassie could hear his business brain whirring behind his calm eyes. After they talked awhile, he paused momentarily and made some quick calculations.

"I've got a counterproposal for you, Cassie doll," he said after reviewing the results of his addition. "How about you take a year's sabbatical. Sort things out up there in Mosquito, and then if you still want to sell out, we'll talk about it. Full pay of course."

"It's Mesquite, Al, not Mosquito," said Cassie, smiling as Al chuckled. "And I can't take full pay if I'm not contributing. That's not fair. Besides, I need the money to pay off the mortgage."

"You drive a hard bargain. All right, half pay. And if it'll make you feel better, you can cut me in on ten percent of your profits once you're in the black. Hey, look, Cassie, don't pour everything down the drain. You've worked too hard for what you've got. Worry about the mortgage if they call it. In the meantime, go off and do your thing. We'll manage for a while."

She was silent for a moment, afraid of choking if she dared speak. "Cassie?"

"Thank you, Al," she stated simply, over the raspiness in her throat. She had always known Al was her friend, but until this moment had not comprehended the depth of that friendship.

After what seemed like hours of discussion Cassie and Al ironed out the details. She would take half pay and work out a contract whereby Al would receive a percentage of any profit Cambridge Stables might show. She would also be available for telephone consultation if anything arose that the staff couldn't handle. She filled Al in on the particulars of projects in progress and gave him tips on how to handle any unexpected events that might occur in trying to conclude the negotiations.

"I'll see you later this week before I go." She got up to go and Al rose to walk her to the door. Before he opened it, she wrapped her arms around him in a big grateful hug.

"Hey, watch that," Al joked. "My wife may burst in here any moment."

"Tell Karen I said hello," Cassie said with a grin. The idea of Karen being jealous was laughable. Al adored her and Karen knew it.

"You'd better tell her yourself. She'll never forgive you if you don't phone before you leave."

Cassie agreed and blew Al a kiss as she left his office.

CASSIE WAS WEARY of rushing, but she had so many things to do and so little time. It had been three days since her conversation with Al, and during that time she had packed most of her belongings, sent her furniture to storage, met with Al and the C&C staff, signed sublet contracts on her condominium and sold her car.

Now she sat on the bedroom floor of her nearly empty apartment and sorted through her clothing, trying to decide what to take, what to discard and what to store. A pile of flimsy lingerie awaited packing, and she wondered if she should take it or buy new, sturdier underwear. Deciding she didn't need the expense, she began placing the lacy garments into a suitcase. Picking up a frilly camisole, she suddenly pictured Trevor's square-tipped fingers slipping a lacy strap from her shoulder. She flushed at the image and returned to her thoughts about the future.

Although she'd presented a determined front to Al, Cassie still had doubts about the decision she was making. What if she failed? Ranch life was often hard, and the skills she'd learned at her father's side were rusty. Could she still train a horse? Of course she could. That was a skill like riding a bicycle. It would come back to her. How about repairing fences? Or shingling a roof? She glanced down at her glossy, polished fingernails and smiled ruefully. Those would be gone in no time at all.

A million such questions darted in and out of her mind and she was trying to reassure herself when the telephone rang.

"Hello." It was probably one of her friends who'd heard she was leaving phoning to say goodbye. She'd received dozens of similar calls during the past few days.

"Cassie? This is Marion Davenport."

"Marion Bradford Davenport," Cassie cried in delight. "I haven't heard from you in ages." Marion and Cassie attended boarding school together and became good friends during those years. When Marion married a successful mortgage broker several years earlier and moved to Denver, they had renewed their friendship. Later, different lifestyles caused them to drift apart but their affection for each other remained.

Marion laughed. "I dropped the Bradford a long time ago. I'm just plain old Marion Davenport these days and loving every minute of it."

The good humor was typical of Marion. Despite Cassie's antipathy for the rest of the Bradford family, Marion was impossible not to like. She was such an enthusiastic and genuinely caring person that she invoked love from all who met her. Even her few detractors called her "too sweet," or "too naive," not quite believing in Marion's accepting nature.

"Well, then, Marion Davenport. How are you? What have you been doing?"

"Having babies. Raising babies. Loving my husband. But that's not why I called. How are you, Cassie? I just recently learned about your father. I am so sorry. It must have been awful for you."

Cassie's throat tightened at this expression of sympathy. "No, it wasn't the best time of my life, but I'm sure you know that."

"Yes, I do. I remember how hard it was for me when Mother died. I'm sorry about your father."

"Thank you, Marion. But it's hard to talk about. Can we change the subject. Like, how are you doing?"

"Yes. I know talking about it can be painful. But I've already covered my entire life. Adam is going on four now and the baby will be two in April."

"Are you planning to have any more?"

Marion laughed, a delightful tinkling laugh, which caused Cassie to smile. "I don't think so. At least not for a while. I've got my hands full these days."

"I'll bet you have." Cassie grinned at the picture of Marion chasing two small Davenports around the house and briefly wondered what it would be like to have a child. They continued into a delightful conversation, reliving old times at the very proper Montclair Boarding School for Girls and updating each other about the events in their lives. As they were saying goodbye a thought occurred to Cassie.

"By the way, Marion, how did you hear about my father?"

"Oh, Father told me. He came down last week to get his car repaired. It has some exotic red paint that they can't get in Mesquite so he drove it here for repair. He mentioned metallic sparkles or something like that. Anyway, I've been trying to track you down since then. Why do you ask?"

Just the mention of Jake Bradford changed Cassie's mood. She again wondered how this marvelous woman could be Jake Bradford's stepdaughter. Even though Bradford blood didn't run in Marion's veins, exposure to that household should have ruined her wonderful disposition. "Just wondering," she answered lamely.

After ending the phone call, Cassie returned to her packing and was intently jamming clothing into a garment bag when the memory of her visit to the Mesquite impound yard flickered through her mind. Sunlight streaming through clouds, striking a red streak that glittered in the light. The image clicked and gelled with the information just received from Marion. *My God, Jake's car is the same color as the paint streak on Papa's car.*

Her mouth turned to cotton and her heart began to race. Although she'd initially suspected Jake of murdering her father, after her emotions had subsided and her reason had returned she'd had to admit she really didn't believe it. Now she had her first shred of real evidence... and wasn't sure she wanted it.

She hastily zipped the overstuffed garment bag and walked back to the phone. When Marion answered on the other end, Cassie squelched her guilt and stated her carefully prepared lie.

"Marion, I sold my car and promised the buyer I'd have a few nicks touched up. Can you tell me the name of the body shop your father used?"

"SORRY, MISS CAMBRIDGE, but the car—or what was left of the car—has been taken away. To the crusher." She was once again in the Mesquite Police Station, sitting across from Captain J. T. Haggarty. He looked slightly uncomfortable as, for the third time, he ran his fingers through his sparse white hair.

"To the crusher? Why? Who authorized that?" The captain's answer had caught Cassie totally by surprise. It had never occurred to her that the car would be gone.

"How did you let that happen without checking with me? I am the next of kin, you know."

"Of course, Miss Cambridge, but . . . well . . . Miss Norwood is also a relative and . . . well, when she ordered it picked up, I just naturally thought she was doing what you wanted."

"Aunt Julia? Aunt Julia asked you to have it picked up?" Cassie looked at him incredulously.

"That is correct. Came in here last week and told me to have it done as soon as possible. So I did."

Realizing that Captain Haggarty had no answers for her, she said, "Well, thank you," and started to leave. Obviously she should continue this conversation with her aunt. But as she reached the peeling door she reconsidered and turned back toward the rotund police officer. "Captain Haggarty, do you have a few minutes? I'd like to discuss something with you."

"Allowing as how Mesquite is not exactly a center of crime," the captain replied, "my time is yours. Have a seat."

When comfortably settled, Cassie reached into her purse and retrieved the paint chip she'd obtained from the body shop in Denver. Handing it to Captain Haggarty, she said, "Do you remember the red paint on the left fender of my father's car?"

THE DRIVE BACK to the ranch seemed interminable. She had so many questions and the trip was taking forever. Her talk with the captain had allowed her to clarify her suspicions but, looking back, she realized that although he had been attentive and interested, the captain was far from convinced a murder had been committed. Jake Bradford was, after all, a respected member of the Mesquite ranching community and his ownership of a red metallic car that had recently been repaired was weak circumstantial evidence at best. Still he had promised to look into it. A promise that did little to put Cassie's mind at rest.

But Aunt Julia had some hard questions to answer. Why in the world had she ordered that car destroyed? The question was eating at Cassie and her mind raced. Julia was like her own mother, and Cassie was sure she must have had a good reason for her actions.

Cassie pressed down on the gas pedal, trying to urge more speed out of the rickety old truck. It was the same truck Trevor had driven when he'd picked her up at the bus station. What a joke, she thought, as she remembered her revulsion the first time she'd climbed inside. She smiled ruefully, while thinking about what her Denver friends would say if they saw her driving this old heap. She would never be able to live down the razzing. Still, it ran, and it got her where she wanted to go. But not fast enough. The drive from Mesquite to the stables always seemed to take forever.

At last the gate of the driveway appeared ahead. She pulled in, parked hastily and ran into the house.

Julia was standing at the kitchen sink, peeling potatoes. Immediately Cassie felt contrite. Julia looked so tired. Her small shoulders were bent forward and her usually lively face was creased. Cassie realized that the past few weeks had drained them both. Her aunt didn't deserve the anger and suspicion Cassie was now harboring. Nor did she deserve any more pain.

Cassie went to a drawer, pulled out another potato peeler and joined Julia at the sink. She studiously examined the potato she'd picked up. Julia smiled a greeting, showing a hint of her normal vitality. Cassie smiled back and gave her a kiss on the cheek. It was settled, then. She wouldn't ask. Leave well enough alone. Most likely Julia had meant to protect her, as though Cassie were still a child. She immersed herself in her task.

"Aunt Julia, why did you tell Captain Haggarty to destroy Papa's car?" Immediately she was angry with herself. But it was too late. The words were out.

Shock registered on the tiny woman's face. She was silent for a moment as she examined the potato in her hand for unpurged eyes. "It seemed like the right thing to do," she finally answered.

"The right thing to do? You knew I thought Jake either killed my father or had him killed. You destroyed the evidence. Why?"

"Cassie." Julia took her hands. "Come over to the table. Sit down. I'll get you some cookies and milk. We'll talk."

"Aunt Julia, I'm not ten years old anymore. I think my father's been murdered. This is not something cookies and milk can cure."

"How I wish it were. Oh, Cass, these past few weeks have been so hard on you. Your papa dying was enough to bear. But more than that, you've lost a dream. A memory. Why do you think George kept you away from here? He knew what this would do to you." She took Cassie's face between her hands, just as she had done when Cassie was small.

"Child, most of your father's life was so full of...of hate and bitterness. He wanted so badly to restore

Cambridge Stables before you ever found out. But he put so much energy into hating Jake, there was none left for the stables. Don't let that happen to you."

"So you and Captain Haggarty destroyed the car to stop me from finding out how Papa died? Is that right?"

"No." Julia shook her head. "No. To stop you from going after it any more. It happened just the way they said, Cassie. He was drunk. He took the corner too fast. The car went off the edge. There is nothing to find out. I thought if the car was gone you would forget it. Let it go, Cass. It will only destroy you. Don't you understand?"

Julia's face was drawn and tense, her forehead wrinkled in worry and Cassie recognized her sincerity. She considered telling her about the paint chip but decided against it. Her Aunt had enough concerns right now. Cassie didn't need to add to them.

She gently pulled her face away from Julia's hands. Somehow she'd get more evidence. Some way she'd prove or disprove her suspicions. But until then she wouldn't add to Julia's burden.

"Okay, Aunt Julia. I'll let it go." *For now,* a voice inside her added.

"Good." Julia smiled in relief.

"I'm feeling restless. I think I'll go riding."

Julia acknowledged Cassie's comment, and Cassie walked to the hall closet and gathered her standard denim jacket, a hat and gloves. Heading to the barn, she tried to sort out her conflicting emotions.

No matter how much Julia pleaded, Cassie couldn't ignore the link between Jake's repainted car and her father's death. Of course, she'd reached an impasse in making a solid case. But if any more evidence came her way, she knew she'd have to pursue it. How to do that without upsetting her aunt was a question she couldn't answer. She entered the barn and led Chauncey from his stall.

Something about horses always soothed Cassie. As she brushed down the handsome stallion, she felt tension leaving her body and the confusion of her thoughts settling into a more orderly progression. Chauncey seemed eager to go, and he nuzzled Cassie gently as she curried his mane.

When she finished the grooming, Cassie checked the saddle she'd used since Chauncey arrived. The worn cinch strap was getting dangerous, so she walked to the tack room to search for a reliable saddle. Like everything else at the ranch, the room showed signs of neglect. Spiderwebs populated the corners and clung to saddles and blankets, creating a moldy, museumlike atmosphere. The musty smell of the air offended her.

She searched the saddle tree for a piece of gear safe enough to use, coughing as the scattering dust floated through the air. She rejected saddle after saddle for one flaw or another and was ready to settle for a bareback pad when she turned to spot a single saddle, mounted on a solitary stand hidden in one corner of the room.

It sparkled like a crown jewel. Unlike the rest, it was well cared for. A restrained pattern of small roses graced the edge of the skirt. One large rose decorated the front corner on the mounting side. Its oiled leather glistened in the dim light and the well-worn suede seat still showed felt, a result of frequent and careful brushing. It was her barrel-racing saddle. How many arenas had she raced through on that saddle? She couldn't remember. But she did remember that she hadn't used it since her last competition just before she'd left for Montclair Boarding School.

Gazing at it in wonder, she knew without doubt that her Papa had done this. For twelve years, among all the decay and neglect, he'd maintained this saddle as a monument of his love for her.

She recognized suddenly that Julia was right. She had to let go. Her father had loved her and now he was dead. It would do no good to carry on a vendetta against Jake Bradford. Far better if she devoted her energy to restoring the stables and getting back their land. Her eyes burned, and for the first time since that awful day at the hospital, tears flowed. Amid the dust, webs and musty air, Cassie laid down her head and wept, allowing all the pain from her loss to flow out of heart, through her eyes and onto the lovingly preserved saddle.

Later, as she rode across the countryside, she reflected on her decision. It felt right, and some of the heaviness that had rested on her heart since her father's death lifted away. The day reflected her mood. The sun was dim, hidden behind heavy clouds, but occasionally it would burst through as if to remind Cassie that hope did exist.

Tightening her left leg, she urged Chauncey south, leaving Cambridge land. The trail was clear but mounds of dirty snow bordered each side, reminding her to stay on the straight and narrow. Chauncey was eager to run and, first checking ahead for ice, she urged him into a smooth controlled lope. His gait was rhythmic and pleasant and she sank deep into the saddle, allowing the cool winter wind to whip across her face.

Suddenly a shot rang out. Chauncey jumped and stopped abruptly, nearly turning a circle with his frightened lunge.

Crack. Another shot. Chauncey whirled and whinnied in terror. Almost unseated, Cassie clutched the saddlehorn to regain her balance. Even though alarmed, she was glad no one had seen her grab the leather.

"Easy. Easy," she said. The frightened animal settled into nervous prancing and Cassie patted his neck lightly murmuring calming phrases. She looked around for the source of the gunshots and said aloud, "Where is that damn fool?"

A low chuckle sounded behind her. Still attempting to calm the uneasy Chauncey, she turned slowly.

"Grabbin' leather?" Standing in a narrow clearing was a tall slim man, his back to the sun. The shadows from the trees combined with the wide brim of his hat hid his face except for the amused smile which played around his lips.

CHAPTER FOUR

"TREVOR AUSTIN!" Cassie's heart gave a little glad thump as he stepped into the sun, still smiling like an idiot. "What do you think you're doing? I could have been thrown."

"I was quail hunting. It wasn't until after the second shot that I realized you were so close." He walked toward her, rifle lowered. In the full sun his eyes blazed like facets of a well-cut gem.

"I'm sorry I frightened your horse." The amused smile again darted across his face. "But it was rather comical seeing an accomplished horsewoman grabbing for the saddlehorn like a city slicker." Something about his grin was infectious and Cassie smiled in response.

His eyes, crinkling at the corners when he smiled, matched the hue of his denim jacket. Their color reminded her of a deep swimming hole where she'd once played. The water had been a dark indigo, just hinting at the pool's hidden depth. "Apology accepted, Mr. Austin. Please refrain from any such actions in the future." She spoke with exaggerated formality.

"My, my, my. Are you going to invite me to tea?" His grin widened, revealing a streak of wickedness which Cassie found both attractive and maddening.

"I guess I deserved that," Cassie replied, amused by his ready flippancy. "Truce?" she asked, thrusting out her hand.

"Absolutely." He walked slowly toward her and when he reached her he enclosed her hand in both of his.

"Actually, I rode out here looking for you. Coming upon the quail was just a stroke of good luck. Well, maybe not so good. I missed. I called your house, and when Julia said you'd gone riding, I thought we could ride together. There's a place I'd like to show you."

Why not? Cassie thought. At least if they were riding he couldn't stand so dangerously close. "Where?" she asked.

"Up in the mountains. It will take about two hours to get there. But," he added, waving his hand toward his horse, a tall dark bay standing quietly ground-tied a few yards away, "I've packed a lunch, a blanket and a couple of warm jackets. What do you say?"

"You're confident, aren't you?" Cassie couldn't help smiling. He had evidently gone to a lot of trouble for her.

"I wouldn't say I'm confident. More like optimistic. So, shall we go?"

"Okay," Cassie agreed.

Trevor took Chauncey's reins and led them over to his horse. "This is Beau. Best horse that ever lived. He'll stand here like this for hours and I can practically go to sleep on his back. Doesn't spook at anything."

"Sounds like a regular stop and go horse. Chauncey's not quite so calm."

"I noticed," Trevor said with a teasing tone. "Takes quite a feisty horse to unseat a rider like you."

Cassie blushed slightly, remembering her earlier embarrassment and with a sheepish grin said, "I'm working on him. But he's still young. He's really a pussycat under all this youthful spirit."

"Sure, sure, that's what they all say." He tossed the reins over Beau's head, not bothering to pick them up as he swung easily into the saddle.

"You think you have all the answers, don't you?" Cassie laughed and swatted at him with her hat. Then they both laughed because Chauncey shied at her sudden motion while Beau stood placidly as though nothing had happened.

"I rest my case," Trevor retorted.

They rode together in relative silence at first. The massive snow-capped Grand Tetons were visible between the trees. Wispy clouds sat above their glacier covered peaks like the halo over the head of an angel. The mountains were so large and formidable that they looked inviting and ominous at the same time.

As they entered a large meadow Trevor pointed to the foothills of Estrella Mountain. "That's where we're headed," he told her.

As they continued to ride he began pointing out particular mesas or meadows, telling Cassie a little bit of their history. For some reason she couldn't fathom, she feigned interest, not reminding him that she already knew the region well. But when he again pointed to the Estrella Mountain and told Cassie it was named after an early settler, she could contain herself no longer.

"I know," she replied. "You've forgotten. I grew up here. Until just a few years ago all this land we're riding on belonged to my family."

"This land belonged to your family? I thought this was Jake Bradford's land."

"It is now." An unwelcome bitterness edged her voice. "He swindled my father out of it. But I'm going to get it back. Cambridge Stables was once the largest breeding ranch in the Northwest. It will be again."

"So you're a modern day Scarlett O'Hara, trying to save her Tara?" Trevor was transparently trying to lighten the conversation but only succeeded in irritating Cassie. She hadn't meant to discuss such a personal matter with him and didn't quite now how to handle the ugly emotions which were once again threatening to emerge.

"Damn it, Trevor. It's not funny and I don't want to discuss it any more."

"I always seem to step on your toes, don't I pretty lady? I'm sorry." He reached his hand across the gap between them and ruffled her hair. His touch was soothing, but she brushed his hand away.

"It's okay," she muttered, replacing her hat so he couldn't touch her hair again. "Let's just change the subject."

"Suits me," he replied much too cheerfully for Cassie. "We're entering some rugged terrain anyway. Hang on to your saddlehorn." Again that wicked smile and then he guided his horse through a hole in the brush.

Past this opening was a narrow trail, bordered on each side by evergreen trees. Their high branches met overhead, creating an enclosed tunnel. A thick carpet of fallen needles covered the ground, which was bare of snow despite a recent storm. The forest floor must be totally protected by the trees, she thought. Indeed, the coverage was so dense that it filtered out any direct sunshine, reducing the light under the trees to a dim glow. "However did you find this trail?" Cassie asked, astounded by its wild perfection.

"I was out hunting and my dog disappeared into that hole through the branches. When he didn't come back right away, I walked in after him, and there it was. But the best is yet to come. Just follow me."

They rode without talking, single-file, along the narrow, steep, rocky trail. The dim light, snapping needles and rustling wind put Chauncey on edge. His ears were drawn forward in peak alertness, and Cassie concentrated on reducing his anxiety.

Soon they passed the densest foliage and stronger light filtered onto the trail. "We're almost there." Trevor shouted and kicked Beau into a lope. Although uncomfortable running Chauncey on unfamiliar terrain, Cassie urged him into a fast trot because Trevor had moved out of sight. Then she rode into the clearing. It was at the top of the mountain: a large meadow covered with beautiful, clean white snow. Small ice crystals had formed on its unsullied crust and they glistened in the sun, creating an incredible fairy wonderland. A pencil-thin trail snaked through the winter carpet and she slowed Chauncey into a cautious walk as she looked around, her mouth suddenly opening in amazement. She uttered an involuntary, "Oh."

At the far edge of the clearing stood a small log cabin. A brick fireplace located at one end contrasted picturesquely with the natural wood. A covered porch ran the full length of its front. Snow covered both the roof and the dormant vines which clung to the porch railing. *A gingerbread house,* Cassie thought. *What a lovely little gingerbread house.* She wondered who lived here.

As she rode up to the cabin, Trevor reappeared, carrying an armload of firewood from behind the house. "Isn't it something?" he asked cheerfully. "What do you say we go in, get warm and have a bite to eat?"

His words reminded Cassie of her cold hands and feet and complaining stomach. She dismounted, removed Chauncey's bridle and loosened his cinch. Trevor gestured toward a small corral to the right of the house where Beau was already standing. Cassie put Chauncey there as well, then followed Trevor into the house.

A small butane stove with a sack of provisions beside it sat on a counter at the far right end. Except for a table, two wooden chairs and a small parsons bench, the room was empty. Trevor busied himself with the stove, and in a minute a delicious aroma filled the cabin.

"Oh coffee! How wonderful," Cassie exclaimed. "Is it ready yet?"

Trevor smiled. "It won't be long. And in the meantime, I'll get a fire going. All the comforts of home, don't you think?" He gestured around the room.

"It's enchanting." She glanced at the flowered curtains. They looked new and the windows were clean. There weren't any cobwebs in the corners either, and the exposed log walls were free from the debris of time. The room looked well cared for. "Does somebody live here? It's so clean."

Trevor put a match to the kindling he laid down, then looked up from where he squatted by the fireplace. He had removed his hat, and his hair curled over his forehead. "It's been abandoned a long time. It was a mess of cobwebs and dust when I first found it, but a little elbow grease did wonders."

"Amazing. And you do windows, too." She walked over to the counter. A pump jutted above a sink. She touched its handle. "Does it work?"

"It didn't at first, but I gave it a little oil and now it's as good as new." He placed a handful of tinder on the brightly burning kindling, then stood up, and shook out a blanket, which he placed on the floor. "Voilà, our picnic," he announced.

"How long do you think this cabin has been here?" Cassie asked curiously.

"I did a little research after I discovered it. I didn't want other people to find out about it, so I went to the library quietly and looked up some records on Mesquite history."

"And...?"

"And...what I found was very interesting." He moved closer and Cassie found herself staring at his lips. They were full and sensual, contrasting with his almost austere face. They seemed softer, more inviting than they had ever seemed before.

"Interesting?" she murmured. His eyes seemed darker, but afire with electricity. She leaned forward to get a better look. A trick of the light, perhaps.

"Yes." He lifted his hand and trailed his fingers through her hair. A delicious feeling of warmth invaded her body. Could something that feels this good do any harm? She tilted her head, inviting his lips to smother hers. Silence permeated the air. The only sounds came from the soft rustling of wind in the trees and the occasional cry of a bird. She swayed forward, her breasts lightly brushing against his wide chest. His hand slid to the back of her neck and he exerted a gentle pressure, pulling her closer.

A piercing whinny shattered the silence. A whinny of absolute terror.

Trevor and Cassie sprang apart and ran for the door. Cassie reached the door first, spied the rifle Trevor had left there earlier and snatched it up before bolting down the stairs.

Cassie looked around nervously. She couldn't see anything, but the horses were very agitated. Chauncey was pacing back and forth, rearing frantically, nostrils dilated, eyes wild. Even the imperturbable Beau was anxiously seeking an exit, snorting with fear.

A rustle came from the nearby brush. Cassie turned toward the sound and raised the rifle. Peering from the brush were two pair of amber eyes over long buckskin muzzles. Coyotes. The rest of their bodies were nearly invisible in the darkness of the dense forest growth. She took aim and pulled the trigger. When the echoes of the discharge subsided, nothing was left in the brush but a few swaying leaves and an empty hole.

"Nice shot." Cassie turned to see Trevor behind her. Lost in fear for her stallion's safety, she'd forgotten about him. All her hopes and dreams for Cambridge Stables were wrapped up in Chauncey. She shuddered, considering what his death or injury might mean.

"Do you think I hit one of them, Trevor?" She lowered the rifle and let it hang at her side.

"I don't think so. I didn't hear a yelp." He took Cassie's arm and led her toward the corral. "And for sure you didn't kill it. I don't think they'll be back, but let's move the horses to the shed just to be safe."

They checked the horses closely for any injuries that might have occurred during their frantic run. Both were fine, and Trevor led them from the corral to a shed near the back of the cabin.

Again, Cassie was impressed. The shed was like a small manger, with four open stalls, two on each side. "Where did this come from?" She pointed at a carefully formed pile of dried grass and grains in the aisle between the stalls.

"I harvested it during the summer." He tied Beau into one of the stalls. "I like to come up here for three, four days at a time. It's too much trouble to haul food for my horse, so I just made it myself."

"Resourceful, aren't you?" Cassie asked as she placed Chauncey into the stall next to Beau. She picked up some hay and placed it in the empty feed bins.

"I used to be a Boy Scout." Cassie looked up to see Trevor sporting that wicked grin. Although it was sometimes irritating, this time it pleased her. She remembered the kiss that almost happened, regretting that it hadn't been carried through. "But you're pretty resourceful yourself. I didn't know you could handle a rifle."

"My papa taught me to shoot straight and ride tall." Cassie smiled with mock self-satisfaction and took a small bow.

"He did quite a job. I'm impressed." Trevor placed a companionable arm over Cassie's shoulder and guided her back into the cabin. "Let's go get that coffee."

It was the best cup of coffee Cassie had ever tasted. Lunch was wonderful, too. Trevor had brought cheese, roast beef and pita bread. They were both so hungry that they ate two sandwiches apiece. "I like to see a woman with a good appetite," Trevor teased.

There were homemade chocolate chip cookies for dessert. "Homemade at the bakery," Trevor quipped, and while they ate he told her the history of the cabin.

"Apparently, at one time in the late eighteenth century, two families warred for control of Mesquite Valley. For several generations they slaughtered each other's cattle, wounded each other's wranglers and, occasionally, killed one another. Then one day, the eldest son of one family, Tom Whitney, asked the head of the other family, Peter Ortega, if he could marry his daughter Betsy. He was bitterly refused.

"But young lovers are not easily thwarted. Betsy had listened from the top of the stairs. She slipped out through the kitchen to a waiting horse and rode to meet Tom."

"Then what happened?" Cassie asked.

"They rode to a nearby town and got married, anyway. What did you think happened?"

"I thought maybe her father caught them and killed Tom."

"He did his best. But Tom and Betsy had made their plans well. They rode high in the mountains and while the weather was warm they began to build this cabin. Both sets of parents hunted far and wide for them, but the one thing that never entered their minds was that these spoiled children would hide in the mountains.

"Then Betsy became pregnant. She had a difficult labor and after the baby, a son, was born, she was very weak. Tom feared for her life, and despite Betsy's protests, he rode to his father for help. At first Tom's father refused but relented when Tom reminded him of his new grandson. Along with the ranch doctor they rode to the cabin, and with proper care, Betsy recovered.

"Tom thanked his father who then refused to leave without Tom, Betsy and the boy, saying the range wars had to stop before the Whitneys and Ortegas began killing their own kin. When they returned, Tom's father took the child and rode to see Peter Ortega. The old man became enraged and denied any relationship to the child until, suddenly, the baby gurgled. Peter stopped midsentence and stared down. Round blue eyes, much like Betsy's, stared back. The baby smiled and Peter held a finger out for him to grasp. He stood there for a long time, his mammoth finger encased in the baby's small hand. Finally he spoke. 'Perhaps we can talk,' he said."

"And so a little child made peace." Cassie blinked back tears, a little embarrassed. After all, she was a modern woman who didn't cry at romantic tales.

"Yes," said Trevor. "A Romeo and Juliet story, only with a happy ending."

Cassie smiled. "First Scarlett O'Hara, now Romeo and Juliet. Do you equate everything to some romantic tale?"

"Maybe I do," he replied thoughtfully. "We modern folk are so immersed in our own problems that we think no one else has lived a life like ours. But if you read enough, you begin to realize that all people have essentially the same experiences—disappointment, joy, obstacles, triumphs, love, hate, birth and death. It's only our reactions that are different."

"You're quite a philosopher, Trevor." She plucked the blanket while she talked, puzzled by her discomfort with the direction of the conversation. "Have you ever thought about becoming a writer?"

"As a matter of fact, I have. That's why I'm in Mesquite. I'm taking a little time off from my real life to see if I have a novel in me. I'm basing it on the Whitney and Ortega story."

"So what do you do in your 'real life'?" Her uneasiness increased. She remembered that twice before she'd pursued the same line of questioning and never received a complete answer. She felt this time was different and that the answer could be terribly dangerous.

"I'm an attorney. As I told you, my practice was in San Francisco before I moved here." Was she imagining it, or did Trevor seem as uncomfortable as she was?

"Why Mesquite?"

There was a long silence. Trevor appeared to be carefully considering his answer. They had been reclining on the blanket. Now he sat up, looking directly into Cassie's eyes. "I think there's something you need to know." Cassie felt a sudden heaviness in her stomach. "I'm here because Jake Bradford asked me to handle some of his legal affairs. They don't take that much time, so I'm able to write. I live at Bradford Ranch."

Cassie looked at Trevor in stunned silence. "You work for Jake? Live on the Bradford Ranch?"

He nodded grimly.

The heaviness in her stomach turned to solid rock. The bright room suddenly became dim and gloomy, even though the same sunlight still streamed through the window. No! Her mind raced for a hundred solutions to this problem. But none was forthcoming. He had spoken the naked truth—a truth that meant he could not be part of her life.

She stood up. "It's time I was going, Trevor." She collected her hat and jacket and walked out of the cabin. She would never, ever, see him again.

But she heard Trevor coming after her. "Wait, Cassie. Why is this so upsetting to you? It's just a job." He had caught up with her and was now grasping her arm.

She wrenched free. "Jake Bradford treated my father like dirt, Trevor. Now my father is dead. Do you think I can forgive that? I want nothing to do with him or anyone associated with him. So stay away from me, Trevor."

"Why? What has he done, Cassie. He bought your father's property honestly. Are you angry because a Bradford instead of a Cambridge is now king of the mountains?" Cassie saw Trevor's eyes turning to steel, reminding her of the cold gray she'd once seen in Jake Bradford's eyes.

"It's more than that. This is not a territory dispute. I have reason to believe that Jake either killed my father or arranged to have him killed. I can't prove it yet but if I ever do, by God, I'll nail him." Cassie's disappointment had vanished and was now replaced by all the blazing anger she'd felt since seeing her father's broken body lying in a hospital bed.

"That's absolutely crazy, Cassie. You don't even know Jake Bradford. He's not capable of murder." Cassie could see Trevor's clenched fists. His shoulders were stiff, and he looked as if he could barely check a desire to shake her.

His posture enraged her further and she clenched her own fists in response. "I know him well enough. I may have been a child but I remember the way he abused Papa. If that wasn't a man capable of murder..." There weren't words to express the depth of depravity that Cassie thought Jake capable of.

She whirled away in frustration and stomped to the shed. Trevor followed at her heels.

"There are things you don't understand about that, Cassie. You were just a kid. Besides, that was over twenty years ago."

"Don't try to defend him," Cassie spat back as she untied Chauncey, led him out of the shed and tightened the cinch. "You work for him, and as long as you do, I can never see you again." With those final words, she was securely in the saddle and, kicking Chauncey, she moved him into a canter across the snow-covered yard.

"You're a crazy woman, Cassie. Absolutely crazy."

With an act of extreme will, Cassie tried to blot out Trevor's shouted accusation. But the words rang in her ears long after his voice was silent.

Once on the trail, she halted Chauncey. In her haste to leave, she'd forgone bridling, but Chauncey wasn't a horse one rode with a simple halter, especially in the agitated condition created by her rough handling and the narrow trail. Goose bumps erupted on her arms as she slid the bridle over Chauncey's head. It was now late afternoon and the air was quite cold in the shadowy forest tunnel. She pulled her jacket from the saddlehorn and slipped into it. Immediately she realized something was wrong.

The shoulder seams came nearly to her elbows and the cuffs hung several inches below her hands. She'd grabbed the wrong jacket. She cursed her stupidity but there was no way she was riding back to retrieve her own, so she remounted Chauncey and rode home, enclosed in Trevor's jacket. The faint scent of his aftershave mingled with the fragrance of the pine, making it impossible to erase Trevor Austin from her mind.

CHAPTER FIVE

"IT'S JUST NOT WORKING, Cassie. Now he wants us to rebuild the entire set." Al was understandably upset. The client he referred to was Sammy Cohen, the owner of a Denver carpet store, who had previously done his own television commercials, using a folksy image for his family owned store. He'd come to C&C because he felt the advertising was no longer effective, but then he'd resisted every attempt to modernize his format.

"He already wants our choreography and music changed. Now this. It will cost a fortune if we have to eat those expenses." The agitation in Al's voice amused Cassie. He was usually so calm and collected. But this was his first venture into client relations and he was obviously stepping out of his comfort zone.

"Stay cool, Al. There's a way out. This isn't the first client to balk. What reason did he give for wanting these changes?"

"He said he wanted glamour, not New Age glitz. The way he said 'glitz' you would have thought it was an obscene word."

"Let me think." Cassie paused for a moment. Glitz. Glamour. There was something significant in those words. "Wait, Al. I think I've got it. Have you changed the choreography yet?"

"No. It's a mime-type thing. The dancers oohing and aahing over the soft carpet, the bright colors. I like it. I like the set, too. It's built of layered geometric shapes covered in various types of carpet. Very space age.''

"How are the dancers dressed?''

"Trendy. Miniskirts, spiked hair.''

"And the music?'' Cassie scratched her head. Yes, the idea was beginning to click.

"Blues.''

"Blues? Yeah, I like that. But try this, Al. Instead of blues music, use a forties tune with lots of wailing saxophone. Dress the dancers in elegant clothing from that period. Pompadour hairdos. Flashy hats. Things like that. Don't change anything else and run a trial tape. See how he likes it.''

"Do you think it will work, Cassie?''

"From what I know of the client, he's very conservative and he grew up in the forties. Probably still attached to that era. Also he loved doing his commercials and is most likely reluctant to give them up. He'll need a powerful reason to do that. Try it. A trial tape will cost a lot less than a new set and choreography.''

"You bet it will. Your idea sounds good. Sure beats anything I've come up with.'' Al breathed a sigh of relief, and Cassie could picture him, hunched over the phone, pushing up his glasses. This wasn't the side of advertising that he loved best.

"You would have thought of something. I have faith in you,'' Cassie told him.

"I'm glad someone does. When are you coming back, Cassie doll?'' Al laughed as he asked the question. He knew darn well Cassie wasn't coming back for quite a while.

"As soon as Cambridge Stables is on its feet.'' Cassie laughed also. It was good talking to Al. She felt at home here, back on the ranch, but she missed the excitement of her job, too. Speaking with Al made her feel she was still involved.

"How are things going there?"

"Moving along."

"Good. I'll be so-o-o happy when you come back."

"I know, Al. I love you, too."

They chatted for a few more minutes. Then Cassie hung up and returned to the courtyard where she'd been sitting before she answered the phone. Julia was at school, teaching, and Cassie had already cleaned the barn and exercised the horses. She sat on a redwood chaise and picked up a contract she'd been reviewing. She looked around and took a deep breath of appreciation.

Spring was finally coming to the Tetons. Brave flowers peeked their heads above the thin blanket of snow, shaking off the sleepiness of winter to welcome the upcoming rebirth. Sprigs of green adorned the barren branches of bushes and trees and the evergreens had shed their white winter coats.

She watched a squirrel scurrying to snatch small crumbs from the leaf-strewn brick patio, the contract completely forgotten. She felt like the wildlife herself, just now awakening from a long slumber. The cloak of grief was beginning to lift from her shoulders and vigor was returning to her body and soul.

Julia and she had worked hard during the winter months, repairing damaged walls, hanging wallpaper, replacing tile, varnishing and painting. She was proud of their work, but as she looked around once again, the magnitude of the remaining repairs hit her full in the face. She could fix damaged posts and broken shutters and prune the foliage. But the ceilings in the house and barns leaked badly and required a roofer. The crumbling porch needed replacement and the corral fences needed to be rebuilt, preferably with steel piping. That would be expensive.

Things would go a little easier if all those pesky problems would stop popping up. First the water line to the horse barn had snapped. For several days they'd hauled water by hand until Mesquite's lone plumber arrived. Next a large tree branch had fallen on the hay shed, breaking one of the supporting posts. After each accident, Aunt Julia had counseled her to sell.

Cassie sighed. She loved her aunt dearly, but she wished that Julia were more supportive of her efforts to restore Cambridge Stables. She seemed to think Cassie's ambitions were little more than a farfetched dream.

She redirected her attention to the contract. She was meeting with a breeder today in town, then registering Chauncey for the Cheyenne quarter-horse show. Winter was over and it was time to show him again and keep those breeding fees coming. Without the fees Cambridge Stables could never be restored. Her savings were dwindling fast.

But if all went well this season, she could make the needed repairs and possibly afford a good mare by winter. And maybe, just maybe, she would find a way to get her property back. Today's meeting should be a good start in that direction.

Recalling she had an appointment soon, snapped Cassie out of her reverie. She hastily finished reviewing the contract, then ran upstairs to get dressed. The breeder was a crusty old man, and Cassie knew he wouldn't be pleased at the changes she planned to request. She'd better hurry. Being late would not make the negotiations any easier.

A FEW HOURS LATER, Cassie walked out of the Mesquite Lodge in high spirits. The meeting had gone well. At first it had seemed they'd reached an impasse. The breeder wanted Chauncey to stay at his ranch for three months, and with the peak show season beginning, Cassie knew she couldn't allow that. Chauncey was in training for cutting-horse competition, and the Golden Cup Futurity, the biggest show of the season, was in July. A three-month hole in the schedule would be disastrous. But she could tell the breeder was adamant. He wanted his six mares in foal to a champion stallion in time for his August auction. And on Cassie's part, at two thousand each, the stud fees were a powerful short-term incentive—twelve thousand dollars would pay for a lot of repairs.

But Cassie was thinking long term and knew how important the Golden Cup was to both Chauncey's value and the reputation of Cambridge Stables. Her father hadn't shown Chauncey consistently. With a few more ribbons his stud fee would increase considerably. She shared these concerns with the breeder, grateful for the negotiating skills she'd acquired during her years in the advertising business.

The man expressed little interest in Cassie's problems, but she persisted. "Perhaps we can work out a compromise that can save me time and you some money."

He'd been packing up his briefcase, but at her words tilted his head in interest. "Tell me more."

"We'll bring your mares to Cambridge Stables. I'll feed them, exercise them and arrange for transportation. In addition, I'll reduce the stud fee to fifteen hundred a mare. Your foals will have their champion sire and I get my show time, both by August. We both win." She smiled in what she'd hoped was her most disarming way.

After a moment of scowling hesitation the breeder returned her smile with an outthrust hand. "You've got a deal, young lady. I never thought a child could get the best of me in business, but it looks as if I was wrong."

So, although twelve thousand dollars now became nine, both purposes were served. Cassie was pleased with the deal and felt so excited that she skipped down the exposed log steps of Mesquite Lodge and nearly ran to her truck.

As she climbed inside she recalled the day Trevor had picked her up in it. A small pang of loss punctured her euphoria. Annoyed that Trevor constantly trespassed in her mind, she was determined to banish all thoughts of him. She had more important things to think about. She couldn't wait to get home and tell Julia to call the roofers. Better yet, she decided, she'd stop at their office in town on her way home.

As she drove down the hill leading away from the Lodge, she could view the entire Mesquite Valley. The change during her twelve-year absence still startled her. Mesquite had been little more than a collection of shabby buildings during her childhood. A school, a post office and a run-down hospital had been the town's principal buildings. Carousing cowboys would drive to Jackson Hole to seek their excitement. But times had changed. Jackson had become a tourist trap, and now Mesquite attracted campers and skiers anxious to escape the maddening crowd. But it seemed as if the maddening crowd had followed them.

Now the main street sported a rustic Western look. Lots of exposed rail, uncut logs and covered wooden sidewalks housed designer clothing stores, ski shops, art galleries and quaint little restaurants. The twentieth century had arrived in Mesquite, and Cassie wasn't sure she liked it.

As she drove down Center Street she noticed a silver-blue Porsche parked in front of the hotel. She frowned. Despite his attempts to contact her, she'd managed to avoid Trevor during the past two months, at least in person. But he still plagued her mind. Memories of that tempting, unconsummated kiss intruded at the most unlikely and unwelcome moments.

The season was too late for skiing and too early for camping, so she was able to find a parking spot easily. Getting out of her truck, she hurried along the wooden boardwalk, her boot-heels clicking, heading toward the construction office. As she passed a deep foyer leading to Chez Teton, a small croissant-and-sandwich shop, she paid little attention to the man standing there and even less to the sounds of his footsteps following behind her.

Suddenly a steely arm enclosed her body, a callused hand muffling her instinctive scream. She struggled with every ounce of her strength, but the man was too strong and pulled her into the foyer, muttering, "Shut up. Shut up."

She shuddered as the man pushed her against the wall, forcing her face to brush the rough-hewn wood. Pulling both arms behind her, he viciously held her wrists together with one leathery hand while yanking her hair with the other. He smelled of strong tobacco, cheap wine and sweat. Revulsion seized her and she couldn't breathe.

*My God. He's going to rape me. Here in Mesquite.
In broad daylight.*

She made another attempt to escape his hold, but he
jerked her wrists upward, sending searing pain through
her shoulders.

Ignoring the pain and getting a grip on her fear, she
gave a high backward kick, aiming to immobilize him.
Angrily, he slammed her against the wall, yanking her
hair until she whimpered. Was he going to break her
neck? Kill her? Suddenly she was numb. No one could
see them in here. Surely rape was inevitable. Even
death.

But instead of heatedly fumbling with her clothes, he
pulled her head back to his mouth. "There are people
who don't want you here," he growled in a whisky
voice, his putrid breath blowing in her ear. "Lots of
people. If you don't leave Mesquite, you'll live to regret it."

He laughed, a short humorless bark. "Or maybe you
won't live," he added, shoving her savagely out of the
foyer onto the walkway. Cassie landed with a thud,
sprawling on the wooden sidewalk, and before she
could regain her footing her assailant disappeared.

A woman ran to her aid. "Are you hurt?" she asked
as she helped Cassie to her feet. Cassie shook her head.
She had a few splinters in her hand but otherwise she
was unharmed.

"It looked like that man pushed you." The woman
wrinkled her brow. "Do you want me to call the police?"

"No, no," Cassie replied quickly, puzzled by her
own words. "I just tripped. I didn't realize the restaurant was closed. That man must have made the same
mistake."

"You're sure?" the woman asked uncertainly, pointing to a couple who'd just opened the restaurant door. But when Cassie insisted it was an accident, the woman finally shrugged and walked away. Her errand forgotten, Cassie headed back to her truck. She knew where the warning had come from and, with a flash of insight, she knew how to stop it.

TREVOR LEANED against the ancient Formica counter in the coffee shop of the Center Hotel, chatting amicably with the waitress. She was a nice girl and she faintly reminded him of Cassie. He was immediately irritated at the comparison. When would he ever rid his mind of that wretched woman?

At that moment he looked up and, with a start, saw Cassie virtually sprinting through the lobby of the hotel. His heart gave a little jump, and he didn't know if it stemmed from delight or from the sight of her disheveled appearance.

Her suit was covered with dust, her blouse partially untucked in the front, and her curls were in wild disarray.

As his eyes moved toward her face he caught the cold fury in her onyx eyes. He didn't like that look. Twice before—at the funeral and again at the cabin—he'd seen her angry, and the recollection almost obscured his memory of other times—times when those dark eyes had widened in surprise, sparkled with amusement and grown misty with desire. He liked those memories a lot better.

He wanted to avoid her. He was uncomfortably embarrassed when he recalled how foolishly he'd ranted during their argument at the cabin. He'd never met a woman before who could reduce him to such a state.

But it was obvious she was heading straight toward him. Better to beat her to the punch.

Informing the waitress that he'd be back, he stepped down from the counter and walked into the lobby. Cassie continued in his direction, fury on her face. He suppressed an urge to grab her and smother those pouty lips with his—that beautiful hundred-pound keg of dynamite looked as if she'd been through enough for one day. He wondered what had happened to her.

This time her fury was contained. "Trevor. Would you step into the courtyard with me. I'd like to speak to you." Soft words edged with steely anger. He agreed and they walked in silence through the back lobby door. The courtyard was quiet and empty.

"What happened to you? You look like you've been rolling in the streets."

"That's an apt description." Still speaking in a cool, ice-laden tone, Cassie quickly described the events in the foyer of Chez Teton. Trevor's fist tightened as she spoke. Who would do such a thing to Cassie? He found himself vitally interested in knowing the answer to that question.

He was about to tell Cassie she could count on his help when she jabbed a finger into his chest, her tenuous control breaking. "Please take a message to Jake for me. Tell him that he can't chase me out of Mesquite with any corny get-out-of-town routine."

"What are you talking about?" Once again, she was throwing him off guard with her insane accusations. He placed a placating hand on her shoulder.

"You know what I'm talking about. Jake is the only one who would have a reason to do something like this. That man wasn't interested in robbery or rape. He just wanted to scare me. So just tell Jake it won't work, and while you're at it, keep your hands off me." She shook his hand away.

As she spoke a large lock of hair fell onto her brow, nearly brushing her inky eyes. "Come on, Cassie." He used his best soothing lawyerly tone, but his words were uncompromising. "You blame everything on Jake. Losing your land, your father's death. Now this. Next I suppose you'll be blaming sick horses and mechanical failure on him. What would Jake have to gain by doing these things?"

"I know what I know, Trevor. Just kindly pass those words along." She turned and started to walk away, her shoulders straight and proud.

Trevor never knew what overcame him. One moment he stood watching her walk away. The next moment he'd trapped her in his arms, possessing her mouth with a brutality that shocked him even as he experienced the first heady taste of her tightly pressed lips.

She twisted her head under his mouth and pounded at him with ineffectual fists, but her struggle only fed his desire. He crushed her closer, wanting to merge with her body and be rewarded by her willing response. With a searching tongue he invaded her rigid lips, feeling the smoothness of her even teeth. Her breath quickened at the intrusion. Her fists ceased pummeling. Her head became still. Then her body relaxed and she seemed to melt against him. Tentatively her lips parted, allowing full penetration of his probing tongue. Suddenly, she exploded beneath his urgent lips.

He tasted her hungrily, welcoming her fiery response and released his bruising hold. He trailed one hand slowly down her perfect back and over her round buttocks. She shuddered deliciously at his touch. Releasing her lips, he trailed his tongue along the curve of her slender neck. Her skin was salty and she smelled faintly of dust and spicy cologne. The taste of her was like caviar and he wanted more.

When her hands moved sensuously up his chest and entered the open collar of his shirt, exquisite impulses shot through his body and he groaned with pleasure. Her ragged breathing told him everything he longed to know. She did want him. As much as he wanted her.

With a gliding motion her hands twined around his neck and she pulled his lips violently back to hers. They were moist and sweet, sweeter still in aggression than in resistance. She parted them greedily as though she could not taste enough of him. Her supple body molded against his and her thigh slid between his parted legs. His loins ignited. He stroked her with hungry fingers, clutching at her rough denim skirt, easing it upward, aching for the feel of her skin. All awareness had vanished except for the bittersweet agony in his groin, the fragrance of her hair and the smoothness of her skin.

Releasing those lips with a reluctant moan, he stroked her wild hair and whispered hoarsely, "Cassie. Beautiful Cassie."

She pulled away as if shot and whirled from Trevor's arms.

"My God!" She backed up slowly, her dark eyes stricken. "I can't believe... This can't be happening." She shook her head, sending curls flying in all directions. "This was a mistake. I shouldn't have come here."

Her protesting words brought Trevor back to his senses. Cassie would never let go of her crazy ideas about Jake. Why couldn't he let go of his need to possess her? It was becoming an obsession. It could never work. Why had he allowed himself to . . . ?

He ruffled his hair in frustration. "You're right, Cassie. It was a mistake. But trust me—there are things about this you don't understand. You're dead wrong about Jake."

"Trust you?" Her voice, hoarse and laced with unbearable sadness, gave Trevor sudden insight into how deeply her imagined betrayal hurt. "What reason do I have to trust you?" She turned and fled into the lobby.

Trevor didn't chase her. Never in his life had he forced himself upon a woman. But something about Cassie drove him to ridiculous behavior. He had to stay away from her. Her fiery response to his kiss told him, unmistakably, that her need matched his own. But the tug of war between her desire and her loyalty to her father's memory would make any relationship between them a living hell. Realization of what he'd just done plunged him into a swamp of self-loathing. And he'd only told her half the truth. He didn't know how to tell her the rest. He knew if he ever revealed the entire story, she would loathe him forever. He laughed bitterly, realizing that Cassie already half-loathed him. He wished he felt the same about her.

THE HEAT of her body was unbearable. The heat of shame. The heat of unconsummated lust. Cassie stumbled to her truck, barely aware that her hair was tumbling around her shoulders and her chest heaving with gasping breaths.

She fumbled in her jacket for her keys. There was a comb in there also. She raked it angrily through her tangled hair as she climbed into the truck, wincing at each painful tug. The discomfort of the comb was an almost welcome diversion from the pain in her heart.

She flopped in the driver's seat and turned the rear-view mirror toward her. Her breath had lost its ragged edge, but the sight of her reflection caused her to gasp. Her hair hung in a wild mess of curls. Her face was flushed and splotchy. She looked as if she'd been ravished and wished she had cold water to splash on her face.

But what shamed her the most was the intensity of her hunger. She had wanted his kiss. Wanted it with a passion she'd never known before. She sank into remorse and humiliation. She had betrayed her father's memory. No amount of rationalization could make it otherwise.

Disgusted, she turned the key in the ignition, backed out onto the street and drove to the highway.

It must never happen again.

During the drive home, she willed her mind to be still, trying to banish all thoughts of Trevor and of what that mindless kiss had done to her father's memory. But as she passed Miller's Curve she wondered what thoughts had raced through Papa's mind the night he drove off the edge.

CASSIE AWOKE WITH A START. The sun streamed across her bed. Vaguely she remembered shutting off the alarm several hours earlier. She looked at the clock through bleary eyes and saw that it was nearly nine o'clock. The tantalizing aroma of coffee drifted into her bedroom.

A steaming shower dispelled her stupor, and pulling on jeans and a light T-shirt, she headed down the stairs, puzzled to hear no hungry whickers coming from the barn.

"Good morning, Cassie." Julia sat at the kitchen table, the morning paper spread on the table. "Sleeping kind of late, aren't we?"

"Yes. I'm beat this morning. Every time I fell asleep my nightmare woke me." She ran her hands through her hair with a weary gesture. "Why didn't you wake me? The horses need feeding."

"It's Saturday. Everyone should sleep in one day a week. Besides, I heard you come up the stairs last night. It was after one o'clock. I thought you needed the rest, so I fed the animals early this morning." Julia wore a worried expression. "You need to take time to relax. I wouldn't be surprised if overwork wasn't the cause of those bad dreams."

"There's so much bookwork, Aunt Julia. With everything that needs to be done during the day, night is the only time I have."

"Give some of the work to me, Cass. All work and no play makes Cassie a dull girl."

Cassie wrinkled her nose at Julia's cliché, causing her aunt to smile. "Not original, I know. But that doesn't make it untrue. Give the books to me, Cass. I did them for your father."

Cassie poured a cup of coffee and sat down in a chair opposite Julia. "You have enough to do, Aunt Julia. You keep this big house up all by yourself and you teach all day. You need your sleep, too."

"Well, then, just give me the financials. You keep the breeding and show records."

Julia's offer gave Cassie a warm feeling of appreciation, but she knew her aunt was more prone to overwork than she was. She didn't want to pile on any more. "I'll tell you what. Why don't you do the breeding and show records. They're a lot less work. When your summer vacation comes, we'll renegotiate." She grinned broadly as Julia responded with a mock-horrified expression.

"So when summer comes you'll just heap the work on my poor weary shoulders. Right?"

"Right." Cassie laughed. "Now read your paper and stop nagging me."

Julia returned to her newspaper with a small chuckle and Cassie idly picked up a section, reflecting on her restless night. The nightmares and hard work were not the only things that had kept her awake. She couldn't get Trevor Austin out of her mind. Just thinking about that steamy kiss brought echoes of the strong passion it inflamed and the shame that followed.

Cassie sipped her coffee and tried to read, but her thoughts kept drifting to the afternoon before. Trevor's face floated clearly in her mind. The cleft in his chin. His strong jaw. The endearing crook in his nose. Above them, dominating his features, were his eyes. Deep blue. Like the ocean. Everchanging, now warm, then cold. Now clear, then opaque. What was worse, his kiss lingered and burned her lips as though it were still happening.

"Julia, what do you know about Trevor Austin?"

Cassie's answer was a long silence broken only by the rustling newspaper. She wasn't certain Julia had heard, so she repeated her question.

"Trevor Austin?" Julia, eyes still directed to the page in front of her, sounded uncharacteristically anxious. "Why do you ask?"

"I'm not sure. It's just... Well, I know he works for Jake but he doesn't seem to fit. He doesn't act like the others... like Marvin or Luke or even Jake."

Julia put down the paper and looked up. "Cassie, you know I don't share your feelings about Jake and I won't pretend I do. But even if I did, you need to judge Trevor on his own merit. He was kind to your father and me and I like him very much."

Cassie recognized the truth in those words. Trevor had shown extreme kindness during that terrible period after the accident. For that reason, his association with Jake puzzled Cassie even more. Perhaps it shouldn't have. Her aunt must have had good reason to think well of Jake, even though they'd quarreled over the subject several times. Julia continually told Cassie that she didn't understand the situation. Maybe she didn't understand, but that didn't mean she had to accept a man who had mistreated her papa so badly.

After her restless night, she was in no condition to resume the argument, so she simply responded, "You're right, Aunt Julia, he was helpful. I'll consider what you said." She lifted the cup to her lips.

"Maybe you'd better consider it now." A faint tone of amusement laced Julia's voice as she glanced out the window.

Cassie turned her head in the direction of Julia's gaze and nearly choked on her coffee. Trevor's Porsche was coming up the cinder drive. With shaky hands, Cassie lowered her cup to the table, causing coffee to slosh over the edge.

Torn between urges to race for the door and to hide under her bed, Cassie stared at the drops in dismay. "It's not that bad," Julia said sardonically. She got up to fetch a rag just as the doorbell rang. "You get the door. I'll get the spill."

Cassie's heart raced as she opened the door and saw Trevor standing there looking just as she remembered. She gaped speechlessly at his mouth, remembering the sensations caused by the pressure from those enticing lips. She fought to regain her composure.

"I came to get my jacket," he explained with an open, candid smile.

She tried to glare at him furiously but anger didn't come. Instead, an unwelcome happiness at seeing him there in person, right before her eyes, flooded her.

"Your jacket?" she asked stupidly.

"The one you took with you that day at the cabin. I have yours." He pulled a blue denim jacket from behind his back and waved it in front of her.

"Oh, right." Cassie didn't move but simply stood there, still staring, still feeling very stupid.

Julia came into the entry hall. "Cassie. Aren't you going to invite Trevor inside?"

"Oh, right," Cassie repeated.

"We were just talking about you, Trevor." Julia beamed broadly, a hint of mischief hidden there.

A flush raced to Cassie's face. She shot her aunt a fierce warning look. Julia appeared not to notice. "Won't you have breakfast with us, Trevor?" she asked cheerfully.

That was enough for Cassie. "Aunt Julia, I'm sure Trevor has other things to do today."

"Not at all." A devilish grin betrayed Trevor's enjoyment at Cassie's obvious discomfort. "Breakfast sounds great. I'm starving."

Julia linked her arm through Trevor's, turning to link with Cassie's also. She led them toward the kitchen with a slightly bullying air. Trevor's smile broadened at Julia's domineering attitude, and Cassie, despite all the reasons she shouldn't, became infected with their good humor. Maybe Julia was right. Maybe she should judge Trevor on his own merits. She couldn't deny he had quite a few of them.

Over breakfast, Julia and Trevor chatted easily and seemed unaware of Cassie's relative silence. Confusion dominated her thoughts. She couldn't deny her attraction to Trevor. Her hands were still trembling and she could barely eat. But his own merits or not, she could find no way to resolve her feelings for him. He worked for Jake Bradford. That couldn't be ignored. Of course, he was only Jake's attorney, not a foreman or wrangler who might be intimately involved in Jake's day-to-day affairs. Also, from what she knew, he hadn't worked for Jake very long. Cassie wondered what her father would do in the same circumstances. She wished he were there to give his advice. She missed him terribly.

After breakfast she and Trevor exchanged denim jackets and he asked her to walk with him to his car.

"Confession," he said. "I stopped by to apologize for yesterday. I know I overstepped my bounds and I feel a little foolish right now. The jackets gave me a perfect excuse to see you again. I hope I haven't upset you even more by surprising you." He was stammering uncomfortably and his failing poise delighted Cassie. He seemed more human, less arrogant. "I'd like us to be friends, Cassie, even if we seem to live on opposite sides of the fence. Okay?"

He thrust out his hand, much as he had done on the first day they'd met. Cassie accepted it and even that brief, impersonal touch sent a shock through her body.

"Okay," she said, "but if you ever pull a stunt like that again . . ."

She knew her pretense at being an unwilling victim was fooling neither of them, but it made them both more comfortable.

"My solemn word." His wicked grin nearly melted Cassie's heart, and as she watched him drive away she wondered if she'd ever regret extracting that promise.

CHAPTER SIX

"You started early today, Aunt Julia." Cassie walked through the door of the study where Julia was sitting at a desk posting figures in a ledger. School was out for the summer and she'd now taken over all the bookwork, but Cassie hadn't expected her to be so hard at work so early.

Julia looked up as Cassie entered. "I just wanted to get these last invoices posted. Then we can have breakfast."

"I don't have time. I just came in to get Chauncey's hauling permit and say goodbye." Cassie walked to a wooden filing cabinet, opened a drawer and pulled out a plastic-coated card.

"At least have some toast and coffee, Cassie. You must be exhausted. You're only going to Cheyenne, and the show isn't until the day after tomorrow. Take a moment and rest."

"I'm too excited to be tired, Aunt Julia. Look how much we've accomplished. The barn is restored, the fences have been replaced and our roof doesn't leak anymore. And the best is yet to come. Chauncey has won every futurity this season. I knew I was right about that stallion, Aunt Julia. He's a true champion. Cambridge Stables is on its way back." New energy filled her when she thought of it. She swooped down on her aunt and planted a perky kiss on her cheek. "All this and now the Golden Cup."

"That's wonderful, but you're nothing but skin and bones." Julia pushed up from the desk and walked over to take Cassie's arm. "Come on. A cup of coffee. A slice of toast. You can spare a few minutes." Cassie laughed at her aunt's bossy manner and good-naturedly submitted to Julia's steering hand. They walked together to the kitchen, and Cassie sat at the table while Julia placed a couple of slices of bread in the toaster. The coffee was fresh and the fragrance wafted under Cassie's nose as she drank.

She looked out the window at the pasture beyond. Several mares ambled across the lush grass, their tails flicking lazily in the morning twilight.

The crusty breeder she'd bargained with at the beginning of summer had only been a start. Cassie had already returned two of his mares, both happily with foal, and ten more mares had passed through the stables in these past three months. At full breeding fees. She now had twenty-five thousand stashed away. Enough to purchase a good mare during the fall auctions. She'd kept two of her father's original mares for working purposes but had resolved to use only the best bloodlines for breeding.

"It's going to be a good week, Aunt Julia," she said. Julia set a plate of toast in front of her. She took another sip of coffee, savoring its rich taste, and nibbled at the toast. It tasted good. Everything seemed good today.

"Is Trevor going to be at the Golden Cup?" Julia sat down across from Cassie and question came out of the blue. Cassie's eyebrows shot up.

"Trevor? Why would I see Trevor at the futurity?"

"Well, I heard he might be there. Jake is showing some horses too, and . . . well . . . he called again yesterday," she blurted, looking into Cassie's startled eyes.

Here we go again, Cassie thought. "And you think I should talk to him. Right?" Cassie asked, exasperated. *Would this woman never let go? For some reason, she thought Trevor was a saint.*

"He's a nice boy, Cassie. He seems to think well of you. Why would he keep calling otherwise? You're not giving him any encouragement."

"You're right, Aunt Julia. He is nice. But no matter how I turn it over in my head, I can't accept his relationship with Jake. It would be disloyal to Papa. That's all the reason I need not to encourage him, no matter how nice he is."

"You can't live your life to please your father, Cassie. He's gone and the rest of life is ahead of you."

Cassie's good spirits deflated like a balloon. The toast suddenly tasted flat and she put it back on the plate. She wanted her aunt to stop reminding her that her father wouldn't return. It was something she didn't want to think about, and every time she saw Trevor she was somehow reminded of that terrible truth.

"There are hundreds of men in this world, so why should I choose one who makes me so uncomfortable? Please, Aunt Julia. Can't we change the subject?" She stood, took a final gulp of coffee, walked to the counter and placed the empty cup in the sink.

Julia must have noticed her change in mood because she followed Cassie and gave her an affectionate hug. "I'm sorry. I'll stop pushing him at you, I promise." Her hug made Cassie feel better and she squeezed Julia back.

"I'm on my way. I'll see you Friday. Behave, and take care of those mares. They're our bread and butter."

"I know one end of a horse from the other." Julia laughed, her black eyes flashing in amusement. "And surely I know which end eats." Cassie laughed, too, and gave her another hug. Despite Julia's sometimes pushy ways Cassie loved the woman.

THE EXCITEMENT of the Futurity competition infected Cassie as she jockeyed her truck for a position near the barns among all the other trucks and trailers. Trainers and handlers, bantering noisily with one another, moved easily through the moving vehicles, unloading horses, carrying big trunks filled with tack, plastic cans of grain and sporting halters slung over their shoulders. The fresh smell of hay floated in the air.

Most of the stables had several handlers for each horse. Cassie had only her trainer, Rick Murphy, and his daughter, Christine, who would ride Chauncey during the competition. Rick and Christine came as a pair and were among the best in the industry. Many stables had also brought several horses. Cassie only had Chauncey.

But Chauncey was enough, Cassie thought, as she gazed at him safely tucked away in his stall. His conformation alone would have branded him champion, but his talent for cutting calves boosted him far ahead of the field. Chauncey, from little Cambridge Stables was the quarter-horse star of the season.

He greedily chomped on the quart of grain that Cassie had poured in his food bin and looked up occasionally, as if to reassure her that he wouldn't let her down. She knew she was getting too attached to this beautiful animal. When she was near him she felt as if she could sense her father's presence, as though Papa would walk around the corner at any moment. It wasn't a sensible attitude. Quarter horses were a business asset, not pets. Someday Chauncey's worth could approach half a million dollars. A rancher couldn't afford to get sentimental with that much money involved. Well, she'd face that problem when it arrived.

"He's in top form, Cassie. Never been better." Rick's friendly drawl brought her back to the present.

She smiled. "Yes, isn't he?"

"And I've never seen a stallion so gentle. If I could cure his spookiness, he'd be the first perfect horse."

"Wouldn't that be something?" She looked back at Chauncey for a moment, scrunching her shoulders to relieve her tension. The drive had been long and tiring and the haze of nightfall was in the sky. "We'd better get some rest, Rick. Tomorrow's going to be quite a day."

"Yep," he replied. "The return of the supremacy of Cambridge Stables. Hooray!"

Cassie laughed delightedly. *The return of the supremacy.* What a flowery phrase for a cowboy. Still laughing she turned and walked toward her quarters.

Her quarters were in her horse trailer, a combination sleeper and kitchenette. While not exactly luxurious, it suited Cassie very well, especially in the morning. Tumble from bed, drink a cup of instant coffee, douse quickly under the hand-held shower, step outside and there she was, in the middle of the show. The lumpy mattress was singing a siren's song as she reached for the sleeper door.

"Hey, babe, what's your hurry."

Cassie whirled to face an antagonistic Marvin Bradford. "Oh, it's you." She spoke with a studied nonchalance.

"Yeah. I've been looking for you." His voice was harsh. His colorless eyes narrowed to slits. With the insight that maturity brings she regretted the crush she'd developed on him during junior high. But even now she recognized a feral masculinity emanating from him, which some woman undoubtedly still found attractive. Thank God, she'd outgrown that type of man.

Rubbing the back of her stiff neck, she reluctantly answered him. "Whatever do you want me for, Marvin?" she asked, drawling his name so it came out M-aa-rrvin-nn.

With an aggressive movement he closed the gap between them. Now he was standing right in front of her, his face twisted into a snarl, whisky breath blowing in her face. She turned her head in disgust.

"Get away from me, Marvin. You're drunk." She gave him a little shove, unbalancing him momentarily and fueling his ugly mood. Regaining his footing, he slammed her against the trailer wall and took her face roughly in his hand.

"Lay off my father," he hissed. Cassie's eyes darted wildly, looking for someone, anyone, who might be walking through the trailer area and could help her, but she saw no one. The yard lights had just come on but all the trailers were dark. The barn area was silent. It was early evening and it appeared that everyone must be out partying. Cassie steeled herself. She would just have to handle this alone.

Marvin tightened his grip. "Look, babe," he growled, "I know what you've been doing. Seeing that Haggarty guy, talking to Trevor and just about anyone who'll listen. Stop screwing with us. If you know what's good for you, you'll get out of town."

Anger bubbled within her like boiling water. What a jerk. Did he think he could scare her with this Humphrey Bogart imitation?

"Babe?" she taunted. "Get out of town? You've been watching too much late-night TV. If Jake has nothing to hide, none of you have anything to worry about." She leaned back against the trailer relaxing against Marvin's grip. When she felt his muscles loosen, she gave a sudden vicious thrust and pushed Marvin backward. With a resounding thud, he fell on his backside, and the sight of him, legs spread, gazing at his gravel-scraped hands with a drunkenly puzzled expression caused Cassie to laugh.

Immediately she realized her mistake. An enraged bull could not have looked more fierce, and as he scrambled to his feet, Cassie frantically fumbled at the handle of the sleeper door and jumped inside before it was barely open, pulling it shut behind her. But not in time. Marvin jerked the door from her hand and grabbed her arm.

She pulled back with shoulder-wrenching violence, but Marvin's grip was too strong. He dragged her from the trailer, ignoring her kicks and protests. As fear and anger warred within her, events began to blur. The sound of tearing cloth, Marvin's rasping breath, crunching gravel. Then he was on top of her, legs spread on either side of her pinioned body. She shouted for him to stop, saw his clenched fist aimed at her face. Then more crunching gravel, the sudden release of weight, a loud thump and the whoosh of forcibly expelled breath.

"Don't you think this is a little primitive, even for you, Marvin?" Through her foggy thoughts, Cassie heard a familiar voice. Relief flooded through her bruised and trembling body.

"Trevor!" Marvin slurred. He had a new target for his hatred. "Keep out of this. This is none of your business." Cassie looked through a haze and saw Trevor crushing Marvin, face-first, against the trailer. She pulled herself to a sitting position. Her hands were trembling. Could this really be happening?

"Everything about Cassie Cambridge is my business, Marvin." Cassie thought she must be dreaming. Trevor couldn't be saying these words. How could he function with such divided loyalties? "Stay away from her. Do you understand me, Marvin?" Marvin answered with a squeal as Trevor gave his arm a sharp upward jerk, then threw him to the ground.

Unsteadily, Marvin climbed to his feet and turned to face Trevor. He straightened his shoulders menacingly, but the wind had left his sails. As he met Trevor's steady gaze his shoulders sagged, and with an air of false bravado he shrugged and backed off. "You can have her, man. She's not worth it. But if that horse of hers wins the futurity, it's on your head. You can answer to Pa."

Cassie realized she had been holding her breath. She exhaled in relief as Trevor bent beside her to ask if she was hurt. A look of real concern showed on his face. His eyes rested briefly on Cassie's chest, then were quickly averted.

She glanced down and what she saw brought a blush to her cheeks. Marvin had ripped her shirt at one shoulder, exposing a full breast, which was barely covered by her lacy bra. She drew herself up, pulling the shirt around her.

"I thought you looked kind of good that way," Trevor teased, lifting her to her feet and sitting her down gently on the narrow step of the trailer. Her blush deepened.

"I apologize for Marvin." He unsnapped his shirt. Cassie froze. What was he doing? "But I'm afraid he may never grow up."

He removed his shirt. Light from a nearby pole reflected off his tanned skin, emphasizing the smooth ripples of his well developed muscles. A narrow line of russet hair ran from his beltline to a larger patch on his chest.

"There's no explanation for why he does these things. Or why he's so full of hate." Cassie sat paralyzed as Trevor bent over her. She couldn't withstand another of his bruising kisses.

But, no. Tenderly he covered her half-naked torso with his shirt, snapping the buttons together and trapping her arms like a bunting. The faint fragrance of musk clung to the light material. Emotions surged within her—emotions she couldn't identify. Relief? Gratitude? Or disappointment?

And then, to her disbelief, tears welled up in her eyes and streamed down her face. What made it worse was that she didn't know why she was crying. She wasn't in pain, at least not physical pain, and Trevor was being kind. Too kind. Had she expected—and even wanted—something else? Something she felt was wrong but that she greatly desired and tried to pretend she didn't.

"I'm sorry," she wailed. "I don't know what's wrong with me. I never cry."

"It's only natural, Cassie. You had a bad scare." He helped her stand, then enclosed her in his arms while she sobbed on his shoulder. As she doused him with tears, he stroked her hair lightly, murmuring, "It's all right, it's okay." It felt so good, so right, so natural to be there, and presently Cassie stopped sobbing and, embarrassed, pulled away.

Did she imagine it or did she see a faint flicker of hurt in his face. Of course not—he must think she was an hysterical idiot. After all, Marvin hadn't raped her. "I'm sorry," she sniffled. "I'm so embarrassed."

"Don't be."

Cassie sniffled in reply, extracting an arm from the shirt-bunting and crassly wiping her nose with the back of her hand. She laughed disparagingly. "I'm a mess."

"That you are." He pulled out a handkerchief from his pocket and wiped her tears and then handed it to her. "Blow your nose."

Cassie gave a few unladylike honks into the handkerchief, looked down at the soggy rag in her hand, then at Trevor, then back at the handkerchief. "I'll wash it and give it back to you."

"Well, I don't want it back that way, that's for sure." He laughed, a deep husky laugh, lightening Cassie's spirits and sparking a responsive laugh.

"That's better," he said. "Now, where are you staying? I'll be your guide."

Still chuckling, Cassie looked at the trailer behind her. "My Hilton of the horse-show circuit."

"Well, milady, your humble servant will show you the way." He bowed with mock formality and opened the door. Nothing in his behavior even hinted that he wanted to be invited inside, and she felt a sinking sensation in her stomach when she realized he was leaving. She put one foot on the step and then turned toward him. There was something she needed to say. Something. But she wasn't quite sure what it was. Just something. In the end all she said was "Thank you, Trevor. Thank you."

"You're quite welcome." He looked deep into her eyes as if also searching for something, then leaned forward and placed a gentle kiss on her forehead. He turned and walked away. Cassie watched him until he was out of sight. She felt empty.

ANTICIPATION. That was the only word Cassie could find to describe what she was feeling as she leaped out of bed. The last day of the futurity. Two days of endless trials, endless eliminations. Now, finally, the last day, and Chauncey held the lead. But just barely. That Bradford mare, Starfire, was only a few points behind. Cassie wasn't worried. Even if Chauncey came in second, which she was sure he wouldn't, his exquisite demonstration of talent over the past two days had assured his reputation.

But Cassie wanted to win. How she wanted to win. Show up those Bradfords and let that SOB Marvin know that not only had he failed to frighten her, he'd also lost to her. She was in Mesquite, and Mesquite was where she was going to stay.

She shivered as she stood under the hand-held shower. The water was only lukewarm, and though it was almost seven o'clock, the sun had not yet risen. She gave a little dance while she briskly toweled herself dry, then poured hot water over instant-coffee crystals. All the comforts of home, she thought.

A knock sounded at the door just as she was pulling on her jeans. "I'll be right there, Rick," she shouted, hastily tucking in her shirt before she opened the door.

Cassie's heart gave a lurch. "Trevor!" Couldn't they be in the same space without this feeling that she couldn't breathe?

"Good morning, milady," Trevor said. "Got time for a cup of coffee before you go out and whip the pants off the Bradfords?"

"Sure. Come in. Rick will be here soon and we'll have to get going, but the water's still boiling." He stepped inside, and she made a big production over the coffee preparation. "Cream or sugar?"

"Black." A wide smile covered Trevor's face. Cassie was sure he'd noticed how clumsy and tense she was, and she became even more self-conscious. "I thought you'd want to rub it in."

"Rub it in?" She handed him the steaming cup.

"Yeah, Chauncey is beating our pants off. Did you forget?"

Forget? My God, she almost had forgotten. She laughed. "Of course not. You bet I'm going to rub it in. With salt." She hugged herself and spun around, her self-consciousness forgotten. "Oh, Trevor! We're almost there. Cambridge is back on the map. Even if Chauncey loses, I've won. His fees will go sky high."

"Is that important to you, Cassie?" His smile had faded, and his brilliant azure eyes became serious.

"Important? Of course it's important. I can't think of anything that matters more. Cambridge Stables has to make a comeback. If it doesn't, my father will have lived his life for nothing."

"You miss him, don't you?"

"Yes." His obvious concern touched her, but his comments brought back that dull ache she'd felt ever since her father's death. "But you know what bothers me most. It's like he fell into a black hole and it just closed over him and . . . and—" her throat tightened, making it hard to talk "—and it's like he never lived. Everything, everyone, all of life, goes on, even though he's gone."

She took a deep breath, suppressing the urge to cry. "That's why I have to rebuild the stables. For him. If the stables live on, so will he. Don't you see?"

He put a comforting arm on her shoulder. "Yes, I see. But don't forget, life does go on—your life, Cassie."

"This is my life, Trevor." She shook her head fervently.

"Then if this is what you want, I hope you get it."

"Cassie?" Rick's Western twang interrupted their conversation. "Are you ready?"

Cassie reached over and opened the door. "Yes, Rick. Come on in." She introduced the two as she prepared Rick a cup of coffee and they talked briefly about the show while Cassie collected her coat and hat.

As she walked with Rick toward Chauncey's stall, Cassie realized she had shared thoughts with Trevor that she had never expressed before, not even to herself.

THE SUN WAS WARM, shining lazily on Cassie's back, infusing her with a feeling of well-being. Well, perhaps it wasn't just the sun. Chauncey was still ahead. So far he had swept the field and only three other horses were left competing: Mueller's Sundance Child,

Kendall Farms' Three-Bar Headlight, and Bradford's Pride of Starfire.

She breathed a sigh of relief at seeing Sundance Child. Capable, but no competition for Chauncey. Three-Bar Headlight would have made a good working horse, but wasn't champion material. Now only Starfire remained. Cassie had not yet seen her. The mare's trials had always fallen right after Chauncey's when Cassie was busy cooling him down. But she'd heard high praises about this mare who, she'd been told, was the only horse capable of outshining Chauncey.

She heard someone murmur that Starfire was next and settled into her stadium cushion, adjusting her hat against the afternoon sun. Then Starfire entered the ring. Cassie shot upright and stared in unabashed admiration. If ever a horse was a match for Chauncey, it was this one. "Close your mouth, Cassie," said the man next to her, a neighboring ranch hand. "I told you she was something."

What an understatement. Gray, with a slight dapple to her coat, Starfire loped smoothly across the ring in fluid grace. Her mane, long and full, billowed behind her head, glistening with unexpected golden highlights, and her tail, arched high, flowed freely behind her. She flicked it lazily, turning it into a gossamer mist.

A shot from a pistol. The calf was released. Starfire's rider urged her into a gallop across the ring. Then she stopped on a dime. The calf bleated and dashed to the left while Starfire easily kept pace, stopping, leaning back on her flanks, moving left, moving right, back feet always planted; concentrating fully on her task, keeping the calf from the herd. There had been no exaggeration—this horse was good.

Cassie's admiration swelled. Nothing was as beautiful as a well-trained cutting horse in action. The precision and grace of their well-timed, purposeful movements matched, and even surpassed, that of the highly trained, highly praised Royal Lippizan dancing stallions, and the breathtaking Starfire was one of the best of the best. Despite her admiration, Cassie's heart sank. Starfire was giving Chauncey a run for his money.

And this was a stubborn calf, a greater challenge than the one that had been assigned to Chauncey, and Starfire was up to the challenge. The calf bleated, dashed, darted, spun and fought, but always the mare was beside it, in front of it, anticipating its next move. Clearly, this horse would take the Golden Cup.

Thirty seconds left in the round. Cassie held her breath, hoping, waiting for the mare to make a mistake. Suddenly, the crowd went crazy—screaming, booing, hissing. Starfire's rider sprawled awkwardly on the ground. The saddle was crazily skewed on Starfire's back, the breast collar trailing. Puzzled, Starfire stopped for a moment, almost losing her calf, and then, although riderless, continued working. Unaware that with no rider she had lost the competition, she just continued to do what she was bred for, trained for and lived for. The rider scrambled to his feet, calmed his valiant mare and led her out of the ring, both their heads held low. As Cassie watched, a lump formed in her throat. Chauncey had won after all. But there was no sweetness in that hollow victory.

"CONGRATULATIONS."
Wherever Cassie walked someone slapped her on the

back with hearty acclaim. Jubilation surrounded her. Rick picked her up and whirled her around in glee. "He's a winner, Cassie. Imagine, the Golden Cup. I knew that horse had it in him."

Chauncey was a champion and Cassie was delighted. But her happiness was dimmed by knowing that Starfire would have won if her saddle hadn't failed. Still, as Rick had told her, those things happened. A faulty breast collar, a loose cinch. Fatal in this kind of precision competition. It was careless of the trainer not to have checked the tack thoroughly before the competition, though. Very careless, in fact. But as everybody knew, it took more than talent to make a champion cutting horse and this was Chauncey's day.

Cassie reveled in the celebration. The cheers of the crowd were like symphony music as she, Rick and Christine led Chauncey into the ring to accept the cup. He was freshly brushed and curried, and wore a silk blanket proudly proclaiming Cambridge Stables. Cassie graciously accepted the cup and the customary kiss on the cheek from the futurity marshal. When she turned and handed the cup to Rick, bestowing a kiss on his cheek, then hugging Christine, the crowd roared. They loved her, loved Rick and Christine, and most of all, they loved Chauncey. It was a David and Goliath story. Or a Rocky story. The little guy wins out. The loser becomes a champion. Cambridge Stables was back, proud and strong, once again a leader in quarter-horse circles.

Cassie's heart almost burst with pride as she led Chauncey back to his stall. She, Rick and Christine chatted excitedly on the way, and though it must have been her imagination, Cassie thought Chauncey stepped higher and arched his head and tail more arrogantly as they moved through the congratulatory crowd.

She stayed with Chauncey quite a while, stroking his silken body, telling him how well he'd done. Rick and his daughter had gone to the postfuturity celebration—beer and hot dogs—and Cassie had told them she'd meet them later. She wanted to be alone and bask in her success, Chauncey's success, and just enjoy the warm glow that her months of hard work had brought.

Still surrounded by that glow, she walked toward her trailer to freshen up before meeting Rick, cutting between two rows of stalls to get there. Halfway down the aisle she could hear voices coming from the far stall, bringing with them the realization that she was walking through the Bradford barns.

"It weren't no accident," said one voice. "The leather on the breast collar was worn clean through...and that cinch was split, too. That trainer, John Collingsworth, woulda never missed something like this."

"That doesn't make sense, Luke. Why would anyone do something like that so late in the competition? If this were deliberate, it would have been more effective during the elimination rounds," said a second voice. Cassie immediately recognized that husky sound. Trevor! She flattened herself against the barn wall. If she were seen, Trevor would think she was eavesdropping.

A third voice, whiny, petulant and very familiar, popped up. "It'd make sense for someone, Trevor. That Cambridge woman. Starfire was the only real competition for that stud of hers." Cassie couldn't believe her ears. It was Marvin, and he was accusing her of fixing the outcome of the futurity. A flush of rage infused her body. How dared he? First he attacked her physically. Now he attacked her character. Only the fear of discovery kept her from storming toward the stall and telling that slimy lizard what she thought of him and his opinions.

But Trevor jumped to her defense. "Cassie?" he said. "Never." There he was, defending her again. Was there no end to the debt she owed this man? "She's not smart enough to pull off something like this." Her defense? And this was a lawyer? He reminded her of the old adage, *With friends like this, who needs enemies?*

"If this was deliberate, and that's a big *if,*" Trevor continued, "it was done by a real pro. There's no way to prove this leather was cut by looking at it. It looks just like natural wear and tear. I'll agree that Collingsworth would never miss something like this. But I know Cassie didn't do it."

"You got the hots for that girl or something, Trevor?" Cassie could hear the sneer in Marvin's tone even from her considerable distance. "That one's nothing but trouble, and even if there's no proof, I'm telling everyone she rigged the futurity."

"What I think about Cassie is none of your business, Marvin. But like I told you the other night, everything about her is my business. Don't talk about her and don't talk to her. Don't even go near her." Trevor's tone was menacing and cold as ice, sending chills down Cassie's spine. But her heart gave a glad jump, and she was immediately annoyed that his opinion of her was so important.

"And how are you going to stop me?" Marvin asked querulously.

"You know how." Trevor's answer was flat and confident.

"Oh, him. Well I know what would put the kebosh on your little romance real quick."

Cassie heard a thud and the reverberation of the metal barn walls. "Damn, Trevor!" Marvin whined. "Damn! You hurt my head."

"I don't like to repeat myself, Marvin, but I will. Just to make it perfectly clear. Stay away from her. Just stay away." Cassie heard the sound of a door opening and pressed even tighter against the barn wall. Trevor emerged through the doorway and began walking away with long angry strides.

"But what about this here broken gear?" the man they called Luke hollered after him.

Trevor turned around to respond and Cassie tried to shrink into nothing. What if he saw her? "Fix it," he answered, then continued his walk to the opposite end of the aisle.

Breathing a sigh of relief, Cassie slunk back in the direction she'd come from. At least they hadn't seen her. But what a confusing conversation. Did someone really sabotage Starfire's tack or were Marvin and Luke just spouting sour grapes? Losers could get awfully bitter. But why had Trevor defended her with that proprietary air? And there was something else Cassie noticed. Trevor treated Marvin more like an equal than the son of his employer. He'd hinted that he had ways to control Marvin. But what ways? And what did Marvin know that would "put the kebosh on their little romance"? Not that they had a romance, but something sinister was hidden in that comment. Lots of questions. Only one thing was certain. If Trevor wasn't for her, he sure wasn't against her. Even if he did work for Jake.

"Cassie." The sound of her name interrupted her thoughtful analysis. It was Tom Saunders, a neighboring rancher and currently futurity marshal. A pleasant man, about forty, he had bushy blond hair and a slight paunch from too much beer. "Hi, champion." He greeted her with a hearty grin. "I wanted to catch you. We're going to have a shindig at Mesquite Lodge on Saturday. In your honor. Thought I'd better invite you. Wouldn't be good to have a shindig and no guest of honor. About eight o'clock. Whaddaya think?"

With a chuckle, Cassie agreed. "Like you said, wouldn't do to have a shindig without the guest of honor."

Tom asked her if she was headed for the celebration. "Everybody's asking about you." At his insistence, she gave up the idea of changing clothes and walked with him to the ramada.

The ramada was packed with rowdy celebrants. Huge ghetto blasters wailed out a mournful Loretta Lynn tune, while dancing couples swayed in harmony with the music. Tom handed Cassie a beer, and while that wasn't her drink, it tasted good, cool and smooth.

She felt as if she were holding court, sitting on a concrete table, while people rushed to her with congratulations and queries about breeding fees. There wasn't even the slightest murmur about sabotage or rigging. Everyone was sincere with praise, and Cassie concluded that Trevor had been successful in squelching Marvin's threat.

She could see Trevor through the crowd, dancing with a blond rodeo-queen type dressed in flashy Western wear, a feather in her straw Stetson. An unexpected surge of jealousy shot through her as she glanced at her worn Levi's, faded plaid shirt and down vest. She knew she would never like that girl. Throughout the evening she tried to catch Trevor's eyes, but not once did he look in her direction. The girl followed him like a puppy dog, and the crush of people crowding around Cassie blocked him from view most of the evening.

As the merrymakers became drunker and louder, Cassie grew tired. The day had been both exciting and exhausting, and her elation was loosing its luster. As she left the ramada grounds, she saw Trevor again, the blonde still in tow. He looked directly at her, smiled and tipped his hat. Her elation suddenly returned. She smiled back, waved, considered going over to talk to him, then glanced at the blonde by his side. Another time, she thought, as she continued walking to her trailer. It wouldn't do to appear too anxious.

CHAPTER SEVEN

"WE'RE THE CHAMPIONS, Aunt Julia! We won!" Cassie clutched the huge Golden Cup to her chest as she maneuvered through the door. Julia was coming down the curving staircase with a broad smile on her face.

Reaching the bottom step, she encircled Cassie in her arms, a difficult task since the cup was nearly as big around as both of them. "As if I had any doubts. I knew you could do it. You can do anything you set your mind to."

Cassie gave a jubilant laugh, set the cup down and gave her aunt a proper hug. "Cambridge Stables is on its way back. We're going to make it, Aunt Julia. I got contracts for nearly fifty thousand in breeding fees. Now we can get a decent mare. With a champion mare and our Chauncey, no one can beat us."

Julia nodded then bent over to pick up the cup. "Let's put this in the trophy case in your fath . . . in the study."

"Good idea." Cassie smiled as she watched Julia lift the cup, pushing away the small prick of loss she'd felt at her aunt's careful avoidance of any reference to her father. It was something Julia habitually did, as though avoiding mentioning him could cause Cassie to forget his death.

"The cup is nearly as big as you are." She followed Julia down the long, wide hallway to the study. It would be of no use to offer help. The offer would just offend her aunt.

As they passed through the door, Cassie's attitude changed from jubilation to reverence. She saw the room almost as a shrine. Her father's study. Everything had been left as it was. Dark wood paneling covered the walls. Hunting trophies, heads of elk, deer, moose, even a wolf were hung at intervals throughout. A locked firearms case stood at one side of a wide shuttered window with its view of the pasture. The trophy case stood on the other side. The shutters were open and the high afternoon sun streamed in, reflecting off polished wood and leather.

Seeing this room stirred memories. Memories of days when Cambridge Stables had been at its best. Now, standing there, looking at the crammed trophy case, Cassie was all too aware of how far she still had to go. One Golden Cup did not make a dynasty of the magnitude achieved during the heyday of Cambridge Stables.

She walked to the case, opened the glass door and rearranged some trophies. Her hand touched another Golden Cup dated nearly fifteen years ago. A lump formed in her throat. "Sometimes I miss him so much, Aunt Julia. Especially in here. It's like . . . like I expect him to walk into the room any minute."

"I know, Cass. I know." Julia placed a sympathetic hand on Cassie's shoulder. "But I worry about you, too. Please remember that all your hard work can't bring him back."

Cassie didn't answer at first. She recognized the truth in Julia's words, but her heart screamed out to reject them. Illogical as it was, she knew that the child deep within her believed if she could make everything the way it was before, she could also erase her father's death. She didn't want to face a contrary view, at least not today. She carefully set Chauncey's award beside the older one, critically checked the placement, then closed the door and turned to face her aunt.

"No," she replied sadly. "It won't bring him back." But even as she said the words, the child inside wailed, *Yes, it will. Yes, it will.*

"DAMN." Cassie cursed the clump of mascara clinging to her lashes and tried to pick it off carefully, cringing when it smudged onto her fingers and cheeks. "Damn."

Julia entered Cassie's bedroom and chuckled at the younger woman's consternation. "You weren't this nervous, honey, when you won your first advertising award. What's the cause of these jitters? It wouldn't be Trevor Austin, would it?" Julia's grin was wide and the lively cadence of her voice exaggerated as she good-naturedly taunted Cassie. "You look white as a ghost."

Cassie turned from her mirror in alarm. "Do I look that bad, Aunt Julia?" She dabbed at the streak of mascara on her cheek, looked down at her emerald green cotton dress, then stood up, still holding the tissue. She stared critically in the mirror and adjusted the off-the-shoulder neckline. Maybe she wasn't tanned enough for this dress. Was it just too, too Western? Her wide eyes looked like dark lumps of coal. "Should I change clothes? Wear my hair down?"

"I was just teasing, Cassie. You look beautiful, absolutely beautiful." Julia took the tissue from Cassie's hand. Her touch soothed Cassie's raw nerves, and she stood quietly taking deep even breaths while Julia finished wiping away the mascara. "There. Now you're perfect." She rearranged a few tousled curls of Cassie's upswept hairdo. "Your hair is so like your father's. You got the best of everything, Cass. A woman of rare beauty."

"Do you think so, Aunt Julia? I've always wished I looked more like Mother, tall and blond. I don't know why I didn't inherit any of her looks." Cassie looked toward a small portrait of the slender, fair-haired woman placed over an oak dresser.

"You look wonderful just the way you are. I wish I could go with you tonight, Cassie, but I have to go to this teachers' workshop. If I don't, it means no raise next year."

Cassie understood. The workshop had been on her aunt's agenda for several weeks now. She expressed those thoughts, and Julia bent to place a kiss on her forehead. "Thanks for being so understanding. I'll be back on Tuesday. Okay?"

"Okay," Cassie replied. "I'm going to miss you tonight, though."

"I'll miss you, too. It's so good having you home with me again, honey." Julia rearranged one of Cassie's errant curls, then left the room.

With Julia's exit, the ball of nerves in Cassie's stomach returned, and it was still there as she walked up the steps to the Mesquite Lodge lobby, her soft, knee-high squaw boots barely making a sound on the wide wooden planks. She concentrated on suppressing that maddening lump and made her way to the Cactus Ballroom.

The lump was maddening because she knew its source. Possibly, hopefully, Trevor would attend tonight. Maybe they would talk. Maybe they would dance. Maybe, just maybe... Cassie didn't want to think about it anymore. She took a deep, calming breath and walked into the room.

The band was playing "Islands in the Stream" as she entered the large, expansive room. Across the empty dance floor, she could see a crowd gathered outside on the wooden patio drinking and chatting in the light of early evening.

Streamers and balloons covered the enormous high ceiling, nearly blocking the exposed log beams from view. Instead of lifting her mood, the colorful decorations caused a faint glimmer, an undefined recollection to invade Cassie's mind, filling her with a nebulous dread. Never fond of large parties, she was accustomed to a momentary reluctance in such circumstances but the anxiety she felt tonight was disproportionate to the cause. She impatiently shook away her discomfort as she saw Tom Saunders crossing the deserted ballroom to greet her.

"Well, well," he said expansively. "The guest of honor has arrived. Now our shindig can begin." Hosting was a role he clearly enjoyed, and he steered Cassie across the floor onto the veranda and led her to a well-stocked bar where he brushed the bartender aside with a "Do ya mind," which brooked no refusal, and commenced preparing "his special concoction," a real "kick in the kiester," he called it.

Neighboring ranchers besieged her, asking about Chauncey, telling tales of their problems at the futurity, many of them hilarious. Again congratulations came, some heartily, others with rueful tones, and though Cassie had at first tried to refuse Tom's "kick in the kiester," it turned out to be delicious, and she sipped it carelessly as she enjoyed the conversation and the joking. Occasionally she stole a covert glance about her, searching for Trevor but seeing him nowhere.

Someone announced dinner, and Cassie again looked for Trevor. He still wasn't there. She sat down among her neighbors and began to eat. The food was delicious. A true Western spread of barbecued ribs, beans, squaw bread and salad, and Cassie ate as eagerly as she drank the delicious fruity drink Tom kept passing into her hand. When a friendly wrangler asked her to dance, she accepted gratefully. She needed to work off all that food, and that drink of Tom's was making her positively lightheaded.

The crowd was rowdy as only hard-working ranchers can be when kicking up their heels, and Cassie danced as she hadn't in a long, long time. Country swing, two-step and pony step, joining in the racy line dances and shuffles, changing partners each time another wrangler cut in with a good-natured tap on a buddy's shoulder. After a particularly breathless shuffle, she felt relieved when the band began a medley of country waltzes. Her present partner was not particularly adept at the more complicated turns of the waltz and his slow pace allowed her breath to return to normal.

Then came another tap, and as she turned to enter her new partner's arms, she looked into Trevor Austin's piercing eyes. Her breath quickened. He enclosed her expertly in his arms, without making her miss a beat. He didn't speak and neither did she. The song had changed to a faster tempo, and Trevor smoothly increased their pace. One, two, three, whirl and turn. One, two, three, pause and wait. Cassie's heart seemed to be beating in time with the music. One, two, three, stopping now. One, two three, starting now. She feared, for a moment, that her heart might stop beating forever. She smelled the faint fragrance of Trevor's musk cologne. Never before had it seemed so sexy.

The pressure of his hand upon her waist felt hot as fire, but she welcomed the heat and melted into Trevor's arms, following each nuance of his lead as they glided around the dance floor. Hard muscles rippled under her hand with each turn, jolting her with delicious electrical impulses, while he looked into her eyes. She returned his gaze openly, drinking in the glorious lines of his face as they twirled and paused, twirled and paused, becoming one with the music and each other. Nothing else existed. Just she and Trevor, the insistent beat of the music and the insistent heat of desire.

They danced for an eternity, a glorious eternity. An eternity Cassie wanted never to end. She felt alive, sensuous, womanly. Moving together over the smooth wooden floor, she seemed to belong here, safely enclosed in Trevor's arms, his thighs inches from her own, his sweet breath on her cheek. She prayed the moment would never cease.

"My turn?"

The interruption was a splash of cold water. Cassie recognized the voice of the young wrangler who had first asked her to dance. His smile was friendly and unaware as he tapped Trevor on the shoulder. As if on cue, the band finished the last bars of the waltz and moved into a lively swing. Trevor looked at Cassie with a rueful grin. She nodded reluctantly, so he graciously relinquished her to the good-natured young man.

Her new partner was an accomplished dancer, and as she followed him through the intricate turns of the country swing, her mind dwelled on Trevor. Her cheeks flushed, and she knew the cause wasn't the strenuous dancing. She fumbled her next step. Her body felt suddenly uncoordinated and her partner smiled. "Getting worn out?"

"Yes," Cassie said. "Do you mind if I sit out the rest?"

"No," he courteously agreed, though obviously disappointed. Unquestionably, this cowboy loved dancing. "Let me get you a glass of punch or something."

"You don't have to." Cassie wanted to find Trevor and as pleasant as her partner was he would just be in the way. "Go on with your dancing."

He smiled gratefully and turned to steal yet another buddy's partner.

Cassie wended her way to the edge of the dance floor, searching for Trevor. The crowd was thinning and in his white Western suit he should have been easy to find. But where? Cassie couldn't see him. A sudden empty feeling filled her belly. Then she saw him near the veranda door, talking quietly with the same blonde who'd accompanied him at the futurity. The girl wore a crimson dress reminiscent of a saloon girl's outfit with a feather artfully placed in her upswept flaxen hair. The feeling in Cassie's belly turned to lead. Who was that blonde? Why did Cassie hate her with a murderous vengeance? Cassie didn't think she wanted to know the answer to either of those questions and abruptly changed her direction toward the table where she'd left her purse. It was time to go home.

Suddenly a deafening clap of thunder sent a tremor through the lodge, nearly drowning out the band. The dancing stopped and, after another thunderclap, so did

the music. A summer storm. Dancers quickly left the
floor. It was time to tend their animals. Teton summer
storms could be deadly, bringing flash floods, cruel
high winds and danger to valuable livestock.

Glad for her head start, Cassie ran down the wide
stairs. In a moment the parking lot would be full of
clamoring cowboys, racing motors and squealing tires.
She slipped into her truck, shivering. The temperature
had already dropped at least fifteen degrees. Large
drops of rain pelted the windshield. Soon the sky would
open with a downpour.

The long drive home was grueling, and Cassie
floored the gas pedal all the way, pushing the truck to
its limits along the winding road. The boarded mares
were in the pasture, undoubtedly panicking, and with
Julia away, no one was there to stable them. Her anxiety mounted as enormous drops skittered off the
windshield with such force the wiper blades could not
clean them fast enough. Her view was nearly obscured. She cursed the truck for its sluggishness and, as
her teeth chattered from the unexpected cold, for not
having a heater.

She sighed with relief when the wide gates of Cambridge Stables came into view, jumped out to open
them and was immediately soaked by the rain. Her
flimsy green dress was no protection from the cold, and
as she climbed back into the truck, she was aware that
her leather squaw boots were already saturated with
water. Ignoring her discomfort, she spun the truck onto
the gravel drive and headed toward the barn and pastures.

The wind was screeching through the trees, whipping their tall, sturdy trunks, making them wave and
sway as though performing an ancient pagan dance.

For an instant, very aware of how alone and how small she was in the face of this awesome power of nature, Cassie felt a pang of fear, but suppressed it as she caught sight of the mares racing frantically around the large pasture. Their terrified whinnies were audible even above the sounds of the fierce storm.

But no sound came from the barn where Chauncey was stabled. Her high-strung stallion was much too nervous to be silent during a raging storm. The mares would have to wait. Something was wrong with Chauncey.

She opened the truck door with a frenzied jerk, dived into the driving rain and ran for the barn, the wind fighting her with a primitive force that at times seemed overwhelming.

She found him lying in his stall, thrashing about and emitting small, whimpering snorts, his black eyes wild with pain. Colic! The scourge of horse owners, killing good stock in their prime. But preventable. How did Chauncey get colic? The thought briefly flickered through Cassie's mind, but the urgency of the moment brushed it away.

She dashed to the tack room, grabbed a halter and dashed back to her pain-racked horse. Slipping the halter quickly over Chauncey's head, she tugged forcibly on the lead rope, trying to bring the agonized animal to his feet. To no avail. Mindlessly, he continued to thrash, unaware that each roll was twisting his intestines, increasing his pain and the likelihood of his death.

"Up, Chauncey, get up," Cassie screamed but Chauncey continued to roll. Avoiding his thrashing feet, Cassie moved to his flanks and pushed. Pushed and pushed. Finally, when her strength was almost drained, he lunged to his feet, whinnying weakly with the effort.

She led him from the stall into the barn aisle. The cure for colic was walking. Either that or a veterinarian, and Cassie was afraid to leave Chauncey to go to the telephone. If she left, he would lie down again. This time, maybe for good. No. Better to walk him around until some of his pain was gone. She thought for a moment about the frightened mares in the pasture. But they would survive without her; if she left Chauncey he would surely die.

After long minutes and hours of walking, the first crisis was over. Cassie again became aware of how chilled she was. Rain had plastered her thin dress against her body, and her soft boots squished as she walked. The driving rain had abated, but the wind still whipped brutally through the brush and trees, occasionally whooshing down the barn aisle, increasing her chill. She led Chauncey toward the tack room, holding the lead tightly so he wouldn't go down again, and snatched a horse blanket and placed it over him. His proud head hung low in agony, his fiery eyes dull with pain. Cassie's heart ached for his pain, and she carefully secured his blanket before searching for a clean saddle blanket for her own protection.

Gathering the blanket around her shoulders, she settled in for a long night of walking. Back and forth. Back and forth. Up and down the barn aisle, they walked. Numb from fatigue, cold and tedium, she continued her trancelike routine, waiting for a sign, any sign, that Chauncey was improving.

A thunderous crack shook her from her trance. Everything went black and she jumped in alarm. The barn and yard lights were out and the grounds were immersed in darkness—a pure deep darkness only possible on a moonless, stormy night in the high country. All Cassie could see through the barn door was an occasional flash of light accompanied by a snapping, crackling sound. The rain had stopped and she knew the sound wasn't thunder. The flashes didn't appear to be lightning. What was causing it? She led her sick horse as quickly as possible to the west barn exit, her heart sinking at what she saw.

A power pole, toppled by the wind, lay fewer than twenty feet from the hay shed. Luckily it had missed the ranch structures, but a loose, live electrical wire danced crazily. It slithered and arched across the wet ground surface like a dragon, flicking its long tongue of white-hot current as it moved toward the neat stacks of hay stored under the shed roof.

Cassie froze, not knowing what to do. That powerful current would knock her from here to Sunday if she attempted to walk onto the wet ground in her soaked boots. Besides, she couldn't leave Chauncey. She stared in horrified fascination as the wire wriggled across the ground, rising high into the air, spewing heat and fire, moving toward the hay, as though guided by an intelligent force. Until today's storm, it had been a dry summer, and Cassie knew that underneath the moist outer layer, the hay lay as dry as tinder, easy to ignite, ready to burst into flames.

Mustering her wits, she thought hard. Rubber boots. The fire extinguisher. Still leading Chauncey, who was too sick to be frightened, she headed for the tack room and rummaged around until she found a pair of her father's knee-high fishing boots. She slipped her feet into them, boots and all, reached for the fire extinguisher on the wall, then headed back for the barn's west end, the ill-fitting boots hindering her progress. Even before she reached the door she could see small flames licking at the dry hay and dark smoke billowing from under the tin roof.

Her mind raced. Every alternative seemed impossible. If she left Chauncey, he could die. If she didn't, Cambridge Stables could burn to the ground. She knew the phone lines went down with the power pole, so phoning for help was not possible.

The wind continued its relentless howling, fanning the flames of the hay fire. Where was the rain?

Suddenly a gust of wind blew the noxious smoke into the barn and Chauncey solved her problem for her. Despite his pain, he whinnied loudly, reared and tore the loosely held rope from Cassie's hand, bolting toward the east exit of the barn. Uttering a silent prayer, Cassie made her decision and ran to the fire.

Fortunately, having left destruction in its path, the wire was now weaving its way toward the gravel drive, freeing Cassie from the fear of electrocution. So far only a few bales had ignited, but the smoke produced from the wet hay burned Cassie's eyes. Huge flakes of cinder, scattering in the wind, peppered her arms with smoldering debris keeping her away from the fire. The saddle blanket! She ran back to the barn, shedding the oversize boots on her way, and grabbed the blanket. Taking it to the water trough she immersed it thoroughly and wrapped it around her head and body.

Thus armored, she returned to the fire, fumbling with the fire extinguisher, desperately trying to remember how it operated. She fiddled with the lever, trying unsuccessfully to read the directions printed on the side in the dim light of the fire. Then, mercifully, a foamy stream issued from the spout.

Coughing and gasping for breath, she aimed the foam at the fire, steadily moving the heavy cylinder in a wide arc, covering every inch of hay. Finally she was rewarded when the hot orange flames stopped their greedy licking and the fire subsided. Just in time. The extinguisher had run dry. Cassie sighed in relief. She flung the empty cartridge on the ground as she stumbled away from the suffocating smoke and sat, exhausted, on the edge of the water trough, coughing and gulping for huge breaths of air to fill her smoke-blackened lungs.

No longer cold, she leaned over the trough and splashed water into her burning eyes, feeling the sheer, animal relief of having escaped danger. With one last look at the hay shed, she turned toward the barn to find Chauncey.

"Oh, no," she moaned.

Flames had reappeared among the charred bundles of hay, and now the extinguisher was empty. Cassie searched frantically for a bucket. There. By the hitching post.

Snatching up the bucket, she scooped water from the trough and ran toward the fire, dumped the water and returned for another scoop. She heaped bucket after bucket on the burning hay, but between each trip the tenacious flames reappeared, as though mocking her efforts to squelch them. Filling yet another bucket, she stumbled and fell on the muddy earth, slipping and sliding at least three feet. Frozen, covered with slime, fighting the loss of her horse and the loss of her property, she sat numbly and buried her head in her filthy hands. It was no use.

Suddenly the sky opened. Torrential rain fell upon the fire, smothering the persistent flames, and soon, even the smoke subsided. She raised her hands exultantly and felt the cool, wet rain pelt her face as it molded her hair and clothing to her body.

She felt like a madwoman, sitting in the mud, making huge gulping sounds as laughter and tears mingled to release the tension from her battered body. But it felt good. Still, there was work yet to be done and she dragged herself to her weary feet, found a pitchfork, and began pulling blackened hay bales from under the shed to soak in the driving rain. As she hauled the final bale, it hit her.

Where was Chauncey? In the urgency of the firefight, she'd forgotten all about him. Dropping the pitchfork, she raced through the barn in the direction Chauncey had fled. She found him near the corral.

He was rolling in pain, his blanket torn off and his sleek coat covered with mud, mane and tail wet and matted. But still alive. Cassie stroked his mud-caked body gently, trying to calm him. His wild eyes stared at her with a mute plea, and he shuddered under her touch. Cassie felt as though her heart would break.

Wearily she picked up the lead rope. Her limbs ached, her chest hurt, and her eyes still burned from the smoke. Afraid she was too weak to raise her sick stallion, she nonetheless pulled and tugged, cajoled and pushed him. Each time Chauncey tried to stand, he lost his footing in the slippery earth. Finally he refused to budge and just lay in the slime, spent, no longer even able to flail.

Beaten, Cassie stared at him mutely. Desolation seeped through her body along with an impotent rage at nameless fate. Consumed by the same emotions that had raced through her after her father's death, she sank down beside his gasping body and laid her head on his matted mane. If Chauncey died, all her hopes would die, too. The future of Cambridge Stables was dependent on him. She would have to abandon her dream.

Tears streamed down her cheeks, mixing with the pounding rain. She made no attempt to control them as she stroked Chauncey lovingly, helplessly, unable to prevent his death.

CHAPTER EIGHT

"CASSIE! CASSIE!"

At first her name seemed a cruel echo on the howling wind, but she wearily lifted her head to see Trevor running toward her. Relief flooded her body. She was no longer alone.

Dragging herself to her feet, she started to say something, but before she could speak, Trevor picked up the muddy lead rope and placed it in her hand. "Hold this tight and pull when I say so." She nodded numbly, grateful for the direction. She couldn't think anymore.

"Pull!" Trevor yelled, pushing hard on Chauncey's flanks. But Chauncey didn't budge. Trevor pushed and yelled again, and Cassie pulled with all her might, but Chauncey just weakly lifted his head.

"This won't work!" Trevor shouted. "We'll have to try something else. Get ready to pull."

Cassie flinched as she saw Trevor aim a vicious kick at Chauncey's flanks, but she steeled herself and pulled mightily when Trevor's boot connected with the stallion's rump. But their timing was off. Chauncey heaved from the unexpected assault then slipped and fell back into the mud.

"Again!" Trevor yelled, and when he kicked, she pulled. Chauncey gave a great shudder, scrambling upward, feet sliding in the slimy muck. Trevor pushed against his flanks to give him traction while Cassie tightened the lead rope. Chauncey's hind feet slipped once more, then he gained his balance and stood upright.

"Oh, thank heaven," Cassie whispered. Chauncey stood in front of her, head low between his hoofs, but standing and able to walk. She led him into the shelter of the barn and turned to Trevor, tears once again streaming down her mud-stained face, and wordlessly thanked him. He moved a wet string of hair from her cheek, wiping her tears away with his hand. Taking the rope from her hand, he said, "I'll walk him. Go call the vet. Walking won't be enough to save him."

"The phone is out," Cassie gestured toward the dead barn lights. "A power pole fell.... There was a fire." She felt the horror of the last hour returning and shivered, both from the memory and the cold.

"It'll be over soon," he said sympathetically, "and then we'll get you warm and dry, but you'll have to drive to a phone." He removed his yellow rain slicker and slipped it on her as though dressing a child. Then he placed the matching hat on her head. "This will keep the rain off your dirty face. Now go."

She followed his instructions, dimly aware that she must look a mess and trudged off to the truck. The rain slicker flapped around her feet, slowing her down, but it offered welcome relief from the piercing cold. She knew, though, that it wasn't just the raincoat that warmed her. Trevor's presence alone would have done that.

HOURS LATER, Cassie followed Trevor mindlessly into her house and up the stairs through her bedroom and into the ensuite bathroom. The veterinarian had come, washed Chauncey's colon and given him a sedative, leaving instructions for Cassie to call the next day. He said he wanted to talk to her about something. Strangely, the fire chief had said the same thing. But now she felt like a child again, warm and protected, and relieved of the need for independent thought.

She experienced no embarrassment or sense of modesty as Trevor slipped the filthy dress over her mud-caked hair. Only vaguely aware that her flimsy teddy clung to her body indecently, she made no attempt to turn away from the flickering glow of the storm lanterns which Trevor had lighted.

The gurgle of running water was pleasant, soothing, and the steam wafting from the faucet looked warm and inviting. Somewhere Trevor had found bath beads, and soon mounds of frothing bubbles sat on top of the steaming bath. He turned his back and instructed her to slip out of the teddy and into the water. She obeyed without question. The warm water felt like a cocoon, the bubbles nestling around her body. He left the room then, murmuring, "I'll be right back," and she lay back in the tub, luxuriating in the warmth that was melting the numbing chill in her bones.

Soon he reappeared with a bottle in one hand and a glass full of a dark liquid in the other. He placed one hand behind her head, supporting her, as he put the glass to her lips. "Drink this."

Blackberry brandy. Swiped from Julia's cooking stock, no doubt. The brandy slid easily down her throat, warming her all the way down to her stomach. What a resourceful man she thought as she took another sip.

She giggled and took yet another sip, or perhaps it was a gulp. It certainly made her feel better. She quickly drained the glass and held it out to Trevor. "Another," she said, giggling again.

Trevor filled it to the rim. "Drink. I'm going to wash your hair." He knelt down beside the tub. She gulped eagerly, downing the drink in a few seconds, then placed the glass on the edge of the tub.

Trevor instructed her to lean forward and, using a jar he'd dug up from somewhere, poured clear warm water over her matted hair. "Beautiful hair like yours should never look this bad." His voice contained an indulgent teasing tone.

Pouring a handful of shampoo, he sudsed her head, his fingers firmly massaging her scalp, her hairline and her neck. The pressure of his fingers, the warmth of the water, and the two glasses of brandy combined to produce a languor in her limbs. All tension had vanished. Her body was relaxed, her mind unfettered and a decidedly sensual longing was overtaking her.

Finished with the final rinse, Trevor dried her hair briskly, then handed her a towel to wrap her head. As she lifted her arms to do so, she became aware that her full breasts were now above the bubble line, fully exposed. Knowing she should feel embarrassed, she wasn't, and was gratified when Trevor's azure eyes darken with arousal. The flickering lamplight highlighted his face, emphasizing the strong angle of his jaw, his arrogant cheekbones and his copper hair, sending a wave of liquid heat through Cassie's indolent body. "Maybe you could join me in here." She impulsively blew on the bubbles, scattering a few across the front of Trevor's shirt.

Brushing the bubbles away, he smiled at her warmly. "Don't tempt me." She saw his gaze rest on her breasts, their erect nipples revealing the extent of her arousal, and she brazenly arched her back, wanting to see, again, the dark heat in his eyes. "It's an inviting idea."

"Isn't it?" She tilted her head to get a better look at his full lips. She remembered all too well the fire they'd ignited when they last touched hers. Then she slumped back into the water and grabbed the glass she had set down earlier. Flopping forward over the edge of the tub, she waved the glass back and forth. "Another? Then come in here with me?" A small voice inside was telling her to behave. She told it to shut up. Trevor smiled patiently.

"The water's muddy. Get out." He filled her glass halfway. "That's the last you get, then into bed with you." He gave her another towel and again turned his back. Cassie began to laugh as she stepped clumsily out of the tub, tucking the ends of the towel together.

"What are you laughing at?" His back was still turned so he couldn't see her.

"You." She spoke very slowly, distinctly, trying not to slur her words. "Being so careful not to look. I remember when you tried to undress me with your eyes." She took another gulp of brandy. "Ya know, this stuff's really good." She drained the glass and set it back down on the tub. "I'm decent now. You can turn around."

Trevor was also laughing, a deep husky laugh that delighted Cassie's ears. Everything about him was so masculine, so virile, so...so sexy. His curly bronze hair, the angle of his neck, the way his damp shirt clung to his muscular back. Cassie stopped laughing and simply stood looking at him, her eyes drinking him in.

Still laughing, Trevor turned to face her. "If I'd known you were such a vixen when you drank blackberry brandy..." She saw his smile fade under her direct gaze, his eyes begin to blaze. "I would have served it to you before," he finished, his voice now softer, slightly hoarse. In one long stride he closed the distance between them and swept her into his arms.

Cassie exploded as the full length of his body collided with hers and her towel fell away, unnoticed. She writhed against his damp shirt, and opened her mouth greedily to accept his tongue. Her hands roamed his body, trying to know every inch, every muscle. She molded herself to his frame, rejoicing in his feverish touch.

He untangled the towel from her head and buried his hands in her hair, holding her face as he rained tiny maddening kisses on her lips, over her eyes and down her neck. Then his hands left her hair, one moving to her breast, stroking and teasing the taut nipple, while the other roamed in tantalizing circles across her back, trailing to her haunches and her thighs.

Consciousness receded as she melted into him, wanting to be closer. Closer. Wanting him next to her, around her, inside her. She couldn't get close enough. His shirt and jeans were an intrusion, frustrating her desire to touch his skin. She tore at his shirt, opening the snaps and pulling it out of his jeans with frantic hands. She rubbed her breasts across his bared chest, brushing against the coarse thatch of hair, but still she wanted more. She reached for his buckle. Her fingers fumbled, pulling and tugging, but it wouldn't release. She moaned as a primitive frustration coursed through her veins. She felt nothing except her passion, her need to join with Trevor in a way she had never known before.

Then, with an anguished sob, Trevor grasped her searching hands. "Don't, Cassie," he moaned. She felt a jolt, as if she'd dived into a pool of ice water, and suddenly consciousness returned. She was deeply ashamed. She had behaved like...like a whore. She turned and broke away from Trevor's gentle hold and leaned against the door trying to control her heaving breath and to avoid his eyes.

Trevor sat on the bathtub edge and lowered his head to his hands. His ragged breathing echoed Cassie's. "Oh, God," he moaned. "I hoped...I prayed. No, I knew it would be like this with us." He raised his head and looked at her, his blue eyes sad. "But not tonight. Not this way."

Cassie bent down to pick up a towel, still not meeting Trevor's gaze. She couldn't talk about this, cooly, calmly, while standing in front of him stark naked. Primly, she wrapped the towel around her as she stole a quick glance at him. He looked so pathetic, sitting there, chin on his hands, the evidence of his desire straining against his tight jeans. Through her own mortification, her heart still went out to him. He obviously wanted her. She knew he did. "Why?" she asked in small voice, directing her eyes to the floor.

"Because you're tired. And more than a little bit drunk. I want you to come to me freely, Cassie. From your own conscious choice. Not take advantage of you."

Cassie nodded. She still ached from wanting him. But she didn't know how to throw herself at a man, and even if she did know how, her pride wouldn't let her.

Trevor rose slowly, conspicuously uncomfortable, and left the room. He returned with Cassie's nightgown. "Here, put this on," he said and left again.

Cassie slipped the flannel nightshirt over her head, the effects of this terrible night and the blackberry brandy overtaking her again. The floating sensation had returned, but desire had vanished. All she wanted to do was lie in Trevor's arms and sleep. But he was going to leave, and as she opened the door she faced that fact squarely.

"Well, good night, then." She stumbled toward her bed. Trevor stood, silently watching her, his eyes were dark. Dark and sad. Cassie wanted to hold him and take the pain away. She slid between the covers, then stretched her arms out toward him. "Come hold me," she said through the fog that was enveloping her.

"For a little while," he agreed, then came and sat beside her, taking her in his arms. "Sleep," he whispered as she cuddled against his broad chest.

"Okay," Cassie replied. "In a minute." She closed her eyes, then opened them quickly. "Who was that blonde?" Then she instantly fell asleep.

The nightmare came again to disturb her sleep, but when she cried out in her childish voice, "What's happening to you," blue eyes, calm as a clear sky, looked down at her and promised her peace and safety. The nightmare faded, and she fell back into a restful sleep.

DARKNESS HAD LONG since surrendered to daylight when Trevor slipped from beneath the warm comforter, disengaging himself from Cassie's light embrace. His gaze fell upon her sleeping form, her dark eyelashes resting on the creamy curve of her cheek, her tousled hair awash upon the pillow, and his desire for her sprang up anew.

Damn, Trevor, you're a fool, he thought with a flash of regret. Nevertheless, he knew he'd done the right thing. She might be angry at him now, but if he'd done what his body demanded the night before, she would have... He wasn't sure what she might have done. Not much for self-deception, he forced himself to recognize that he was more frightened of what he might want from her if they ever consummated the ravenous desire sparking between them.

One thing for sure, she wasn't the type for a one-night stand. At least not for him. Maybe another man could love her and leave her. But Trevor knew he couldn't and wasn't sure where a relationship between them might lead. He decided to drop this line of thought. He pulled his damp socks and boots over his feet, snapped his rumpled shirt shut and tucked it into his pants. Black mud stained his pants legs. White suits didn't lend themselves to romps in the mud or to being slept in. But he supposed the horses wouldn't mind what he looked like as long as he brought food.

Cassie moaned and tossed in her sleep. He looked at her and knew she would want him to wake her. She wouldn't let something as unimportant as fatigue stop her. Last night he'd witnessed her strength of character in action. The very qualities that irritated him were also the ones he admired the most—her determination and persistence, the way she hung on when others would have given up. He'd felt like a knight in shining armor, coming to her aid last night, but knew that if he hadn't been there, she would have managed without him. Well, he'd let her sleep this morning. He still remembered how to feed a horse.

He smiled, then, thinking how cute she'd sounded as she tried so hard to speak distinctly and felt a twinge of pleasure remembering her jealous question about the client he'd been with last night.

Stepping outside, he took a deep breath, drinking in the fresh morning air, washed clean by the storm, and savored the sweet fragrance of the early blooming flowers. Only chirping birds and the occasional rustle of a scurrying squirrel disturbed the silence. Trevor was suddenly glad to be alive. Glad to be in Mesquite, away from the endless noise of car engines and horns. Glad to breathe pure air—air that didn't contain noxious gases and pollutants. Mesquite Valley in the summer was as close to heaven as a man could get on this earth.

He walked to the hay shed. The horses were going to be hungry this morning. Bringing those mares in from the pasture had been quite a chase. Agitated by the violent storm, they had charged feverishly around the pasture. He and Cassie had chased them one by one, driving them into a corner, murmuring soothing sounds, until finally they were all captured. All this while rain drenched them. It had been exhausting, and Cassie had already endured more than one person should ever have to take in a night, but she'd kept going and wouldn't even consider his suggestion that she go in the house and let him catch the mares. She said they were her responsibility.

The charred remains of the burned hay bales surrounded the shed, and the electrical wire lay quiet and disarmed just a few feet away. Linemen from the power company were returning today to restore the power. He kicked a couple of blackened bales out of his way and began loading hay into a small wagon. Then an unfamiliar sound intruded on his quiet morning.

He turned to the source of the noise and saw a portly man bending over the broken power pole. Deciding he must be a lineman, Trevor walked toward him, wanting to satisfy his curiosity. High winds or not, it was strange the way that pole had fallen. These poles were made of hard ash and buried deep in concrete, not easily bent to the will of high winds, rain or snow.

As he got closer to the crouching figure, he realized it wasn't a lineman. Captain J. T. Haggarty was bent over the pole, inspecting it intently. About three feet above the ground was a ragged break. The fallen portion of the pole was still attached by a few fragments of wood. It looked like a matchstick broken by a giant hand, carelessly discarded on the ground.

Haggarty looked up at Trevor's approach. "Just inspecting the scene of the crime," he said with a wry smile.

"Crime?" Trevor asked.

Haggarty nodded. "Got a call from the power company this morning. Then just a few minutes later the vet called. Seems they have reason to believe what happened here last night wasn't an accident."

Trevor nodded. For some reason he couldn't explain, the news wasn't surprising. "So what's the verdict, Judge?" He tried to conceal the uneasiness that was creeping over him.

"Someone cut this pole partway through with an ax. See the marks here." Haggarty pointed to a clean, smooth surface on the stump. "Guess the perpetrator thought the fall could conceal his handiwork—or maybe he didn't much care if we guessed this wasn't an accident. Yep, I'll stake my career on it, such as it is. Somebody wanted this pole to fall. Wouldn't have an idea who might want that, would you?" He looked up at Trevor, wearing a guileless expression on his round, rosy face.

"So you want me to play amateur sleuth, J.T.?"

"Nope. Got enough volunteers for that role already. But you do work for Bradford, and Miss Cambridge has been saying all along that Bradford wants her out of here."

"I'm his attorney, J.T. Even if I did know something, which, for the record, I don't, it would be privileged information. And you know it." Trevor's face broke into a wide, knowing grin.

People underestimated Haggarty. His Columbo act was convincing. But Trevor had known J.T. when he was a vice cop in San Francisco. The seamy street scene had finally gotten to him and he'd come to Mesquite to "settle down in a small, dull town, arresting drunks and vagrants." But he hadn't forgotten his subtle, persistent, questioning methods, and Trevor was once again witnessing his genius.

"What are you doing out here so early?" Haggarty suddenly changed the direction of his questioning. "From what I hear, it was kind of a late night for you."

Trevor kept his face impassive and replied, "Cassie's exhausted. I drove over to feed her horses."

"You dressed for the occasion, too, didn't you? You might have laundered your pants first. Would have made a better impression." Lumbering to his feet, he pointed at the mud-spattered legs of Trevor's white dress slacks. Trevor grinned sheepishly.

"Look, J.T., we were both exhausted. I fell asleep here. Can we leave it at that?"

With a knowing smile, Haggarty nodded. "It will be our secret. But come here, there's something else I want to show you." He led Trevor to the barn.

The horses whinnied entreatingly as the men entered. "Getting hungry," Trevor commented.

"You can feed them in a minute. I want you to see this first." Haggarty entered Chauncey's stall. Cassie had transferred the horse to a fully enclosed box while he was recovering, and his usual stall now stood empty. J.T. picked up a flake of hay. "Do you think Miss Cambridge is in the habit of feeding her horses moldy hay?"

Trevor stared at the flake in Haggarty's hand. It was black and musty smelling. He knew that Cassie would never give an animal feed that was so obviously sour. A gnawing uneasiness came over him.

"But that's not the worst of it," Haggarty continued. "Deeper down. Look at that." Trevor peered closely. Embedded in the hay were small reflective fragments. He pinched a few leaves between his finger and thumb and his finger began to bleed.

"Ground glass," he said incredulously. Someone had deliberately tried to kill Cassie's stallion.

"Ground glass, all right. The vet said that the stallion's stomach must have cramped at the first taste of mold, so he quit eating. But there were signs of blood, and if he'd eaten any more he would have been a goner. Good thing he's a high-bred horse, used to better stuff than this, or Miss Cambridge would have had herself one dead stud."

Trevor knew exactly what Haggarty was getting at. "So you think there's some truth in Cassie's allegations? Right J.T.?"

"I'm not so sure about George and the way he died. But it sure looks like somebody wants her away from here. At first I thought she was just paranoid. A little hysterical over her father's death. The feud between

George and Jake has been public knowledge for years, of course, but that didn't mean George was murdered. Now, I just don't know."

"And you want me to help you look into it. Isn't that what you're getting at?"

A grin played around Haggarty's lips. "Follow your conscience, Trevor. But if you care about the girl..." He didn't finish, and Trevor knew Haggarty was confident the seed was already planted. Perhaps it was even beginning to sprout.

After Haggarty left, Trevor hauled the hay into the barn and talked softly to each horse as he laid some in the feed bins. After feeding the mares, he went to the tack room, got the medicine the vet had left for Chauncey and headed for the sick bay. Chauncey was lying down in his stall, his eyes a little bleary, but otherwise looking healthy. He lunged to his feet at Trevor's approach, nestling him as he lowered hay into his bin. Trevor gave him an affectionate pat and dumped the healing powder on top of the hay, then waited to be sure he ate.

Chauncey greedily assaulted the hay, and feeling assured the horse would finish his meal, Trevor walked away. It would have been a sin if Cassie had lost a horse as fine as Chauncey. His anxiety was definitely chomping away at his innards now, taking huge bites out of him. He knew he had to do something, but his loyalties were divided. Not only his loyalty to Jake as his employer, but the other loyalty, the loyalty he was trying to avoid.

"If you care about the girl..." Haggarty's words bounced through his head as he drove the winding road back to Bradford Ranch. Deep down, he knew who had the most to gain if Cassie left Mesquite. It wasn't

Jake. He already had it all. Against all odds, Jake had raised Bradford Ranch from the small run-down boarding stable he'd inherited from his father to one of the largest ranching empires in the west.

He now owned most of the land in Mesquite Valley, including the bulk of the Cambridge Stables estate. He also owned a cattle ranch in Montana, apple orchards in Washington and an Arabian horse ranch in Arizona. He had enough holdings already to keep him from lusting for more. Or did he? After all, he'd had a long-standing feud with George. Then again, he and George had pretty much patched things up before George's death. At least it had appeared that way. But why would he want to drive Cassie away...unless it was for Julia's sake?

No, it had to be Marvin. He had the most to gain. If Cassie gave up the stables, the Evergreen trust would revert to him. Trevor had set up the trust as confidential. Jake, George and Julia had been adamant that Cassie should never know about it.

But Trevor had witnessed the confrontation between Jake and Marvin in which Jake had told Marvin that if Cassie abandoned or sold the Cambridge property it would go to Marvin. Trevor remembered being very disturbed about that breach of confidence. Once Marvin had left the room Jake had looked at Trevor apologetically. "The boy has so little going for him," he'd muttered, giving no other explanation.

But Marvin would profit from Jake's promise only if Cassie failed to keep Cambridge Stables. Chauncey's performance at the Golden Cup Futurity was a big step in assuring her success. Yes, Marvin had a lot to gain if Cassie failed.

As Trevor drove into the ranch yard and pulled into the spacious garage that was large enough for six cars, he was highly aware of the contrast between Bradford Ranch and Cambridge Stables. The Bradford property showed the gleam of constant attention. Everything was spit and polish: the pastures and corrals enclosed by whitewashed steel fencing, the barn walls brushed clean of debris, their eaves offering no home for roosting birds. The drives and parking areas were paved, and the gravel area raked and free of leaves. It took a lot of labor and money to keep such large grounds in this condition.

The irony of it struck a philosophical chord in Trevor. Material success was so fleeting. Just a generation ago, Cambridge Stables had known this type of care. Now it was a degenerating heap of building and fences, which Cassie was desperately trying to maintain. He wondered if the next few decades would be as cruel to the Bradford ranch.

He walked toward the house while he thought, and as he started to climb the wide stone steps to the entrance he caught sight of Marvin entering the nearby barn. Perhaps it was time for a showdown. He changed the direction of his stride.

Marvin was in the tack room, examining the underskirt of a saddle when Trevor finally caught up with him. Marvin flopped the skirt down hastily when he saw Trevor enter the room and greeted him with his customary sneer. "Trevor, how good to see you. You been mud-wrestling with the sexy blonde I saw you with at the futurity?"

Trevor glanced down at his soiled suit and decided to ignore the comment. "Somebody tried to poison Cassie's stallion last night, Marvin. I don't suppose you know anything about it?''

Marvin let out a derisive whoop. "Hip, hip, hooray! Someone else is finally after that mouthy broad."

"You didn't answer my question, Marvin. What do you know about it?"

"Not a thing, Trevor. But if I did, would you expect me to tell you? It's nothing more than she deserves, anyway."

"Does she deserve having her barns burned down, too? Whoever poisoned the stallion also cut the power pole. It started a nasty fire. I'm asking you again. What do you know about it?"

Marvin widened his stance, as though bracing himself for an assault. "Oh, I get it. You were mud-wrestling with Cassie. How nice for you, Trevor. Was it good?"

Trevor's patience snapped. It had always been thin where his stepbrother was concerned. Ever since they'd first met as teenagers, Marvin had goaded, connived and lied, and eventually Trevor had beat the tar out of him. It was maddening that at twenty-nine years of age, Trevor could still be pushed into a childlike rage by Marvin. With that thought he took a menacing step forward. Marvin shuffled back, fists raised, brushing the saddle he'd been handling. It fell to the ground with a thud, upside down.

Trevor stepped over the saddle and grasped Marvin by the collar. It was time he got some answers.

"Damn, Trevor." Marvin pushed at Trevor's arm. "I was just joking. You can do whatever you like with that Cambridge broad. I don't care."

Trevor glanced down and suddenly his quarrel with Marvin was forgotten. There was something funny about the brand on that saddle. He peered more closely, still loosely holding Marvin's collar. Marvin's eyes followed Trevor's, and he tried to squirm loose while Trevor's attention was diverted. Trevor tightened his grip.

"What's that?" Face twisting in anger, Trevor shook Marvin violently.

"What?" Marvin's eyes darted back and forth, avoiding Trevor's livid face.

"The brand on that saddle." Even in the dim light of the tack room, Trevor could clearly see the deep capital C over a rocking horse rocker etched in the leather. The brand was from Cambridge Stables. "Where did you get this saddle, Marvin?"

He had a good idea where it came from. It was identical to the saddle worn by Starfire at the futurity. The saddle that had broken during the competition. Rage bubbled within him.

Marvin was silent for a moment and Trevor gave him another vicious shake. His reply came instantly. "Damn, Trevor. How should I know. I was just looking at it myself when you walked in." It never ceased to amaze Trevor that Marvin was all bravado and no guts. One moment an abusive bully, the next a fawning coward.

"You're lying." Trevor drew back a threatening fist and Marvin broke free from his single-handed grasp. "Don't, Trevor. I'll tell you."

Trevor lowered his fist. "Talk."

"I took Cassie's saddle at the futurity. We have one just like it and I swapped the saddles so she wouldn't miss hers. I weakened the cinch and was going to return it the morning before the competition. I figured her trainer wouldn't have time in the morning and would check the rigging the night before." The words tumbled in a rush from Marvin's mouth. "I wanted to make sure Chauncey didn't win. But something happened. Someone moved the saddle and the next thing I knew it was on Starfire's back."

Trevor stared at Marvin in disgust. "So you were trying to fix the competition?"

"Yeah. Funny thing is, I didn't have to. Starfire would have won if that cinch hadn't broke." He punctuated the sentence with a short, bitter laugh. "Trevor, we've got to get Cassie out of Mesquite. Can't you see this? She's going to ruin everything."

"Only your plans for owning Cambridge Stables. Now, I want the truth. What do you know about last night?" Trevor crouched, ready to lunge at Marvin if he didn't like the answer, and Marvin's frenzied eyes showed he knew it. He cringed, placing one hand in front of him to ward off a blow.

"Nothing, Trevor. I swear to God, I don't know anything about it." The naked fear in Marvin's voice turned Trevor's stomach, and he relaxed his threatening posture. He wasn't sure if Marvin was telling the truth but he knew he wouldn't get any other answer at this point. Marvin was only interested in getting out of a beating.

"Okay, Marvin, I'll accept that. But leave Cassie alone. I told you that once before. I meant it then. I mean it now." Trevor's momentary feeling of triumph had vanished, replaced by disgust. Damn that woman, she was shattering his carefully cultivated self-control. All his life he'd tried to control his temper, and he'd been quite successful during the past few years. But since he'd met Cassie, he'd quarreled with Marvin three times. Not that Marvin wasn't easy to quarrel with, but there were better ways for a man to handle a problem. Trevor didn't know what was getting into him.

"I get the message." Marvin rubbed his shoulder and widened the distance between them. "That little gal's got you lassoed and hogtied. And you know what I think, Trevor? I think—"

Trevor didn't give a damn what Marvin thought and continued to walk away, but Marvin's next words, delivered like a curse, hit Trevor more forcibly than a fist.

"I think you're in lo-v-v-e."

CHAPTER NINE

THE SUN streaming across her bed signaled that morning was nearly over. Cassie looked at the clock on her bedside stand. Its face stared at her blankly and she concluded that the electricity must still be out. Scrambling to a sitting position, she tried to find her watch, then noticed the indentation left by another body on the bed. Trevor! The events of the night before flashed in her mind, and a warm flush of embarrassment invaded her body.

My God! Had she really behaved that way? Memory followed memory and the heat intensified. She wanted to crawl back under the covers and hide her head in mortification. But underneath the embarrassment was another emotion. Joy. She could almost feel the cool, smooth texture of his skin. The tickle of the russet patch of hair on his chest against her breasts. His breath upon her cheek, her neck.

His touched filled her with overwhelming happiness. Never had she desired a man with such intensity, and deep inside, she knew she would endure greater shame, greater rejection and even greater pain just to experience that wondrous emotion once again. She forcibly buried her sudden flash of insight and, having located her watch and noted the time, crawled wearily out of bed.

The horses would need feeding, but surprisingly no whickering sounds of hunger were coming from the barn. She scrambled into some jeans and a flannel shirt, not bothering with underwear, and slipped her feet into a pair of loafers. The animals usually ate early. She was also anxious to check Chauncey. His medication should have been administered hours ago.

Cassie was relieved when Chauncey poked his head over the edge of the stall, ears cocked, and whinnied at her approach. Although caked with mud and exhibiting a noticeably lower energy level then usual, he appeared to be recovering. She reached over the railing and stroked his matted coat.

Chauncey didn't act hungry, which puzzled Cassie until she looked into the feed bin. Small bits of hay rested in the bottom, along with evidence of a fine, powdery substance. Trevor must have fed him.

She headed in the direction of the mare's stalls, and as she passed the tack room, she saw a piece of paper speared on a hook next to the door. Plucking the note from the hook, she saw it was from Trevor and told her that he'd fed the horses and given the medicine to Chauncey.

A wide smile crossed Cassie's face.

She worked outside most of the day, cleaning up the damage caused by the storm. She gave Chauncey a long leisurely bath, hosed down the mares, raked the drive, filled potholes and removed leaves. Although she was fatigued, the hard work felt good and it helped discipline her mind. She tried not to think of Trevor or her embarrassing conduct the previous evening. Sometimes though, without warning, a sudden undisciplined thought raced through her mind before she could squelch it. A stray speculation about a possible future together. A random flash of desire. A quick picture of his chiseled profile. But each thought also provoked memories of her father's broken body, or a crumpled car streaked with red paint and of Jake's angry face as he'd insulted her father many years ago.

The memories made her rake harder, scrape harder and haul faster. She was so engrossed in her present task, scraping burnt paint from the shed eaves, that she didn't hear a truck pull into the drive, and when she turned and saw a man walking toward her she jumped convulsively, nearly hitting her head on the eaves.

"Captain Haggarty!" Regaining her balance, she placed the scraper on the top step of the ladder and stepped to the ground. "What brings you this way?"

"Just checking my territory," he said, "and thought maybe I could talk you into fixing me a cup of coffee."

"My pleasure." Pleasant conversation would keep her mind off. . . that other thing. She chatted amiably with the captain as they walked to the house.

Once inside, she poured them both a cup of coffee and joined him in the breakfast nook, sinking into the soft cushion of the wicker chair. The captain was already comfortably settled and thanked Cassie as he took the cup from her hand. They spoke easily about current Mesquite events—a new colt at the Ames Ranch, a wrangler who'd changed employers, an upcoming marriage, and he congratulated her on winning the Golden Cup.

Cassie thanked him graciously, then added, "But I didn't win it, Chauncey did."

"Suppose so," replied the captain. "I hear you had a little problem with him last night."

Cassie nodded. "Colic. A bad case, too. I nearly lost him."

The captain was momentarily silent. "Did the vet call you today?"

"No. He said he wanted to speak to me, but the power was only restored a couple of hours ago, and I haven't got around to phoning him yet."

"How about the fire chief?"

Cassie shook her head. "But he said he wanted to speak with me, too." Suddenly those requests seemed ominous, and Cassie realized that the captain was leading up to something. "Okay, out with it."

A grin poked at the corner of the captain's mouth. "You don't miss much, do you?" He laughed and his round stomach shook from the reverberation again reminding Cassie of Santa Claus. "All right. I guess it's time to come to the point."

He told Cassie about his early morning visit and what he'd found. Cassie concentrated on every word and was aghast when she heard about the glass in the hay. She shuddered to think how close she'd come to losing Chauncey.

When he'd finished, she said, "So you finally believe someone wants me out of Mesquite? What about my father's death? After what happened, do you still believe it was an accident?"

The captain rubbed his chin thoughtfully. "I'm sure someone wants you out of Mesquite, Miss Cambridge. The jury's still out on your pa's death. Most of the evidence points to an accident. But I can't think of any reason for someone to want you to leave unless from fear that you might stumble on the truth about your pa. I'll be keeping an eye out, I promise you." He took a swig from his coffee cup, set it down with an air of finality and lifted his bulk from the chair. "Well, I'd better be on my way."

Cassie walked the captain to the door. "Have you found anything more about the paint on my father's car?"

"Only that Jake did, indeed, have his car repainted. Nothing yet on how it got damaged. But I'm still looking into it."

Cassie thanked him for his help, then returned to her work, reflecting on what the captain had just told her. Deliberate. All the events of last night had been deliberately caused. The knowledge was almost more than she could digest in one moment.

Although the captain hadn't said he suspected the Bradfords, he'd hinted at it. Certainly he had no better suspects. Who else would want Cassie to leave Mesquite?

She thought of the previous evening. Without Trevor's help, Chauncey would have died. Trevor had proved again and again that he was her ally. But this just made his being employed by Jake bother Cassie even more deeply. How could she look at him without thinking of Jake? Or her father? She felt guilty, and her warm feelings for Trevor seemed an affront to her father's memory. She needed to stay away from him until she could sort out her conflicting thoughts.

DAYLIGHT WAS FADING and Cassie's body ached when she quit working for the day and walked into the house. Since the captain's departure she'd repainted the shed, exercised the horses and cleaned all the stalls. Busy. Just keep busy and all the anxiety monsters would leave her. She was lonely without Julia and wanted to talk to her about the previous night's events. Maybe now she would see that the Bradfords were dangerous.

Cassie took a hot shower, allowing the beat of the water to revive her overworked muscles, then towel-dried and combed out her freshly washed hair. Slipping into a terry-cloth bathrobe, she headed downstairs to fix something to eat.

Not truly hungry, she prepared a light dinner of scrambled eggs and bacon and had just finished the last bite when she saw the headlights of a car coming up the drive. Low headlights. Like those of a sports car. Her breathing stopped and immediately she was angry at herself. The last person she wanted to see was Trevor Austin. At least that's what her head told her. Her heart, wildly beating in her chest, told an entirely different story as she reluctantly walked to the door.

"What a surprise, Trevor." Cassie opened the door with feigned nonchalance, hoping her coolness hid her throbbing pulse.

He smiled wryly. "Ah, Cassie, my sweet." He stepped inside without waiting for an invitation. "I was hoping for an impassioned pledge of undying love. Have I done something to offend you?"

She wasn't expecting his flippancy and it caught her off guard. His oblique reference to the previous night brought back vivid memories and she flushed deeply. Lowering her head, she said, "You caught me at a bad time."

"Milady is upset. What can I do to appease her?"

Although Cassie was aware that Trevor thought she was still annoyed about his rejection the previous night and was just attempting to tease her out of it, his light attitude ignited a fuse. He worked for the man who'd tried to kill her horse and here he was trying to... She wasn't sure what he was trying to do. She snapped her head up and leveled a cool stare in his direction. "You can tell me who tried to kill my horse. That's what you can do."

He immediately abandoned his teasing attitude. "You heard from Haggarty today?"

His question surprised Cassie. "How did you know?"

"I saw him this morning before I left. He was investigating and showed me what he found."

"Did he tell you he suspected Jake?"

Trevor ran his hand across his forehead before answering. "Not in so many words. He did imply that Jake was the only one with a motive. But I don't believe it."

"Why did you come here last night, Trevor?"

"I knew Julia was gone and I thought you might need help because of the storm."

"Is that the only reason?"

"No..." Trevor removed his hat and ruffled his hair as though thinking. Suddenly his eyes flashed with understanding. "You think I had something to do with what happened, don't you?" His tone was now hard with controlled anger.

Cassie turned away from him, wanting to avoid the accusation in his eyes. "I don't know what to think, Trevor. All I know is that someone's trying to hurt me, and I'm afraid. And that I almost lost Chauncey."

He grasped her shoulders and abruptly turned her to face him, looking at her with blazing eyes. "But you didn't lose him. We saved him, didn't we, Cassie?"

She nodded mutely, suddenly mesmerized by the light reflecting from his fiery eyes. She stared in fascination as the fire of his anger mellowed, ripened and changed to the deep blue of desire. Almost instinctively she slid her arms around his waist and tipped her head back as, pulling her tightly against his chest, he lowered his lips to hers.

They were soft. They were hard. They were bruising and caressing. Firecrackers exploded. Brilliant blue. Radiant red. Hot. Cold. Glorious light filled her consciousness, and she was no longer aware of anything but the pressure of Trevor's mouth and the touch of his wild hands roaming her body with a hunger matching her own. She only dimly noticed when he momentarily broke away, kicked the door shut and stripped off his boots and pants. When once again he pulled her into his arms, she yielded to the weakness in her legs and sank to the floor with him, clinging helplessly.

His breath was sweet and ragged against her face as he gently untied the belt of her robe. A small moan escaped his lips when he gazed at her naked body. Then he pulled her against the full length of him. The thrust of his manhood came alive against her aching loins. She wriggled against him, placing small frantic kisses on his chiseled cheekbones, nibbling at his ears, tasting the curve of his neck and the powerful muscles of his shoulder.

His kisses tantalized her. His tongue moved across the soft underside of her lower lip, grazing her teeth, sending exquisite sensations throughout her body. She drank in the musky scent of his cologne, running searching hands through his thick hair. Her skin tingled as each strand caressed her fingers, and then she sought the different texture of his smooth bare back. His hands skillfully searched her body. They seemed to touch everywhere at once and ignited a storehouse of desire that Cassie had kept locked for so long. She responded joyfully, returning his kisses, kiss for kiss; his touches, touch for touch; wanting to join his body and lay waste to any walls standing between them.

She rolled on her back, opening her body, welcoming his response to the demand that they be joined as one. She cried out his name when he entered her, then enclosed him in an all-consuming embrace as together they rode to the top of the flame.

Afterward they clung to each other for a long, long time, breathing heavily at first, allowing the fire of their passion to subside to embers. Cassie luxuriated in the weight of his body on top of hers and traced small patterns on his back with her fingers. He took one hand and kissed the palm, sending electric tingles to the very center of her soul. "I knew it would be like this," he said, finally breaking their intimate silence. "It's as though we were meant to be together."

"I know," she said in an aching whisper. Reality was intruding, dowsing the flames, and Cassie wanted to return to the fire. "What are we going to do, Trevor?"

"I don't know. But let's not think about it for a while." He sat up, despite Cassie's small moan of protest, then slid between her legs, lifting her on his lap and wrapping her legs around him. He buried his hands in her hair and pulled her mouth to his in a bittersweet kiss....

Later they lay in her bed, spooned together, and he told her about Marvin. His hand absently drew small circles over the curves of her breasts while he spoke.

"You mean that saddle was meant for Chauncey?" She turned on her back, brushing his hand away. It was hard to concentrate when he was doing that.

"Yes. If you go through your tack room, I'm certain you'll find a Circle Y saddle with the Bradford brand on it. Starfire's trainer took your saddle away before Marvin had time to switch them again."

Cassie sat up abruptly. "One more piece of evidence. Papa always said that Jake rigged horse shows. This just proves it."

Trevor put up his hand in protest. "Whoa, Cassie. I didn't say Jake had anything to do with it. This was Marvin's doing. Only Marvin."

"What would Marvin have to gain by acting on his own, Trevor? Jake had to be behind it. Why are you always defending him?"

Trevor reached out to pull her close. She rebuffed his hand testily. Seeing his eyes flicker with pain, she immediately regretted her action. This cool, calm man was suddenly vulnerable, and she realized that she was the source of his vulnerability. An overwhelming tenderness suffused her. If only she could fully trust him.

She leaned over and placed a light kiss on his mouth. "Quit working for Jake, Trevor. Please."

He buried a hand in her hair and ran his finger along the curve of her jaw. "I can't, Cassie. Not right now. I've never met a woman like you and I cherish what we have together. But I have commitments that I just can't walk away from."

"You could work for me. You could replace Harry Teitelbaum."

A wry grin played at his lips in an obvious attempt to cover his painful conflict. "Do you think I could live on the one hour of legal work you generate each month?"

She could see the logic of his statement. They were at an impasse. She knew Trevor didn't share her opinion of Jake, and the man was, after all, a wealthy employer. With a sigh she flopped back down beside him on the bed. "I guess not," she conceded sadly. "But it tears me apart, knowing you work for a man I hate."

He gathered her in his arms. "It won't be forever, Cassie. Let's just enjoy what we have right now."

She cradled her head on his shoulder. "Sleep," he said. "It's late." She nodded and began to drift into a gentle slumber when a question popped in her mind.

"Trevor, how did you get Marvin to tell you about the saddle?"

The first answer was a long silence, but finally he chuckled deeply and said, "I have my ways."

"What ways?" A delightful suspicion was forming in her mind. "Did you and Marvin have a fight?"

"I wouldn't exactly call it a fight. It takes two to make a fight. Let's say we had a confrontation."

"You did!" she exclaimed, breaking into laughter. "I'm ashamed of you. A grown man fighting." She teased him between bursts of laughter. "I hope you beat the tar out of him."

"I wouldn't say it went that far," he replied with an answering laugh, hugging her tightly against him. "But I'm always a champion of ladies in distress, especially this lady."

And despite all her doubts, Cassie believed him. Believed him deeply. But she also knew she believed only because she wanted to.

THE ALARM intruded on her deep peaceful sleep, and as she rolled over to hit the snooze button she was surprised by the hindering arm around her waist. But only for a moment. A smile lighted her face as she turned to see a drowsy Trevor smiling back. She slapped the alarm button and snuggled up next to him, savoring the warmth of his body, and he wrapped her in his arms and went back to sleep. For a while, she lay next to him, then she slipped quietly out of bed and into the bathroom for a shower.

When she returned to the bedroom Trevor was shaking off the last vestiges of sleep. "Where are you going in such a hurry?"

"There's still lots of work to be done," she said, gazing affectionately at his sleepy face. "The storm blew some shingles loose and I have to tack them down before the roof leaks. Also, the horses need working."

He reached out a hand toward her. She moved closer and took it in hers. Even the touch of his hand sent delicious chills down her spine. "Why don't you hire someone to fix the roof, Cassie? And we'll play hooky today."

"Can't. The weather report says another storm is coming, and I'm operating on a shoestring, remember?"

"All work and no play makes Cassie a dull girl," he teased, slowly untying the belt to Cassie's robe. She giggled and pretended to fight him off.

"Where have I heard that before?"

"What?"

"That's what Aunt Julia always says. So you think I'm dull, do you?" She bopped him on the head with a pillow. With mock fear, he lifted his arms to ward off her blows.

"No," he pleaded. "I didn't mean it. Not dull. Definitely not dull." Snatching the pillow from her grasp, he threw it aside and enclosed her in his arms, rewarding her with a generous, delectable kiss. "Most definitely not dull," he repeated after releasing her lips. Then he captured them again.

Cassie thought she'd spent every ounce of her passion during the previous night, but the touch of his lips, the sweetness of his fluttering tongue, sent millions of miniature explosions through her body, and soon she answered him with a matching fervor. She wanted to taste every inch of him, slowly, savoring his sweet flavor.

Restraining the high tide of passion that rippled through her, she tore her lips from his and poured small kisses over the strong line of his jaw, his neck. Moving down his shoulders and chest, she tasted his erect nipples, evoking a shudder from his hot body. She continued down, savoring the salty tang of his skin. When she touched the solid center of his pleasure, he arched his back and she yielded to the urgent need to taste him fully. An aching moan escaped his lips and she clung to him, reveling in his cries of pleasure.

And when she thought she could hunger no more, he brought her around to face him, grazing her mouth with soft, moist lips and whetted her appetite again, his marvelous hands taking her to a banquet of sensuality where she was fully satiated in every way.

Still panting, Cassie rested against his shoulder as he stroked her hair with such tenderness she thought her heart would break. She felt complete, as if, with Trevor beside her, nothing was missing in her life. She basked in the afterglow and prayed it would never end.

But as their breathing returned to normal, small doubts poked at her mind. She was frightened of falling in love, yet knew her thoughts were already becoming long range. And how did Trevor feel? She didn't believe he loved her, though she wanted to believe it. If she allowed herself to sink into this relationship, could she survive if he left her?

Becoming irritated at her own thoughts, she banished them to a corner of her mind. They were ghosts she would exorcise on another day. Reluctantly she slipped out of bed. "I'll have to take another shower," she teased, enjoying the sight of Trevor reclining on the bed.

"I'll join you." His eyes sparkled with devilish good humor. "I'm wide awake now."

They shared a playful shower, splashing water and scrubbing each other's back, then went downstairs, where Cassie prepared breakfast, frying eggs and bacon, while Trevor made toast and coffee. They ate slowly, trying to delay their inevitable parting, and Trevor attempted, several times, to persuade Cassie to take the day off.

But even though she ached at the thought of his leaving, Cassie refused. There truly was much to do, but more than that she needed some time to herself. Time to sort out her raging emotions and put things into perspective. So, with many gentle kisses, she finally led him to the door and shoved him outside, agreeing to have dinner with him that night.

Cassie shut the door softly, returned to the kitchen, and refilled her coffee cup. The kitchen was one of her favorite places. It brought back hazy memories of her early childhood when her family ate breakfast here. At times in this room, Cassie could almost smell her mother's flowery fragrance, see the tiny print on her beautiful dressing gown and the lovely golden tresses piled upon her head.

It was a rustic room. Rough-hewed terra-cotta tile covered the floor and the pattern on the long counters picked up the color beautifully. A chopping counter stood in the center of the kitchen beneath a round copper wheel from which pots, pans and utensils were suspended, ready for instant use.

She walked to the breakfast nook with its huge bay window hung with tied-back curtains. She placed her cup upon the rattan table and sank into a chair with a soft green flowery cushion matching the curtains. The pattern, once bright, was now faded, and the subdued shade added to the charm and the timelessness of the nook.

For some reason Cassie could always think clearly in this place. She gazed out the window, allowing her eyes to roam over the rolling pasture and into the distance where the proud icy Tetons stood, snow capped even in summer, jutting their majestic heads above the lesser mountains of the Mesquite Valley range. The racing questions in her mind were slowing, coming down to manageable speed. In a few moments she could face the situation. Just as she felt a measure of calm overtake her, she saw Julia's dilapidated Volkswagen putter up the drive.

CHAPTER TEN

As CASSIE walked down the front steps, she saw Julia wrestling with a suitcase jammed in the storage compartment behind the front seat of her little car. "Need some help?"

"No, no. I've got it." With a final yank, Julia freed the case and pulled it out the door.

Cassie took the bag from her hand, set it down and gave her an elated hug. "I'm so glad you're home."

"I got here as fast as I could, Cassie. I worried about you when I couldn't reach you by phone after the storm. Did you have problems?"

Cassie nodded. "Bad problems." She began telling Julia of the events of that stormy night. Her aunt listened quietly, brow furrowed, as Cassie briefly told her of Chauncey's illness and the fire caused by the downed power pole, making no comment until Cassie reached the part about Trevor's help.

"I like that boy," Julia interjected.

"You like that boy?" Cassie repeated incredulously. "The whole world caves in and all you can say is you like that boy? Besides, he isn't a boy."

Julia responded with a sheepish grin. "I know what's important, that's all. A man like that only comes along once in a while."

"Oh, is that so?" Cassie said in a sassy tone. She was so delighted to see her aunt that nothing could annoy her.

"That's so." Julia bobbed her head definitively, as though there was nothing more to discuss.

Cassie laughed and threw her arms around the petite woman, giving her a large kiss on the cheek. "I'm just glad you're here. I missed you."

Julia gave her a sly look. "But not too glad, I imagine."

Cassie, slightly hurt by her comment, asked what she meant. "I passed Trevor's Porsche as I was driving out here."

Cassie lowered her head to hide the flush that was inexorably appearing. She didn't know what was wrong with her. Blushing had never been her style. "Um...yeah...uh...he stopped by to make sure everything was okay here." She hated lying, but it was embarrassing to discuss her love life with her aunt.

Julia gave her a knowing wink and Cassie's flush intensified. "Like I said, a man like that doesn't come along very often."

"Aunt Julia!" Cassie replied indignantly. "He is just a friend, and besides that, it's none of your business."

"Everything about you is my business, Cassie. I want to see you happy." She picked up the suitcase, took Cassie's arm and started heading for the house. "Have you eaten?"

"Yes, I have, thanks. But if you haven't, I'll fix you breakfast."

Julia laughed. "You cook for me? That'll be the day."

Cassie laughed, too, and slipped her arm around Julia's waist. "We'll see about that," she retorted.

"You sit. I'll cook. I need to talk." And she did urgently need to talk. To talk about Trevor. The Bradfords. Her feelings. Her fears. She just didn't know where to begin.

They walked companionably into the house and went into the kitchen. Cassie parked Julia in one of the wicker chairs and started breakfast. While preparing the eggs and bacon she asked Julia about the conference.

"Same old thing," Julia answered. "Rules, rules and more rules. So tell me, Cassie, what's on your mind?"

Cassie turned the eggs on to a plate. "It's complicated, Julia. I'm not sure how to start." She speared bacon from the pan and transferred it to the plate, adding a couple of slices of toast.

"Why don't you start at the beginning," Julia responded. Cassie walked to the table and set the plate in front of her.

"Good idea," Cassie agreed, and while Julia ate, Cassie poured out the events of the past few weeks. She told Julia, again, about the fire and Chauncey's illness and about Captain Haggarty's visit. Julia's eyebrows shot up when Cassie talked about the evidence that pointed to a deliberate act. She started to make a comment, but Cassie raised her hand to indicate more was coming, continuing on about the man who'd pulled her into the entryway of Chez Teton, and Marvin's violent attack at the futurity.

Her eyes suddenly glistening with tears, Julia took Cassie's hand. "Why didn't you tell me about any of this before, Cassie? I feel as if I've let you down." She blinked the tears back and looked at Cassie intently.

Cassie sighed and rubbed her face. "You were so worn out after the funeral and . . ."

"And?"

"Well, Aunt Julia, you've been so dead certain that I was wrong about Jake. I just thought I should handle it myself." She hated being so direct, but she'd felt so alone without Julia's support and it seemed important now to make her understand.

Julia nodded thoughtfully. "Yes, I see why you'd feel that way." She released Cassie's hand and toyed with the collar of her tailored shirt. They were silent for a moment. Then Julia looked up, her eyes shining with love. "I *have* let you down, honey. I see that now, and I truly regret it. I never believed you were in any danger." With a thud, Julia slammed her fist against the table, shocking Cassie thoroughly, and added vehemently, "We have to find out who's behind all this!"

"Who? Jake Bradford's behind it, that's who." Suddenly Julia's refusal to face Cassie's feeling about Jake Bradford incensed her. "Who else would have reason to cut that power pole or put ground glass in Chauncey's feed? I already know it was Marvin who tried to sabotage Chauncey's performance at the futurity."

"What are you talking about?" Julia's puzzled expression made Cassie realize she hadn't mentioned the saddle yet.

"Marvin swapped saddles at the futurity." Cassie explained wearily. "We have identical roping saddles. He took mine and weakened the cinch and breast collar. He was planning to put the damaged saddle back in our tack room before the competition but something went wrong."

Julia's face flushed with enlightenment. "So that's why Starfire had the accident you talked about." Julia's expression changed to mirth and then she dissolved into gales of laughter. Cassie stared at her in disbelief. This wasn't an amusing subject. "Oh, that's funny," she said between laughs. "He was trying to make sure you lost and instead ended up losing himself." Julia bent over to hold her sides, unable to stop her laughter.

One of Julia's most endearing traits was the ability to see humor in almost everything, and caught up in the infectious bubbles of her laughter, Cassie gave a small chuckle. Then, as Julia's laughter began to subside, the irony in the situation hit home and she, too, began laughing. Releasing the tension she'd carried for the past two days she became lost in hilarity, completely unable to control her giggles. She felt like a young girl again, sitting in the kitchen, laughing with Julia.

The giggling fit finally ebbed and Cassie lifted her head, wiping away the tears still streaming down her face. "I hadn't looked at it that way. Until now."

"You haven't been laughing enough these days, Cassie. Ever since you came home you've been so intense, so set upon proving something. You need to have fun. Laugh more."

Cassie was now totally relaxed and found herself able to see the wisdom in Julia's words. She was about to reply when Julia leaned across the table and took both her hands.

"I love having you here, honey. It's been so long since you've been home and I've missed you so. But I don't think this place is good for you. I think you should sell Cambridge, Cassie. Go back to Denver. I'm so afraid that staying in Mesquite will bring you nothing but heartache."

Although Cassie was astonished at Julia's directness, her words struck a chord deep inside. She suddenly had a glimmer of how grim and single-minded she'd become. Perhaps it was time for a change, for her to reexamine her goals, her priorities. She gazed out the window, drinking in the beauty of the rugged land.

The pasture lay before her eyes. Stolen by her ancestors from the silent, eternal, rock, it was a monument to her family's determination to bend wild nature to its will. She realized then, that though it was only a piece of land, she truly loved Cambridge Stables for itself, and it was this enduring love that formed the bedrock of her confidence. She couldn't leave. So maybe the time had come to begin enjoying this place that was her home.

She returned her gaze to Julia. Her abiding affection for the woman who had been the only mother she'd ever known welled up to almost overwhelming proportions. She squeezed Julia's hands. "I see what you're saying, Aunt Julia—probably for the first time since I've been here. I do need to lighten up. But I can't sell Cambridge Stables. I can't leave yet. I will promise to relax more, though. Would that make you happy?"

Julia gave a sad little smile. "Maybe you wouldn't have to sell, Cassie. Maybe you could just hire someone to run it."

"Eventually. After all, I promised Al I'd come back to the business. But the stable isn't on its feet yet. Besides," Cassie added hesitantly, "there's Trevor."

"Trevor?" Julia's eyes gleamed with interest. "Tell me more."

So at last Cassie opened the subject that had really been uppermost in her mind, and over several cups of coffee, she poured her heart out to Julia as she had so often done long ago when she was a child.

CASSIE FELT SOFTER SOMEHOW, less brittle, as she went through her closet, searching for something to wear to dinner with Trevor. Most of her wardrobe was still in the garment bags she'd packed so hastily when she left Denver. Needing only jeans and workshirts, there had been no reason to unpack them. Now she leafed through the various bags, hunting for something appropriately casual and dressy. Casual and dressy. Now that was a contradiction in terms, she thought as her hand found a blue silk jumpsuit.

She extracted it from the bag and examined it critically. The top had loose dolmen sleeves and an overlapping Grecian neckline. The bodice and pants gathered softly at the waist, leading down to slim legs loosely tucked at the ankle. Perfect. She stroked the nubby, brilliant fabric with one hand. Now a belt. She rummaged some more, unearthing a pale violet belt with a lovely shell clasp. The contrast was perfect, and she searched again, coming up with the matching shoes.

Strange, after all this time, to be fretting over her choice of clothing again. It was also fun. Talking with Julia had left her relaxed and accepting. Julia had advised her to let go of her anger and let love take its course. Cassie thought she just might take that advice and hummed softly to herself as she slipped into her clothing. It was nearly eight o'clock and Trevor would be arriving soon. She wondered if he were the punctual type and realized that despite what had passed between them, she knew little about him. It looked as if this was the time to change all that.

The doorbell rang and she hurried to complete the finishing touches. A little blusher on the cheeks and a quick comb through the hair. Inspecting herself critically, she had to admit she didn't look bad. Trevor had seen her at her worst. If he liked her then, surely he would love her now. Love. Lord, how she hoped he loved her.

Julia rapped on the bedroom door and stuck her head in, beaming broadly, as though there were an unspoken conspiracy between them. "Trevor's here."

Julia didn't conceal her approval of the relationship, and Cassie was somewhat embarrassed as they walked down the stairs and Julia presented her as though she were a debutante at her first ball. "Doesn't she look pretty?" she asked, taking Cassie's hands and twirling her around in a small circle, then presenting her to Trevor. Trevor whistled.

"Pretty? Beautiful, I'd say." He took Cassie's hands from Julia's and held her at arm's length so he could get a better look. "Breathtakingly beautiful," he added in a lower, huskier voice. Cassie basked in the glow of his open admiration and thought how handsome he looked. The diffused light of the entry hall chandelier softened the angular lines of his face, making it appear almost boyish, and his eyes were a brilliant dancing blue, sparkling with anticipation.

He had abandoned his Western clothing for the evening and wore a turtleneck pullover, casual slacks and a navy blue sports jacket. He looked so handsome that Cassie suppressed a wave of desire, remembering how he looked even better undressed.

"You two be on your way now." Julia had gathered Cassie's jacket and held it for Cassie to slip into. "Have fun," she added, opening the door and virtually pushing them onto the porch.

Cassie laughed as she closed the door and Trevor looked at her, an amused if somewhat puzzled look on his face. "What are you laughing about?"

"Aunt Julia. She's acting as if she's sending a slightly unmarriageable daughter out to be courted. I wonder if she's counting my dowry."

"Unmarriageable, huh?" Trevor looked at her with mock disapproval. "That'll be the day. You, pretty lady, are immensely marriageable, and don't you forget it."

"Is that a proposal?" she asked flippantly, then almost bit her tongue. What a dumb thing to say.

Trevor looked at her out of the side of his eyes. "We'll see," he replied cryptically, a sphinxlike expression on his face, though his eyes sparkled.

Everything seemed faintly amusing to Cassie, and the thinly veiled arrogance of his remark struck her as funny. She laughed a bell-like peal and poked Trevor playfully in the ribs. He clasped her hand and put his arm around her shoulder. "I can see I'm going to have my hands full keeping you under control tonight."

"You betcha, mister," Cassie bantered back. They had reached his Porsche, and Trevor opened the door, sticking his tongue out at Cassie as she slid in the seat. As soon as he was also seated inside, he stuck his tongue out again, then reached over and gathered Cassie in his arms, his eyes darkening in that now familiar way. She encircled his neck with her own arms and hungrily welcomed his approaching mouth.

Her lips softened at his touch and parted at the pressure of his insistent tongue. What wonderful uses we can make of tongues, Cassie thought irreverently as she sank into the delicious warmth of his embrace.

Time ceased to move as they caressed, tasted and stroked each other, but finally Trevor broke away.

"We'd better stop this," he said hoarsely. "Or Julia will wonder why we spent the whole night in the driveway. Is the Ol' Watering Hole all right?"

"Fine," said Cassie, confessing that she'd never been there. In fact, except for the lodge, she hadn't seen any of the night spots of Mesquite.

"It looks like I'm going to have to reacquaint you with your own hometown."

"I can think of worse prospects."

They continued bantering until the came to the restaurant. Trevor parked the car and once again stole a tingling kiss before tearing himself away. "Hardest thing I've ever done," he murmured as he slipped out of the car. He gave her another light peck on the mouth as he helped her out and they walked inside arm in arm.

The restaurant was a unique blend of the formal and informal. Walls of coarse dark wood, exposed beams and copper lamps greeted her eyes as the tuxedoed maître d' escorted them to their table. In contrast to the homespun architecture, the table was formally set.

Carefully arranged napkins were placed in silver rings on the serving plates. After sitting in the high-backed traditionally upholstered chair in which the maître d' had seated her, Cassie removed the ring and settled the napkin in her lap.

"Do you like it?" Trevor asked after a prompt waiter had taken their drink order. He seemed anxious for her approval and this small chink in his defenses touched Cassie.

"It's charming." As they sipped their wine and perused the menu—hers without prices—her gaze roamed the Oriental rugs, artfully laid upon the wide plank floor and the beautiful rectangular stained-glass windows that ran around the entire room beneath the high ceiling.

They ordered dinner and soon the salad course arrived. As they ate, Cassie asked Trevor why he had left his law practice. "I know you're writing a novel, but what made you reach that decision? It couldn't have been easy to leave a successful practice."

He talked openly about what must have been a very difficult time in his life and told her about defending thieves and murderers and how disenchanted he had become with the lack of true justice in the court system.

He continued talking at her urging. The flickering candle shed a pulsating light across Trevor's face and the table, creating a feeling of isolation even in the large room. She wanted to know everything about him, and when he said he'd lost an important case, Cassie commented, "All attorneys lose a case now and then, Trevor."

"Yes, they do. But this one was different." He had defended a woman who had murdered her husband after enduring years of physical and mental abuse. "The woman was a broken shell, Cassie, and prison killed her before I could bring the case to appeal. She was sentenced to ten years, while hordes of scum walked free because I was able to have charges dropped on technicalities. Yet I couldn't save one pathetic woman who had been driven to the edge of madness." He spoke with an intensity Cassie had never seen before. "That's when I decided to come here."

Cassie understood, and she recognized, for the first time, that they were much alike. They both believed in justice. They both felt the effects of injustice intensely. Unfortunately, she reminded herself, when it came to the Bradfords they saw justice in a different light. She pushed that thought from her mind.

The waiter interrupted to clear the table and asked if they would like dessert. They both declined, but ordered Keoke coffee, which was presented with the same dispatch as the entire meal. Cassie took a sip of the sweet liquid and leaned back in her chair. Filled with well-being, she felt she could sit there forever, sipping coffee and drinking in the sight of Trevor's face.

"But your situation is different, Cassie. Why did you leave the glamorous world of advertising?" His question hit a tender spot since it touched on the subject of her father's death.

She forced a smile. She didn't want anything to spoil this evening. "I'm not planning to stay forever, Trevor. Just until Cambridge Stables is financially sound."

"What will you do if you can't make that happen?"

Cassie's eyes began burning and she didn't answer, for fear her voice would crack. She turned her head away to conceal her emotion, knowing Trevor saw. He leaned across the table and lifted her hand into his. "I'm sorry, Cassie. I didn't mean to hurt you. It's just that I want to know everything about you."

"I can't fail, Trevor. I just can't." Her voice was a choked whisper. "If I let Jake Bradford win, it will mean my father's life was lived in vain."

"Win what? Domination of the quarter-horse circuit?"

Cassie checked her tears and turned her head back. "Yes," she said defiantly. "That, and...and I want our land back."

"I don't mean to sound pessimistic but it's just a dream, Cassie, and I'm not even sure it's your dream."

"If it isn't, I'll make it mine."

"But it will never happen. Jake has worked too hard getting that land. He'll never give it up."

"Yes, he worked hard," Cassie replied, bitterness dripping from her voice. "He worked hard at destroying my father. Then in the end he killed him."

Trevor looked at her as if she were demented. "Why are you so convinced that Jake killed your father? Do you have any evidence?"

She gave him a sullen look. "I feel like I'm being cross-examined, Trevor. Isn't what happened the night before last evidence enough? And what about that man who attacked me in Mesquite with his ridiculous 'You'll live to regret it' line? What further evidence do you need?"

Cassie was answered with a long silence. She toyed with the little straw in her drink wondering what Trevor would say next.

"I'm sorry, Cassie." She was relieved by Trevor's sincere tone. "It is obvious that someone is trying to get you to leave Mesquite, but no matter how I run it through my mind I can't see any reason Jake would be involved. He simply has no motive."

"You're right, Trevor. There is no obvious motive, but there is a connection. There was a streak of red paint on the fender of Papa's car. The next week, Jake had that little red sports car of his repaired and re-painted in Denver."

"Oh, that." The tension immediately left Trevor's face. "Marvin hit a fencepost while he was driving the car. It's common knowledge. Jake was really hot about it and read Marvin the riot act. He took the car to

Denver to be sure of getting a perfect paint match. Besides, it gave him a chance to see Marion."

Cassie also felt tension leaving her body. She realized suddenly that she no longer wanted to believe that Jake killed her father. To do so created an almost insurmountable obstacle to developing a relationship with Trevor, and he had stated his explanation with such sincerity that Cassie believed him—or at least she believed that he believed. "And that's the whole story?"

"The whole story, Cassie. There were witnesses." She wanted to believe also, but inside her a small voice wondered. If Trevor's explanation was truly common knowledge, why hadn't the captain heard about it? She stilled the voice, wanting to ignore its message. Wanting, instead, the sweet intimacy they had shared earlier.

She gazed thoughtfully into her coffee cup. "Everyone—you, Julia, the captain—everyone thought I was wrong. Now they believe that someone's out to sabotage me, but not Jake. Maybe they're right. Maybe it's time I listened. But if it isn't Jake, who is it?"

"I don't know, Cassie. I wish I did. But there is one thing I do know. Something very special is happening with us and if Jake Bradford comes between us, we're the ones who'll be the losers. I know you have a dream, Cassie, and parts of it are wonderful. But a dream based on hate can never bring happiness. Let's build our life on..."

He lowered his gaze and stared intently into his cup as though searching its depths for his next word.

Love.

Cassie's heart stopped. Her breathing ceased. For a moment, just one crazy, hopeful moment, she thought

Trevor was going to say he wanted to build a life with her, based on love.

"On something else," Trevor concluded, drawing a tantalizing finger across the back of her hand.

Her heartbeat and breathing returned to normal. Disappointment burst the balloon of her soaring hopes. Still, it was such a romantic speech, and the realization that he was referring to a future together with her left some of her hope intact. It is time, she thought. Time to let go of hate. Time to look to the future instead of the past.

"You know what I'd like to do, Cassie. I'd like to dance with you again. Feel you next to me and get lost in the music."

Leaning across the table, Cassie ran her finger down Trevor's nose. "Sounds wonderful." Trevor grasped her finger, drew it across his full lower lip, then placed a tender kiss on the tip, locking eyes with her.

"Then let's blow this joint, milady." Still holding her hand, he stood to help her out of her chair. Cassie rose. Trevor's intoxicating nearness made her heady. She leaned her head against his broad chest, oblivious to the other diners.

"We'd better leave," Trevor murmured. "Or we'll never be able to come back here."

They drove to the Mesquite Lodge, secured a table, then danced until the closing lights came on. They walked hand in hand to Trevor's Porsche and, once settled inside, Trevor gathered Cassie in his arms. "It's been driving me crazy, being so close to you and not being able to touch you...like this." He trailed his hand across the swell of Cassie's breasts, visible above the deep V of her bodice. "And like this." Electricity shot through her. She sighed deeply, arching her head against the seat as he deposited butterfly kisses behind the path of his hand.

"And this gear box is driving me even crazier." His kisses moved across her shoulder, up her neck and onto the curve of her cheek as her body slowly dissolved into liquid desire. With difficulty, she attempted to return to reality.

"The accommodations do leave a little to be desired." Her voice sounded as if it were coming from someplace far away.

"Come to my place with me, Cassie."

Cassie cringed at the request. Reality became very clear. Trevor lived on Bradford Ranch. As much as she wanted to be with him, as much as she wanted to give up her anger, she just couldn't. "I'm sorry, Trevor, but you're asking too much."

"I have my own entrance. You won't have to see..." His voice trailed off, as he obviously realized the enormity of his request.

"Yes, I suppose it is too much to ask." He released Cassie and sat upright in his seat, running his fingers through his thick hair. After a long silence he said, "I'll just have to get a place in town."

Cassie's face broke into a delighted smile. "You'd do that for me?"

"You're worth it." His lecherous grin brought highly dramatic pleas for mercy from Cassie, which he smothered with a delicious kiss. Leaving the lodge parking lot, they drove to a secluded spot near one of Mesquite Valley's many lakes, and for the first time in her life Cassie made love sitting up in the front seat of a very tiny car.

CHAPTER ELEVEN

CASSIE HAD NEVER been happier. The next day, she and Trevor found his new home. It was a charming little house across from the grammar school. Because it had been built when fire was the only source of heat, there was a fireplace in every room, and the bedroom opened on to a patio filled with flowers and bushes.

Trevor had no furniture, so they rummaged through the gloomy ballroom at Cassie's house, discovering a serviceable sofa and chair in a misty blue color and a tapestry ottoman that coordinated nicely. More digging unearthed a large Oriental rug "to tie the room together," as Cassie put it. The only bed was twin size, but Trevor just smiled his lazy smile and said that he wouldn't mind being closer to her, so they took it anyway.

They haunted little shops and boutiques for accessories, even driving into Jackson in search of the perfect item. When she bubbled to Julia about the brass coatrack they'd found on their latest expedition, Julia asked, "Are you planning on moving in with him?" Cassie dismissed her comment with an amused wave of her hand but realized that she found the idea rather attractive. With each new acquisition, Trevor took her to his new home for a "celebration."

Cassie had kept in frequent contact with Al, and the C&C Agency seemed to be thriving without her. The news gave Cassie a little twinge of regret, as she realized she wasn't indispensable. But her ego had been given a boost when Al had told her how much Sammy Cohen had liked the forties theme she'd suggested for the commercial. According to Al, the little man had kept repeating, "Now that's glamour!" and had given the commercial his broadest blessing. Acceptance. Since then Al and the staff had handled any subsequent crises without Cassie's help.

Business was going well for Cambridge Stables, also. Since the futurity, breeding fees had rolled in, and she hired a town man to come out daily to maintain the grounds. She was looking forward to the day when she could renovate the bunkhouse and cabins and have live-in help again.

Trevor spent mornings working on his novel, visiting Cambridge Stables in the afternoon. Sometimes he helped her work the horses. Sometimes they rode to the cabin, which they had stocked with food and sleeping bags. Other times he stayed for dinner and they drank wine in front of the fireplace in the great room. And many evenings they spent at his place.

One night after dinner at Trevor's house she began talking about her plans for Cambridge Stables. "It will be just like the old days," she said happily. "Now, if only I could find a way to locate the people behind Evergreen trust, everything would be perfect. I'd like to buy it out. It makes me nervous, having that trust hanging over my head." Trevor nodded at her comment but made no suggestions and for a moment seemed to fade away.

"Hey, Earth calling Trevor," Cassie joked.

"Huh?" For a moment he looked at her as though seeing her for the first time. Then he smiled. "Oh. Guess I was in outer space, wasn't I?"

"I was talking about the Evergreen trust. You're a lawyer." She smiled provocatively. She never got tired of looking at him. "Help me."

He noticed the invitation in her smile and responded with a wan grin. "I'll look into it, Cassie. I promise," he said, giving her an absentminded pat. His obvious preoccupation disturbed her.

"Is something wrong?"

"No." But Cassie caught a note of hesitancy in his voice.

"Are you sure?" she pressed. If something was bothering Trevor she wanted to know about it. Wanted to help in any way she could.

His eyes roamed the room, momentarily unfocused. Then he stood up, got a poker from the hearth and began stoking the fire. "What is it, Trevor?" Her voice was low, just barely a whisper.

He replaced the poker in the stand and turned to face her. "It's nothing, Cassie, honest. Sometimes I get so wrapped up in my novel that I have trouble coming back to reality. That's all it is." He sat back down beside her and began tickling her lightly. She fought him weakly, then wrapped her arms around his neck and submitted to his friendly kisses, soon forgetting her earlier concern.

She recalled the conversation several times, wondering if Trevor was being totally honest with her. Also, she hadn't yet called Captain Haggarty to verify Trevor's story about the car. For some reason the memories always came as a pair but then drifted away without her taking action on them and were soon forgotten.

She was thinking about this very subject as she sipped her first cup of coffee and glanced up in the middle of her musings to see Julia standing by the stove, staring intently in her direction. Something about her expression made Cassie anxious. What was going on with the people in her life? Why did they have these blue spells? Wasn't everything going along beautifully?

"Aunt Julia, is something bothering you?"

"Bothering me?" Julia sounded uncharacteristically evasive. "Why do you ask?"

"I'm not sure. It's just that sometimes you appear...worried."

"Oh, I see." There was something in Julia's words that Cassie couldn't quite put her finger on.

"What do you mean, 'you see'?"

Julia aggressively scrubbed an imaginary spot on the stove and the sound grated on Cassie's nerves.

"Nothing serious, Cassie. I'm happy for you and Trevor, but sometimes it's just not easy seeing my little niece all grown up. Even though you're twenty-six years old with a life of your own, I still think of you as my little Cassie."

Cassie smiled. So that was it. Of course. It would be natural for her aunt to feel this way. She got up and walked to Julia, who was still furiously scrubbing away and wrapped her arms about her aunt's slender waist, resting her head on her bent shoulders. Julia stopped scrubbing, straightened and leaned back against Cassie.

"You're worried that if Trevor and I get married, there won't be a place for you here anymore, aren't you?" Cassie asked.

"I suppose that's part of it."

"Well, stop worrying. It's premature, anyway. We haven't even discussed marriage. But if we did, there will still be room for you here. I love you. Trevor loves you. This is your home."

"I hope you always feel that way, Cassie," Julia answered with a sigh, as though there were doubt in her mind.

"Always," Cassie repeated, turning Julia around to face her. "So stop worrying." She wagged a finger near Julia's face, the way her aunt had so often done to her when she was small. "Hear?"

Julia broke into a smile at Cassie's teasing imitation. "The child becomes the parent. Okay, honey, I'll stop worrying." Then she assumed her usual brisk tone. "Now go finish your coffee. I've got an errand to run in town and the account books to bring up to date before I go."

After planting an affectionate kiss on Julia's cheek, Cassie obeyed. "I've got a busy day, too," she commented. "Rick will be here soon to work with Chauncey. We've got to get as much schooling in as we can before the first snow falls. From the looks of today, that could be anytime now."

Julia agreed and resumed her chores while Cassie refilled her coffee cup and went upstairs to get dressed. The doorbell rang, signaling Rick's arrival, and they both went outside to work with Chauncey. The session was going very well and Cassie became engrossed in Chauncey's performance, taking only dim notice when Julia called out and said she was leaving.

Cassie glanced at her watch and noticed it was nearly lunchtime. Her stomach growled, and she asked Rick if he was hungry. "Starved," he replied, so she went inside to prepare a lunch.

She was poking around in the refrigerator, looking for leftover friend chicken when the phone rang.

"Cassie?" a familiar voice asked. The raspy twang was recognizable even over the phone.

"What do you want, Marvin?" Why would Marvin be calling her? He was the last person on earth she wanted to talk to and he knew it.

"How did you know it was me?" he asked.

"You have a singular voice." And that singular voice was already setting Cassie on edge. Would he get to the point?

"Huh?"

"Forget it. Why are you calling, Marvin?"

"I'm calling about Evergreen Enterprises. Trevor told me you wanted to find the people behind it and I thought I could help."

Her interest flickered at the mention of Evergreen, but so did her suspicion. "Why would you want to help me? We haven't exactly been the best of friends. As a matter of fact, the last time we met was decidedly un-friendly."

Marvin slipped into his habitual whine. Combined with the twang, the sound was nearly unbearable. "I know, Cassie, and I'm sorry about that. I had too much to drink and sometimes I get like that. I shouldn't drink so much."

Cassie couldn't listen to any more of his sniveling excuses, and she interrupted. "What do you know about Evergreen?"

"Actually, I don't know anything. But my dad does and I set it up for you to talk to him."

"Talk with your father?" The idea was astounding. As much as she disliked Marvin, those feelings were minor compared with her feelings toward Jake. "Why?"

"Like I said, he has information about Evergreen Enterprises. He said he could see you at one o'clock. At Bradford Ranches. Can you be there?"

Cassie hesitated for a moment. It might be a waste of time, but if Jake truly did know something about the trust, it could be worthwhile. She swallowed her distaste. "I'll be there, Marvin. But I still don't understand why you're helping me."

"I just think we got off on the wrong foot. I'd like to make it up to you."

Keeping in mind that she wanted to make peace with herself and her neighbors, she took Marvin's comment at face value. Perhaps she was being too harsh in judging him.

"I'd like us to become good friends. Real good friends," he added. That was carrying it a bit too far for Cassie.

"We'll see what time will bring," she said cooly. "But thank you, Marvin. Tell Jake I'll see him at one o'clock."

She hung up and ran outside to tell Rick his lunch was on the table but that she had to leave, then scurried up the stairs to change clothes. She wanted to dress appropriately to face Jake. The clothes she'd worn in her business world would do just fine.

IT WAS GETTING LATE when Trevor pulled his Porsche into a parking place near the hardware store. A leaky faucet at the house was getting on his nerves and he wanted to fix it today. He glanced at his watch. It was nearly noon and he was meeting with Jake at one o'clock. He'd better hurry. As he stepped out of the car, he noticed a woman who resembled Julia hurrying along the boardwalk. She slipped into the entry hall of Chez Teton. She must be meeting someone for lunch, he thought. He passed the entry on his way, didn't see her, and since he wasn't certain it was Julia, anyway, he continued to the hardware store.

He picked up the washers he needed, paid for his purchases and glanced at his watch again. Twelve-thirty. It was over a thirty-minute drive to Bradford Ranch. Time to hustle or he'd be late.

Out on the wooden sidewalk, he tucked the small package in his jacket pocket, and when he looked up saw Julia standing in the entry talking to Luke, the wrangler from Bradford Ranch. He was a slippery worm, that one, and Trevor wondered what business he would have with Julia. He stopped, planning to say hello, when he heard Julia's voice increase in volume, full of agitation. He knew he was eavesdropping, but if this man was upsetting Julia, he wanted to know why. He stepped closer to the wall to avoid being seen.

Straining to hear, he leaned slightly forward but they spoke in hushed tones, despite Julia's obvious distress, and only an occasional word drifted to his ears. "Cassie... Denver... Information." Disjointed words that contained no coherent meaning. Then suddenly Julia's voice rose sharply and her words were crystal clear.

"I'll get the money somehow, Luke. I've got to take care of Cassie before she finds out everything." Julia's face had an agitated expression.

Shock reverberated through Trevor's body. He couldn't believe his ears. Julia? Was Julia behind the things that had happened to Cassie? Why? Trevor suppressed an urge to jump into the entryway and shake them both and make them confess their plot. But that wouldn't help. A few snatches of overheard conversation was not evidence. Better to confront Julia alone. Obviously, Luke was working for her. Trevor felt sick at this sudden knowledge. He didn't want to believe what he'd heard. Luke spat out a derisive laugh and mumbled something more about the money.

"I told you, I'll get the money." Julia spoke in an impatient tone and pushed the scrawny man out of her way. They both began walking toward the sidewalk.

Trevor turned, feigning interest in the merchandise displayed in the neighboring store window while keeping sight of Julia and Luke. He saw Luke reach out and grab Julia's arm. "When? When am I going to get it?" he said.

"Don't touch me," Julia snapped, brushing his hand away. "I'll get hold of you as soon as I raise it."

"How long?"

"A couple of days, that's all. Now, I'm leaving before I vomit."

"If I don't hear from you, lady, you'll hear from me," Luke called after Julia as she walked away, head bowed low. Trevor kept track of her destination but waited until Luke went back into the restaurant before chasing after her.

"What's going on here Julia?" He spoke sharply as he caught her arm. She flinched at his touch and whirled around.

"Trevor!" Her voice was a horrified whisper and she stared at him with dark, frightened eyes.

CASSIE HURRIED to her truck. A chill permeated the air, and she gathered her blue velvet blazer more tightly around her body. Climbing into the cab, she was grateful she'd repaired the heater, recalling the freezing drive from Mesquite the night of the storm.

It still seemed like yesterday, even though it had happened almost two months ago. A smile crossed her face. That night had been the proverbial blessing in disguise. If it hadn't happened, she would never have known what a wonderful man Trevor was. Her mood was almost euphoric as she pulled the truck onto the highway and drove toward the Bradford ranch. The only blots on the perfection of her life were Evergreen Enterprises and the mysterious events that happened after her arrival in Mesquite. But there'd been no further sabotage since the night of the fire, and now she had an opportunity to find out who was behind the Evergreen trust. She hummed out loud. No one deserved to be as happy as she was.

The purr of tires on the pavement was soothing and the heater breathed warm air. Cassie felt enclosed in a warm, comfortable cocoon, complete with warm, comfortable thoughts. No matter how bleak and threatening the outside world might be, nothing could touch her. She had love, hope and her dreams to protect her.

Lost in her pleasant thoughts she was surprised to see the gate to the Bradford ranch appear. It seemed as though she'd been driving no time at all. The gate was open and Cassie slowed to make the turn.

A small twinge of apprehension poked at her sense of well-being. Facing Jake was not going to be easy. Her shallowly buried resentment toward his ownership of former Cambridge land clawed its way to the surface of her mind. She tried to control it. If she discovered Jake could help her with the Evergreen problem, carrying a chip on her shoulder wouldn't aid smooth negotiations.

As she pulled through the gate she noticed the Bradford brand suspended from an arch connecting the iron posts of the gate. The Circle Bar B—a *B* underlined by a bar and enclosed in a circle. Once, just the sight of that brand would have stirred Cassie to an impassioned desire for vengeance. Today she felt only mild resentment. With a pang of guilt she realized she hadn't thought of her father in weeks, or of the mystery surrounding his death. Worse, she couldn't even arouse the old need to avenge him. She felt traitorous, but justified her feelings by telling herself that salvaging Cambridge Stables would settle the score more fully than open warfare. Keeping that thought in mind, she continued up the drive.

She rounded a corner and the ranch house came into view, shattering a long-held belief. In her mind's eyes, the Bradford ranch house had always been a mansion, dwarfing the Cambridge house—a mansion with high ceilings and hundreds of rooms, each with a cavernous fireplace and luxurious ornate furniture.

Instead, she saw a modest one-story brick house nestled among a stand of trees in the hollow of a small valley. Two chimneys jutted above the Spanish-tile roof. So much for a fireplace in every room. It was a long sprawling structure, and at first glance appeared enormous, but as Cassie drew closer she saw that much of the space was devoted to garages. In reality, the Cambridge Stables house was much larger, though not nearly as well maintained. As she pulled into the driveway, she could see just how carefully the house was cared for.

It was surrounded by a low white fence, and a long covered porch with a waist-high railing ran the full length of its front. Cassie felt a stab of pain as she remembered that the Cambridge house had looked much like this when her mother was alive—with bright flowers and white rails and cheerful curtains hanging at the windows.

She felt as if she'd been taken back twenty years, and at any moment expected to see her mother running out the front door, eager to take her in her arms. For the first time Cassie fully realized how badly Cambridge Stables had deteriorated in the years since she'd left, and an unexpected anger at her father erupted inside her. How could he have let it happen? She didn't—couldn't—understand. She wasn't sure she ever would.

Well, this was no way to meet the enemy. Although, for a moment, she was no longer sure who the enemy was. She stepped down from the truck and smoothed her gray-blue tartan skirt, rearranging her white sweater around her hips. The blazer and soft blue suede boots she wore completed her outfit. She was pleased with her choice. It was businesslike, but not too crisp, the sort of thing she would have worn to a meeting with some young entrepreneur. Perfect for a confrontation with a Wyoming land mogul. She ran her fingers nervously through her hair and marched resolutely up to the front door.

As she rang the bell, her stomach quivered, and the hair stood up on the back of her neck, bringing to mind one of Julia's favorite expressions, "Somebody walked over my grave." A frightening premonition raced through her mind, a feeling that once she stepped inside, her world would never again be the same. She resisted an impulse to turn and run.

A voice interrupted her eerie thoughts. "Hello?" A young woman of Spanish descent stood inside the opened door.

Feeling foolish at having been caught daydreaming, Cassie stammered, "I'm here to see Jake Bradford. My name is Cassandra Cambridge."

"Cassandra Cambridge?" The girl looked slightly puzzled. "To see Mr. Bradford?" She had a heavy accent and spoke in a singsong, ending each sentence as though it were a question. "You mean Mr. Marvin?"

"No, Mr. Jake Bradford." Cassie repeated.

"Okay, I go find him. You wait here." The girl closed the door, leaving Cassie to stand on the cold, drafty porch. She shivered. What odd behavior. Surely, Jake was expecting her. Marvin had said that he would be.

The door opened. "Cassie, what a pleasure to see you." Jake greeted her in a rich, full voice. "I'm sorry Marti left you standing out here. You must be freezing to death. Come in, please." The eyes she'd remembered as cold gray steel were soft and kindly.

"Thank you," Cassie replied, disarmed by his obvious concern and the warmth that emanated from him like the glow of a well-tended fire. "I am a little chilly."

"Come into my study and I'll have Marti bring you some coffee, or perhaps you'd like hot chocolate or even tea?"

"Coffee would be nice, thank you. Black." She was taken aback by her own easy acceptance of his hospitality. She was forgetting too easily that he was an adversary.

He led her into a spacious room with a hardwood floor covered by a braided rug in tones of rust and slate blue. He directed her to a chair while he left the room to request coffee. She chose one of a pair of slate blue chairs, which sat across from a comfortable looking print sofa. She looked around nervously. An enormous oak desk sat at the other end. Like the rest of the room, it was neatly kept, and only a few papers and a pen lay on its surface. A case crammed with trophies stood behind the desk.

The walls were paneled in deep rich oak and covered with photographs and certificates, all framed in heavy brass. She was curious but too uncomfortable to get up and look more closely, but most of the photographs appeared to be of the family. Some of the older portraits were tintypes or black-and-white photos. Jake's ancestors, she concluded. They surrounded a grouping of modern color portraits of Jake, a woman Cassie presumed to be his late wife and three children. Cassie recognized the childish faces of Marvin and Marion, but the third picture was of a young boy with tousled rusty hair and a lazy smile. Something about the photo tugged at her memory. She wondered who he was. She remembered hearing that Jake had a son from a prior marriage. Undoubtedly the photograph was of him.

"Here we go." Jake walked into the room, carrying a silver tray with a small silver coffee pot and two cups. "Marti was too busy. I don't get no respect around here." An indulgent smile covered his face, revealing a tolerance that momentarily impressed Cassie. But then she decided it was an act to make her think he wasn't such a bad guy after all.

He set the tray on the oak table between them, settled his bulk onto the sofa and poured the coffee. "What brings you here Cassie? Your visit is quite a surprise."

"A surprise?" His question was confusing. "Didn't you know I was coming?"

"No." An eyebrow rose quizzically. "Was I supposed to know?"

Cassie ran her fingers through her hair, feeling very awkward. "Marvin phoned and told me to see you at one o'clock. But it appears you weren't expecting me." It took every ounce of Cassie's will to keep from squirming under Jake's questioning gaze.

"Marvin said I wanted to see you?"

Cassie nodded.

Jake scratched his balding head, his eyes directed upward, as though expecting an answer from heaven. Apparently none was forthcoming, and he shifted his gaze back to Cassie. "He must have forgotten to tell me," he offered as a weak explanation. "But leaving that aside, it's obvious that you came on a mission. So, back to my original question—what brings you here today?"

"Marvin said you have information about Evergreen Enterprises, the trust that holds my ranch." She spoke in a faltering voice. "I want to buy it out, but I've been unable to find the individuals involved. He said you might know." She was losing the calm, professional composure she had envisioned when imagining this encounter.

Jake looked at her incredulously and again scratched his shiny head. Cassie thought it was no wonder he was loosing his hair. She exerted superhuman effort to maintain her poise. Why didn't he say something? She was beginning to feel very foolish.

Jake finally broke the silence, speaking slowly, as though carefully measuring his words. "Cassie, I don't know what to say to you. Yes, I know about the Evergreen trust but I need to phone someone first before we talk about it. Can you excuse me for a moment?" Cassie said she would, and he left the study.

Restless, she rose from her chair and roamed the room, inspecting Jake's certificates. She hadn't realized that Jake was president of the Montana Cattle Breeders' Association or that he was so active in charities. A letter from the Mesquite Fire Department thanked him for donating a fire truck. He was also a CPA. The wall presented quite a different picture of this large, lumbering man than the one Cassie carried in her heart.

She moved on to the family picture grouping. Marvin had been an engaging child. What a shame he had to grow up. Marion's physical homeliness started in childhood but her spiritual beauty stared out even from an ancient photograph. The third child intrigued her. He was so cute. Why did he seem so familiar?

Jake reentered the room, closing the door behind him. He seemed disturbed. "No answer," he said. "I'll just have to use my own judgment. Sit down, Cassie."

His tone was casually directive, the tone of a man used to giving orders and having them obeyed. Cassie returned to the blue chair and sat. "You have information for me?"

"Yes. I'm just not sure where to start. The beginning is a good place, I imagine." He unfolded his large frame in the other chair and slumped down wearily. "The person I was trying to reach was Julia."

Cassie wrinkled her brow in confusion. "Why would you need to talk to my aunt?"

"To get her permission to tell you about Evergreen. But as I said, I couldn't reach her and I've made the decision to tell you, anyway."

"I still don't understand what Aunt Julia has to do with it." The eerie feeling that she'd experienced on the porch was returning. Goose bumps rose on her arms, though the room was cozily warm.

"You will. Now just let me speak. When I'm done I'll answer your questions. Agreed?"

Cassie nodded.

"Evergreen Enterprises was set up for a number of reasons, none of which are very flattering to your father. Julia and I are the other partners. Your father was forever in need of money, Cassie, and he was selling the land almost faster than I could afford to buy it. Julia was afraid he'd sell it all, so we concocted the trust, with all its hooks, so he couldn't sell the last of it. The thirty-day notice saw to that. His sudden death put us in an awkward position, and we didn't know how to dissolve the trust without your knowledge."

Dumbstruck, Cassie opened her mouth to speak. Jake raised his hand to stop her, but it was totally unnecessary. No words came out. "Julia wanted Cambridge Stables for you, Cassie. No other reason. And I love Julia. I want to see her happy."

She was frozen, unable to move. Aunt Julia and Jake? She didn't believe it. Her father's death put them in an awkward position? Cassie still believed Jake engineered the accident, but now...

"But what did he do with the money?" Her rediscovered voice came out in a thin squeak. The money was the least of her worries, but there were so many questions that she didn't know where to start. So many. Her head reeled.

Jake slouched forward, placing his face in his large hands. "He was your father, Cassie, and a good man in many ways. But with money... Money, women, booze. They were your father's downfall."

Anger spewed like molten lava from the depths of Cassie's soul. Anger. Denial. Hate. She leaped to her feet. "I don't believe any of this. Aunt Julia? Why would Aunt Julia involve herself with you? You hated my father. I remember that clearly. I still believe you had him killed."

"Yes, Cassie, I did hate your father." He looked up at her with sad eyes, speaking softly in spite of her undeniable rage. "So much that it almost poisoned me. But that's in the past for me, the distant past. I had nothing to do with your father's death. It was an accident. You must believe that. For your own sake, for Julia's, and for Trevor's."

At that instant, the door burst open. "Dad!" Cassie was instantly confused. The voice was familiar, but it wasn't Marvin's. It was rich and husky and ...

"We have a big problem, and I—" Trevor stopped in his tracks. Deadly silence followed as both Cassie and Jake turned to stare at him.

CHAPTER TWELVE

DAD? DAD! OH, DEAR GOD!

The blood drained from Cassie's face. Everything was spinning. Disoriented, she turned to face the picture wall, fixating upon the photo of the young stranger. Now she knew why the boy seemed familiar. Her hand shot to her mouth. "Trevor?"

The questioning word was a mere whisper. Trevor's bronze skin paled and his shoulders sagged under her horrified scrutiny. The brilliant blue eyes, which Cassie loved so much, faded to a dim lusterless hue. With outstretched arms he took a hesitant step in her direction.

The room tilted crazily and her vision became a continuous blur. A tornado roared through her head, wiping out all sound. Steadying herself on the chair arm, she struggled to gain control.

"Lying bastard." His betrayal, his deception, resurrected the hate she felt for the Bradfords, and now in those two words, she hurled the full force of that hatred toward Trevor.

"Cassie, please let me explain." He moved toward her. Jake slipped discreetly out of the room and closed the door behind him. Cassie only vaguely noticed his departure as a myriad of emotions warred within her.

"How could you keep this from me?" Even as she asked, she knew the reason, and now she wished she'd never discovered the truth. Her ears pounded as the tornado continued to blaze a trail through her head.

"I tried. Oh, God, how I tried. But there was no way to tell you without the risk of losing you. I was afraid to take that risk." He stopped a few feet from where Cassie stood, as though he feared to step any closer.

"And what about me? What about my father? What would he think if he knew I was involved with Jake's son?" As Cassie asked these questions, she felt traitorous, knowing that she wanted Trevor, anyway, regardless of his connection to Jake. But she couldn't. To do so would mean admitting the possibility that the tales about her father might be true.

"Cassie, your father is dead. He's been dead nearly ten months now. Why can't you face that truth? My relationship to Jake has nothing to do with your father or with us." Although Trevor's words were blunt, he spoke with extreme tenderness and closed the distance between them, brushing the back of his hand across her face. "Remember us? It's been good, hasn't it, honey?"

"Yes, it's been good." She nodded almost reluctantly. "But it's not enough. I know my father is dead, Trevor. But I won't destroy his memory. You're all against him. Jake talks of his drinking, his women, his spending. I'll never believe those things. How can there be an *us* with this..." She shivered with apprehension and almost unbearable pain as her jumbled words trailed off.

"I'm not asking you to believe anything about your father. I'm just asking that we talk."

Cassie lowered her head and rubbed her temples. "All right, Trevor. But, please, not now. I can't discuss this anymore. I have a blinding headache." She felt as if she were talking through a fog. The whirling inside her head had become almost deafening.

"When?" Trevor asked as Cassie began walking to the door.

"Tomorrow. Call me tomorrow." All she wanted to do was get out of there.

She squelched the urge to break into a run and tried to move at a dignified pace to the outer door. Relieved that Trevor didn't follow her, she broke into a run as soon as she stepped outside. Reaching her truck, she jumped inside, locked both doors, backed out of the driveway and aimed the truck toward home. Glancing in the rearview mirror, she saw Trevor standing in the driveway watching her leave, hands at his side, face ashen and drawn. Jake was beside him.

And from the porch, slouched against the railing, Marvin watched, too. He wore a smug, self-satisfied smile and lifted his hand in an insolent wave. Suppressing an urge to retch, Cassie pressed the accelerator to the floor and tore her eyes from the mirror. Marvin must be very pleased with himself, she thought bitterly.

A WAVE OF NAUSEA washed through Trevor as he stood on the blacktop watching Cassie drive away. He ran his hand restlessly across his face and turned to speak to his father. "Damn! I could kick myself for not telling her sooner."

"Do you think she would have reacted any differently, son?"

"Maybe not, but at least she wouldn't have thought I'd deceived her." Trevor looked into Jake's eyes. The empathy he saw in them surprised him. It was as though Jake truly understood the difficulties a man's stupidity could lead him into. "Why was she here, anyway, Dad? Cassie always swore she'd never come to our ranch."

Jake turned his head toward the porch, and Trevor followed his gaze until his eyes rested on Marvin, who was slithering down the steps. "Marvin told her I knew something about the Evergreen trust."

"Marvin!" Trevor bellowed as the beefy man broke into a jog, heading toward the garage. Trevor sprinted after him, Jake right behind, and snagged Marvin's arm before he could enter the garage.

"What do you know about this?" Trevor pulled back his fist ready to slam it into Marvin's flat nose but Jake captured his arm.

"Whoa, Trevor. That temper of yours is getting out of hand again. Let's go back in the study." Jake forced Trevor's rigid arm back to his side and gave Marvin a look that clearly commanded him to follow.

Once inside the study, Jake directed Marvin to one of the blue chairs and Trevor to the other, then settled himself on the sofa. "Marvin, why did you tell Cassie I wanted to see her today?"

"I didn't tell her nothing like that."

Trevor's nausea returned as he watched Marvin crouch in his chair. That weasel turned his stomach, and he couldn't figure why Jake always defended him. It wasn't as if Marvin were his own son.

"Don't lie, Marvin!" Jake's sharp tone prodded Marvin into an upright position and surprised Trevor. He didn't think he'd ever heard Jake speak to Marvin that way.

"Okay, okay," Marvin whined. "I'll tell you. I knew Cassie didn't know Trevor was your son, and I thought if I could get you all together, I'd find a way to let the cat out of the bag." He looked at Trevor and barked derisively. "I never figured you'd work it out so neat for me."

Jake's eyes narrowed to slits. "Marvin, I want to know why you did that."

"We've got to get her out of here, Pa. Out of Mesquite. She's ruining everything. All my plans. With the way she and Trevor were going at it, I knew she'd never leave."

"I should never have promised you Cambridge Stables, Marvin. It wasn't mine to give, and that property has caused so much heartache already." Jake leaned back with a sigh. "And what was so important that you rushed into my office, Trevor, without finding out if someone was with me?"

"In town today, I overheard Julia and Luke talking," Trevor began, and went on to tell Jake about his confrontation with Julia.

"It looks like Marvin isn't the only one who wants Cassie to leave," Trevor concluded. "It seems Julia hired Luke to scare Cassie away, but he took the job too seriously. First he cut the water line to the barn. Then he weakened a tree branch so it would fall on the hay shed. When that didn't work, he manhandled Cassie while she was in town. When Julia found out he'd also chopped the power pole and tried to kill Chauncey, she told him to stop. But he told her he had another employer."

Marvin began squirming in his chair during Trevor's story and upon hearing the word *employer* gulped audibly. Trevor gave him a curious look. "Luke demanded Julia pay him blackmail or he'd continue until Cassie was dead," Trevor went on. "And Julia was very frightened, but when I asked her why she'd hired Luke in the first place, all she said was 'Ask Jake.'"

Trevor noticed that both Jake and Marvin had blanched. Jake's eyes filled with sorrow, while Marvin looked terrified. The silence was palpable until Marvin started speaking distraughtly.

"Luke did it all by himself, Pa. I didn't want anything to do with it. I told him so but..." Marvin buried his hands in his head.

"What?" Jake spun his head toward Marvin, his voice full of incredulity, and Trevor sprang from his chair.

"What the hell is going on?" Trevor grabbed Marvin by the collar and shook him until his teeth rattled.

"Stop it, Trevor," Jake ordered, then directed a withering glare at Marvin. "Now what are you talking about, Marvin?"

"Luke's been blackmailing me, too," Marvin sniveled. "He was with me the night George died. That's when your Alpha Romeo got wrecked. Luke told me I ran George off the road, and he made me promise to give him a partnership in Cambridge Stables when I finally got it, or he'd report me to the police. I knew about the fire and the poisoning but I swear, Pa, I don't know anything about any plan to kill Cassie."

Trevor shook his head in confusion. "But you wrecked the Alpha when you hit the post. There were witnesses."

"Me and Luke staged it to cover up the dents. It was already wrecked the night before."

Jake stood over Marvin, hands clenched, his face white with fury, saying nothing. When he finally spoke his voice was cool, even, deadly. "Did you run George off the road, Marvin?"

Marvin slumped over, covered his face and wailed,
"I don't know, Pa. I was so drunk I can't remember."

CASSIE TOOK A DEEP breath exhaled slowly and demanded that her heart stop pounding. She had to sort
things out. So much. So fast. So many unanswered
questions. One question she couldn't answer: how
could she live without Trevor? She shoved it away by
examining yet another piece of information, asking yet
another question.

Cassie drove as she thought, heading toward home.
She needed to talk to Julia. Only Julia could answer her
questions. Cassie didn't believe even for a moment that
Julia could be involved with Jake. But her partnership
in the Evergreen trust cast a shadow on that certainty.

Cassie's concentration was so intense that she had
been ignoring the shimmy of the steering wheel in her
hands, but now the truck was shuddering and re-
sponding poorly to her efforts to steer. A rhythmical
rattle intruded on her consciousness. She braked and
pulled the truck slowly over to the shoulder and
stepped out, gasping when she saw the front wheel toed
in at an alarming angle. She was so close to Miller's
Curve and could never have made that hairpin turn
with that loose wheel. She shuddered, remembering the
way her father had died.

Reaching behind the seat, she pulled out a tire iron
and jack and walked to the wheel. As she pried off the
hubcap, two lug nuts clattered to the ground. Nearly
frozen with fear, Cassie bent over awkwardly to retrieve them. She couldn't imagine how the nuts could
have come that loose, even though the truck was very
old and overdue for a tune-up. Shaking off her dread,
she positioned the jack and methodically pumped. She

then tightened the wheel judiciously, checking each nut carefully before getting back in the truck and continuing on her way.

At long last the turnoff to Cambridge Stables appeared. With a pang of disappointment Cassie saw that Julia's Volkswagen was not in the driveway. Unwelcome tears rushed to her eyes, and she dashed them away. This was no time to cry. She had to keep her mind clear. No matter which way she looked at it, she couldn't believe the loose wheel was an accident. A suspicion kept poking at her mind. She'd been lured to Bradford Ranch, and after she'd left, her car had a mechanical failure. Could the same thing have happened to her father?

She desperately wanted to talk to Julia. There was no one else to turn to. Trevor was Jake's son, and now she had reason to believe that all her suspicions were true. Someone wanted her to leave Cambridge Stables, and all of Trevor's careful rationalizations about Jake fell apart in the face of her knowledge of their relationship. She was all alone except for Julia.

She gripped the steering wheel angrily, then slumped forward and rested her head upon her arms. Suddenly an idea sprang fully formed into her mind. She could go to the cabin. There was plenty of firewood and lantern fuel. Trevor had seen to that on their last visit. He'd also stocked the little lean-to stable full of hay. If she packed a little food, warm clothes, oats for Chauncey, she could be on her way in thirty minutes.

The more she thought about it, the more appealing the idea became. She could think clearly in the mountains, and after two or three days she might be able to sort out the confused jumble of her thoughts. She'd promised Trevor they would talk tomorrow, but she wasn't up to facing him. Maybe later, but not right away. The pain of contemplating a life of never again joining with Trevor's warm body or laughing with him in front of a fire hurt deeply. She took large breaths until the pain subsided, then made her decision. She would go to the cabin.

Cassie stepped out of the truck and hurried into the house, hoping her aunt would return soon. Cassie wanted to tell Julia where she was going, but if she waited too long she couldn't make the cabin before nightfall.

After packing hastily, Cassie went to the barn. Chauncey danced with excitement when she approached his stall, snorting little puffs of steam into the cold air. Cassie saddled him quickly, threw the saddlebags over his back and deftly tied them in place.

Looking up at the sky, she saw that a storm was approaching, but the weather report had said it wouldn't hit until the next day. She glanced at her watch. Four o'clock. Plenty of daylight. She could be at the cabin well before dark, and a few days of being snowed in wouldn't hurt her at all.

She flipped Chauncey's bridle over his neck and started to mount, then realized that she hadn't packed a rifle. Although it was unlikely, she might encounter a rattlesnake or wild animal in the hills and it wasn't wise to travel alone without protection. She remembered also that she'd forgotten to leave word for Julia that she'd be gone. Although she was anxious to leave, these were two compelling reasons to return to the house.

As she exited the barn she saw her aunt's car parked in the driveway. The sight made her feel safe again, and she hurried to the house.

"Aunt Julia?" she called as she stepped into the hallway. There was no answer, so Cassie headed for the study to get the rifle before looking for Julia. She crossed the room quickly, stopping at the desk to get the key for the firearms cabinet when she noticed it was already open. How strange. The cabinet was always locked. She reached inside, picked up a hunting rifle, bullets and a case, checking for missing guns as she did so. There were several empty slots where the handguns were stored, but Cassie couldn't remember how many guns had been there in the first place. All the rifles and shotguns were accounted for, so she shrugged and locked the cabinet. As she turned to leave the room, the phone rang.

She reached to answer it, suddenly nervous. What if it were Trevor? Knowing she couldn't ignore him forever, she picked up the phone and heard Julia's voice as the receiver touched her ear.

"Julia?" said another voice, a man's voice.

"Jake, oh, Jake," Cassie heard her Aunt respond.

Jake? Cassie suppressed a gasp. Julia sounded so relieved to hear from him. What if everything he'd said was true? She held her breath so Julia wouldn't know she was on the extension.

"Cassie just left here," Jake reported. "She was very upset and she already knows too much. You've got to do something, Julia." Jake sounded agitated and tense. "She found out about Trevor."

A small sob erupted from Julia. "No. Please, no." The words were a mere whisper.

"Calm down, Julia. You're becoming hysterical. Why didn't you tell me things had gone this far?"

"It's something I had to handle on my own. I've got a gun, Jake, and I know what to do."

"Julia." Jake's voice became very soft. "Please listen. It's all taken care of. Just take care of Cassie. You can't put this off any longer."

"Oh, God, Jake, I can't."

"You have to."

There was a long pause and when Julia spoke again the quaver had left her voice. She spoke with steely determination. "You're right, Jake. I have to."

She hung up then and Cassie stared at the phone in her hand, wondering what Jake and Julia had been talking about. All she knew was that somehow it concerned her and she wanted some answers.

She hurried from the study, leaving the rifle leaning against the desk, and walked to the stairs. Julia was coming down, dressed warmly, as though planning to go out.

"Do you mind explaining that phone call, Aunt Julia?" Cassie couldn't identify the emotions she felt. Anger, fear, confusion and some vague suspicions she couldn't pin down. "I heard it all."

Julia's eyes widened in alarm. "You heard everything?" She looked as if her mind was whirling, trying to remember what had been said.

"Everything. And I didn't understand any of it. What is this all about?"

"I can't talk about it, Cassie." Julia spoke haltingly as though breathing were difficult. "Let me go to the study and get something. Afterward, we'll talk. But not now. Wait here. I'll be right back."

Julia passed Cassie and walked down the hallway. Impatient to understand the meaning behind the overheard conversation, Cassie had every intention of following, but suddenly her mind began clicking in a chain reaction. The loosened nuts on the wheel of the truck. Trevor's concealed relationship with Jake. Julia's frantic words on the phone: *"I can't... You're right... I have to."*

Even as her brain reached the conclusion, her heart denied it. Her aunt, the woman who'd raised her since early childhood, would not, could not, plan to kill her.

But her aunt's words haunted her. *"I've got a gun,"* she'd said... *"I know what to do."* Oh, Lord, Cassie thought. The unlocked firearms cabinet. Could she? Would she...?

An uncontrollable tremor shook Cassie's body. The puzzle pieces came together with an ugly jolt. Julia! Jake! Trevor! They must be in this together. Whatever their plan, she was now certain that it had cost her father his life. Her realization was followed by a blast of shame. She'd been all too willing to believe the horrible things Jake had said about Papa. Willing to believe almost anything if it meant she could be near Trevor. Now a telephone conversation hinted she might be the next victim. But Aunt Julia? No! It couldn't be.

Cassie had known fear before, but now she was struck with pure, stark, terror. Unable to move, she stared down at her trembling hands, trying to erase, to undo, the conclusion she'd just reached. Then she heard Julia's footsteps in the hall. She turned and ran pell-mell through the door, across the gravel driveway and to the stables. She ran faster than she had ever run in her life. She jumped on Chauncey's back and kicked him into a full gallop. Her first plan had been a flight from confusion. Now she was running for her life.

"THAT TAKES CARE OF LUKE." Jake rubbed his hands in satisfaction as he and Trevor left the Mesquite Police Station. "Feel better now, Trevor?"

Trevor nodded even though it wasn't true. Cassie had walked out of his life, and while knowing she was now safe from danger eased his mind, he wasn't sure he could ever make up for his deception. Until now there hadn't been time to think about her.

After the conversation with Marvin, he and his father had searched for Luke. They'd found him in the barn and forced him to accompany them into town to see Haggarty. Luke had not been willing, but when Trevor trained the barrel of his rifle on him, he'd seen the wisdom of their suggestion. Before they'd left the ranch, Jake stopped to make a phone call, and Trevor had almost hoped the man would try to escape while they were waiting. His fingers had itched against the trigger. He forced that thought from his mind. It revealed a side of him he didn't like.

"Dad," Trevor asked after a while, "why do you always defend Marvin, no matter what he does? Even today you were making excuses for him."

"Well, Trevor, Marvin has always resented you because you were my natural son and he wasn't. He never saw that he had the benefit of my love and guidance, while you didn't."

Trevor knew that Jake's confession of neglect was difficult for him, but it nonetheless resurrected his long-buried resentment of his father's early abandonment. "That's the truth," he replied bitterly.

The sorrow in Jake's eyes burned through Trevor's resentment, and suddenly he realized that his father also had regrets.

"Marvin reminds me of myself when I was young, Trevor. He's such a fool, always overlooking the good and concentrating on what he doesn't have. If I'd recognized those traits in myself when I was younger, your mother might have stayed with me. And I wouldn't have lost you. When I married Marvin and Marion's mother, she helped me see how wrong I was. She was such a good woman. So much like Marion. I owed it to her to help Marvin.''

Trevor thought of his stepsister with her cheerful and giving ways and could see why Jake would love and feel loyalty to a woman with those same traits. But there was another question on his mind.

"Are you saying that if you knew then what you know now, you wouldn't have left us?''

"Your mother left me, Trevor." Trevor's mouth dropped open in surprise. This news contradicted everything he'd ever been told about his parents' divorce. "She remarried less than a year later and gave you her new husband's name. For the longest time she wouldn't let me see you. She told people I left her and she wanted nothing to do with me. In her eyes, I suppose it seemed true.''

"What do you mean?''

"She thought I was having an affair with Sara, George's wife, and she became insane with jealousy. As far as she was concerned I had deserted her then.''

"Were you having an affair with Sara?''

Jake paused as he opened the door to his low car. He slid in and waited until Trevor was settled before answering.

"Oh, I loved her, all right. She was everything I wanted. Vivacious, elegant, beautiful. Your mother was just an ordinary person. Very human. A little shy. I wanted a princess.''

Trevor snorted, remembering how abruptly his life had changed since the day his mother left his father. Until then he'd been an adored only child. Afterward, neither parent wanted anything to do with him. His mother sent him to boarding school and built a new life with another man. Jake had been cool and distant when he'd visited, giving more love to Marion and Marvin than to him. He'd felt robbed.

But now Trevor thought of his mother in light of Jake's comments. Hair always perfectly coifed. Expensively and elegantly dressed. At home in every environment from a palace to a fishing shack. With irony, he recognized that she had become the woman Jake had wanted, and because of that, he understood her better. He also understood more about Jake and realized he wanted to increase that knowledge.

He ruffled his hair. He was avoiding the most important subject. Why was Julia involved in this horrendous situation?

"Dad, when Julia and I talked this afternoon she refused to tell me why she wanted Cassie to leave Mesquite." Trevor saw Jake's impassive eyes flash with pain. "She said to ask you. What is it? It has something to do with the letter George gave her, doesn't it?"

Jake looked at Trevor sharply. "How did you know about the letter?"

"I saw George give it to Julia at the hospital. She was crying when she read it, so I knew it had upset her."

Jake frowned pensively, undeniable pain reflected upon his face. "The crimes of youth, son. The crimes of youth."

"What the hell does that mean?" Trevor was suddenly angry, at Jake's evasiveness. He wanted answers *now*. "I ask you a serious question and all you have to say is 'the crimes of youth'?"

Jake's expression didn't change but he gave a sigh of resignation. "Yes, you do deserve answers, Trevor."

He lifted his shoulders as if to ease his tension and then continued. "We managed to hide it all these years. Now George is dead and doesn't have to face it, so he's forcing Julia and me to deal with the truth from beyond the grave. Isn't that funny?" He gave a short bitter laugh.

"Not particularly," Trevor responded, failing to see any irony in this yet unexplained situation. "So what is Julia trying to hide? What was in that letter that was so important that she'd put Cassie's life at risk?"

"It happened a long time ago, the same night your mother decided to leave me. It shattered all our lives. Your mother's, George's, Julia's, mine. Even yours, Trevor. Only Cassie was protected. She doesn't remember. But now she has to know and I'm afraid the knowledge will devastate her."

"Remember what? Know what?" Trevor asked impatiently. This whole conversation made absolutely no sense.

"Julia killed Cassie's mother, Trevor."

Trevor choked in astonishment and was trying to regain his composure when Jake's next sentence sent him reeling.

"And Cassie, little three-year-old Cassie, witnessed everything."

CHAPTER THIRTEEN

"JUST A LITTLE FARTHER, Chauncey." Cassie ran her gloved fingers through his ebony mane. Holding the reins loosely in her other hand, she led the stallion through the nearly concealed opening to the path toward the cabin. It was almost as dark as night in there, the sky blocked by the overhead branches, and Chauncey walked nervously behind her, streaming vapors from his dilated nostrils. The storm was moving in faster than she'd anticipated and, darkness or not, she was grateful for the protective tunnel that would shield them from the biting wind.

She unwrapped her woven wool scarf from her face. Small particles of ice had formed on the outside and she shook them loose. Chauncey jumped at the unexpected motion and pranced restlessly, looking nervously from side to side, as though expecting a sudden attack. Despite the cold he was lathered with a foamy sweat.

"Easy." Cassie spoke softly as she remounted. She didn't resent his spookiness or the approaching storm. Chauncey's behavior helped keep her own terror under control and the storm would keep them from following.

Them.

What a funny word to use to refer to Julia and Trevor. The two people whom, until an hour ago, she had trusted beyond all others.

She realized now that her terror had subsided, that she might have reached the wrong conclusion about Julia. She prayed she had. But she was afraid to go back. What if she wasn't wrong?

But even if she'd misinterpreted the phone conversation, there was no longer any doubt that Julia had a deep relationship with Jake. So now Cassie no longer knew what to believe. Her father a drunk? Her aunt the mistress of her father's bitterest rival? What was true? What was false?

The darkness of the tunnel was waning, signaling that the cabin was near. She breathed a sigh of relief when they entered the clearing. Snow was falling in large, gentle flakes as she approached the cabin, reminding Cassie of the house in a glass ball she'd owned as a child. She'd often stared at it for hours, shaking it each time the snow began to settle. For a moment she experienced the same deep peace she'd known during early childhood. She took refuge in that feeling, refusing to think, at least for the moment, about her dangerous situation.

She rode Chauncey to the shed and dismounted. His edginess evaporated as soon as he saw the cabin, and he lowered his head, grazing calmly while Cassie removed the saddlebags. Daylight had nearly vanished and the snowflakes were getting smaller and harder. She'd better hurry. She quickly unsaddled, stabled and fed Chauncey, then checked the wood supply on the porch and decided there wasn't enough. Five trips later, she began carrying the heavy wood inside. If the advancing storm was as fierce as the threatening sky suggested, even the porch wouldn't keep the firewood dry.

Once the logs were stored, she knelt in front of the fireplace, reaching to open the flue. When she pulled the handle it creaked loudly and spewed ashes onto the floor of the firebox, scattering them into her face. Her hands flew to her burning eyes. Suddenly it was all too much and she fell back on her haunches and let out a string of curses, which bounced off the cabin walls as she pounded her fists violently upon the floor.

She thought of Trevor's deceit and Julia's betrayal. Wild thoughts darted through her mind. Malevolent thoughts, which she had never before experienced. A lonely howl sounded in the distance and the wind screeched against the cabin walls, as though the forces of nature had joined in her anger.

Eventually Cassie's rage subsided, and she rolled onto her back, her eyes turned upward. Her loneliness was a physical ache in her chest.

Once again the plaintive howl drifted on the still night air. Although back in control, Cassie felt so empty that the howl seemed to whip through gaping holes in her soul. She rose listlessly and began placing wood in the fireplace. There was no use freezing to death.

Soon flames blazed high and she warmed herself briefly before attacking the little butane stove. For once it didn't balk, and she placed the coffeepot on top of a burner. She didn't feel like eating, though she knew she should. Her stomach was still in knots and she was overcome with lethargy. She sat on an open sleeping bag in front of the fire and waited.

As she was taking her first sip of coffee, another howl reached her ears, closer than before. A second howl joined the first in a strange symphony. The plaintive wails were followed by a frightened whinny. Cassie shot to her feet, nearly overturning her cup. Damn, she had left the rifle in the study. But she could hang a lantern on the lean-to. That should keep the coyotes at bay. She didn't want Chauncey chasing around that lean-to, risking possible injury.

Slipping into her down jacket, she unbolted the door, grabbed a lantern and ran down the stairs. Blind to everything outside the circle of light cast by the lantern, she could nonetheless hear Chauncey whickering frantically and slamming against the makeshift railings of the shed. She worried that the wood might snap at any time under the assault of his powerful body, and she quickened her pace, softly calling Chauncey's name. Another howl erupted, but as the light of the lantern reached the lean-to, it stopped short.

Coyotes seldom hunted live game and certainly nothing as big as a horse, but Chauncey didn't know that. Cassie murmured his name repeatedly and ran to the corner of the shed to hang the lantern. He reared and plunged crazily inside the flimsy structure and seemed deaf to her repetitive calls. Planning to restrain him before he seriously injured himself, she spied the halter she'd tied to the rail earlier.

As she stretched across the railing to release the halter, she heard the coyotes rustle in the underbrush. Reminding herself they were scavengers, probably hoping she was bringing out garbage, she stilled a nervous voice inside her. She had to deal with Chauncey. Fear was making him crazy. She walked to the gate, continually looking over her shoulder. As though finally aware of her presence, Chauncey stopped lunging and lapsed into an agitated jog around the edge of the stall. Cassie formed the lead rope into a makeshift lariat and opened the gate, clucking monotonously, ready to slip the loop over Chauncey's head.

She continued clucking, forming the loop into a large circle. As Chauncey jogged past her, she threw the rope over his head. It tightened about his throat and he stopped. Cassie relaxed, certain everything was under control. But suddenly new howls erupted from the brush and Chauncey reared with a pitiful shriek. Caught off guard, Cassie failed to move quickly enough to control the frantic stallion. He spun around, crashed through the wooden gate, and sent Cassie flying into the corner post. Her head struck with crippling force and she felt herself floating. Brilliant light flashed before her eyes. From very far away, she heard Chauncey's galloping hoofbeats, and the coyotes howled again. Then everything was dark and silent.

TREVOR URGED BEAU FORWARD, pushing the placid animal along through the narrow beam of light cast by the electric lantern he carried. Trevor's blood boiled with anger. Why was Cassie so impetuous? Coming up here in the face of the first storm of winter was the most damn fool thing she'd ever done. He indulged his anger, realizing that if he dwelled upon the quicksand of his underlying worry, he would soon sink below the surface.

Beau's ears pricked forward and Trevor became alert again. He could hear a faint rustling, a rattling of the brush, and a dull, rhythmic pounding. Like a horse racing down the trail. Trevor frowned. Something was wrong. Cassie wouldn't be crazy enough to race a horse down a dark, narrow trail. Especially Chauncey. He

reined Beau to a stop and lifted the lantern. The sound
was getting closer.

Then Chauncey plunged headlong into the beam.
Even in the weak light, Trevor could see the flashing
whites of Chauncey eyes and the froth on his coat. But
the stallion's frenzied appearance wasn't the cause of
Trevor's worry. Chauncey was scared of his own
shadow. No, it was the sight of the halter tied loosely
around Chauncey's neck that aroused Trevor's concern. Obviously the horse had broken loose while Cassie was trying to snare him. Forming the rope into a
lariat shouldn't have been necessary, since Chauncey
normally haltered easily, so that meant Cassie had
shared the horse's fear. Trevor had to reach her. But
first he had to stop her horse.

Trevor edged Beau around until he stood across the
trail, blocking Chauncey's path. Most horses settle
down in the presence of other horses, and Trevor was
counting on Beau to calm the stallion. But instead,
Chauncey stopped about ten feet short and began
pawing the ground, snorting and twisting from side to
side.

"Whoa, boy, whoa." Trevor inched Beau carefully
forward trying to calm the frightened animal. But with
each step forward, Chauncey moved back, scraping the
ground viciously with his front hoofs. Deciding he
would never catch him on horseback, Trevor slipped
quietly out of the saddle, ground-tied Beau and positioned him to block the trail. Lowering the lantern,
Trevor walked slowly forward, crooning gentle words
with each step, his free hand outstretched. Gradually
Chauncey's pawing slackened and his flattened ears
began to relax. Trevor was only a few feet from him
now.

Just as Trevor's outstretched hand touched the dangling halter, a chilling wail broke the soundless night. Screaming in response, Chauncey reared, leaped forward and slammed into Trevor with his powerful withers, sending him rolling into the bush. As he tumbled, Trevor saw Chauncey force Beau aside and continue his breakneck course down the mountain path. *Damn,* Trevor thought. *I'll never catch him now.*

He pulled himself to his feet and, finding no injury, retrieved his lantern and walked back to Beau. He had to get to the cabin fast. Spooky natured as he was, Chauncey had never behaved this way before. Cassie could be in real danger.

He kicked his horse into a slow jog and breathed a sigh of relief when the clearing appeared. A lantern hung from the shed and illuminated the cabin grounds in a yellow glow. Snowflakes fluttered through the light, glistening like specks of gold before touching the ground. Then he saw Cassie lying immobile inside the pool of light. Blood trickled from a gash across her head. With a sharp gasp of air, Trevor pushed Beau into a full gallop across the remaining distance to the shed. How badly was she hurt? He was almost afraid to know.

Reaching Cassie's inert body, he knelt beside her. She was so white. The gash above her hairline was like a dire crimson omen and contrasted sharply with her skin and the snow-covered ground. He closed his eyes and, with a small childhood prayer, touched her neck at the pulse. She moaned, a soft kittenlike mew, and Trevor's heart flooded with relief. He squelched a desire to press her against his chest as a small sob escaped his lips. Only then did he admit to himself that he'd been terrified he had lost her. He placed his lips on her forehead. She opened her eyes at the pressure and looked at him hazily.

"Trevor." A sweet smile crossed her face.

She wrapped her arms around his neck, placing her face next to his. She felt so sweet in his arms that Trevor wanted to hold her forever, but then her grip loosened and she went limp. With a trembling hand, Trevor checked her pulse again, relieved to find it coming regularly. Releasing her gently, he let her slip back to the ground. At least he knew that neither her back nor neck were broken and he checked carefully for other broken bones. Finding none, he began formulating a plan to get them out of there.

Climbing to his feet, he bent over to lift Cassie. Although she was petite, her unconscious body was unwieldy as he struggled with her dead weight. Finally she was safely gathered in his arms and he carried her inside the cabin.

Trevor placed Cassie on the sleeping bag and covered her as best he could. Pulling a handkerchief from his pocket he walked to the sink and jerked at the pump until it finally began spewing water. Wetting the soft cloth, he returned to Cassie and dabbed at the gash near her hairline.

The low light from the fireplace bathed her face, creating a reddish glow on her lovely cheeks. The cut on her forehead had stopped bleeding and Trevor sighed in relief. It was merely a surface wound. Her eyelashes flickered then opened. "Trevor." She smiled again.

Trevor smiled in return. "So you're awake. How are you feeling?"

"Fine. Did we fall asleep in front of the fire?" Trevor frowned. Something was wrong.

"Where are we, Cassie?"

She seemed amused at his question. "We're at the cabin, silly. Why do you ask?"

"No reason." She was obviously disoriented, and Trevor decided, with a quick flash of insight, not to set her straight. Doing so would most likely revive other memories. Memories that neither of them needed to face right now. "But a snowstorm is coming. Do you feel up to riding back?"

"I think so," she replied and sat up. "O-o-h!" She dropped her head on her hands. "My head aches."

Trevor nodded. "You hit it earlier. Don't you remember?"

"No. How did I do that?"

Trevor recognized the signs of concussion. He had to keep her calm and warm, and most important, he had to get her back to the ranch.

"You ran into an open cupboard." She seemed so vulnerable, gazing at him with that puzzled expression and Trevor wanted nothing more than to gather her in his arms and kiss her pain away. But there was no time. "Just sit there a moment."

He stood, removed his shirt and jacket, took off his undershirt and tore it into strips.

"I thought you wanted to take me home." Her expression contained such sweet desire that Trevor almost succumbed to his earlier impulse. Only the sound of the increasing wind outside the warm cabin kept him from doing so. The storm couldn't be far away.

"I want to tie you to me while we ride to your place. You may be a little weak."

"Am I to be your captive slave, then?" Cassie teased.

As worried as he was Trevor couldn't help but grin at the idea of Cassie being anyone's captive salve. "Ah, if only you were," he answered. Finished with his work, he replaced his clothes and walked over to Cassie. "Can you stand?" He reached to help Cassie up.

"Sure," she replied blithely, but swayed against him as she reached her feet. "Maybe not," she giggled.

"Lean on me." Trevor forced a smile and tried to make his voice sound as light as possible. The last thing he wanted to do was reveal how worried he was. Cassie appeared to have regained her balance and as they talked, he loosened his grip to see if she could stand alone. "You okay?"

She spread her arms and giggled again. "I guess so. Here I am standing up all by myself." This time Trevor felt a genuine smile cross his face. If she could stand and joke, her concussion couldn't be too bad.

"Stay here. I'm going to get Beau ready." He sat Cassie back down on the sleeping bag, then walked out the door.

The wind whipped at his face as he stepped onto the porch but the snowfall was light, just barely dusting the ground. There was still time to beat the storm, and his optimism returned as he walked to the shed.

He led Beau to the front porch, went back inside and gathered some blankets. "We have to hurry before the storm comes," he told Cassie as he guided her out-side. With a gentle shove he boosted her into the sad-dle, then wrapped her in several blankets. When she was safely perched astride, he slid on Beau's back and settled behind the cantle. He wrapped the makeshift rope he'd fashioned from his undershirt around Cas-sie and himself and knotted it securely. Now, even if she fell unconscious, he would have no difficulty keeping her in the saddle. He clucked his horse forward and started for the tunnel.

As they entered the tunnel, Cassie turned to him in confusion. "Why do we only have one horse?"

Trevor pulled her against his chest. "It's going to be a long, hard ride, Cassie. Don't worry about anything now. I'll explain when we get to your place."

To his surprise, Cassie didn't argue. She simply rested her head on his shoulder. "I'm so tired," she murmured, and then she was quiet. Trevor breathed in the scent of her hair mixed with the cool night mountain air and, for a moment, just enjoyed the rhythmic pressure of her body as Beau's steady steps rocked them together in the saddle.

His heart ached for her and the pain she was about to face. Because of her physical condition Julia and Jake would undoubtedly delay giving her George's letter. But they couldn't delay it forever. Once she read the letter and learned of Luke's arrest, she would begin asking piercing questions. The ugly truths she would soon know would be even more devastating than the one she had learned today.

He didn't want to think of what might happen when Cassie remembered that he was Jake's son. He cursed himself for not telling her sooner. He had tried, but not hard enough, he knew, and his cowardice disgusted him. Trying to push these thoughts from his mind, he decided for now to simply concentrate on the sweet smell of Cassie's body and getting her safely home.

The closer they got to Cambridge Stables, the faster and heavier the snow fell. Trevor held Cassie so tightly that his legs ached in protest, and he pushed Beau mercilessly through the blinding snowfall.

It seemed forever before the shimmering yellow glow of the Cambridge yard lights finally appeared through the dancing flakes. The lights seemed so close and yet so far away, and he prompted Beau into a gallop. The poor obedient horse didn't balk or falter, but hammered the ground valiantly until finally the barn and the house were clearly visible even through the whirling snow. Trevor breathed a deep sigh of relief. Cambridge Stables had never looked so good.

Jake and Julia were standing on the porch as they approached the house. "Cassie. Trevor," Julia called with outstretched arms as Jake ran down the steps.

"Thank God, you're home, son."

Trevor slipped from the saddle, holding Cassie steady until Jake lifted her down to carry her to Julia's waiting arms. Never in Trevor's life had the word *home* sounded so good. Almost mechanically he uncinched the saddle, pulled it from Beau's back and carried it to the porch. Dropping it, he returned and led his weary horse into the small courtyard.

Jake and Julia had already disappeared inside with Cassie, and with his last ounce of strength Trevor dragged the saddle behind him as he entered the house. Once inside, he pulled it to the ballroom, opened the door and threw it on the cluttered floor.

Julia appeared behind him carrying a steaming cup. "Irish coffee." She led Trevor to the base of the stairs and gave him a gentle downward shove. "Drink."

Trevor sipped the warm brew gratefully, not caring that he hadn't even closed the ballroom door. The hell with it, he thought. For, at that moment, he truly realized what the important things in life were. An unclosed door was not one of them.

CHAPTER FOURTEEN

A THOUSAND SOLDIERS, wearing cleated boots, were tromping through Cassie's head. She crept down into a dark tunnel in her mind trying to escape the pain. But something pushed her up and the tromping continued. Faces peered at her, familiar faces, but she wasn't sure whose they were. And she was afraid. Something—somebody—was trying to hurt her. She had to escape.

"Cassie." A voice called her name. The husky sound soothed her fears, and she tried to reach its source, tried to see the face connected with it. She opened her eyes. Ten worried faces with bronze hair looked at her and she willed them to merge. But nothing happened. She closed her eyes again and slid back down the tunnel.

"Our baby is afraid," said a melodious voice. Cassie scrambled back toward the tunnel opening. Suddenly it wasn't safe down there, either. "Cassie, don't run away." She tried to reach the top, but the stomping boots pounded at her. "Mama. Papa. What's happening to you?" She burst out of the tunnel and opened her eyes, clinging to the warm body next to her.

She found herself enclosed in a comforting embrace, and she sobbed against a firm broad shoulder. Trevor sat beside her. She was in her own four-poster bed, in her own bedroom and Trevor was whispering softly in her ear. "Thank God, Cassie. Thank God you're awake. I was afraid you'd...afraid I was going to lose you."

"The dream," Cassie said. "Was it all a dream? The wheel? The phone call? How did I get here?" She clutched at his shirt, her head buried against his chest and spoke a muffled whisper. Her heart began beating erratically as memories flooded over her. Suddenly her mind was clear. Reality and illusion were no longer entwined. She remembered everything.

"Where are Jake and Julia?" She hadn't given Trevor time to answer her first questions, and he placed his finger over her lips.

"Shh. One at a time." He started to answer but Cassie interrupted.

"Trevor. Are they here?"

"Yes. They've been waiting for you to regain consciousness."

His answer confused Cassie. Waiting? Why? What were they waiting for?

Of course. At first she had thought Trevor might be part of it. But now she realized he couldn't be. If he were, she'd be dead now. "You've got to get me out of here." She wrapped both her hands in his shirt. Her voice was hoarse with fear.

"I can't, Cassie. We're snowed in."

"No," she cried. "We can't wait. You've got to get me out now. Jake and Julia are planning to kill me."

Trevor's expression grew incredulous. "Cassie, you've just had a nasty knock on the head and it's the middle of the night. Rest for a while. As soon as the roads are clear, I'll take you to the hospital." He placed his hands on her shoulders and tried to force her to lie on the bed, but she resisted and he stopped his effort.

"But the wheel of the truck...the phone call..." Could she possibly be wrong? Could she have misunderstood?

"What wheel? What phone call?"

Cassie rubbed her eyes, trying to clear her thoughts. She looked up at Trevor, praying she could trust him. There was no one else left.

"After I left your ranch yesterday my truck started shaking. When I got out, I found the nuts on my front tire were loose." A sudden flash picture of the truck veering off the ledge at Miller's Curve made her flinch. "Trevor, I don't think it was an accident. Jake and Julia are trying to kill me."

Trevor tried to gather Cassie in his arms, but she didn't yield to his gentle pressure. Someone was trying to kill her and she would not have her fears kissed away as if she were a frightened child.

"Cassie, I have some new information that explains all the horrible things that have happened to you. You're in no condition to hear it tonight. But trust me, darling, Jake and your Aunt Julia have nothing to do with it."

Cassie brushed his arms away vehemently. "Aren't you listening? You are always defending that man. Your father." She spat the words at him. Here he was again, handing out rational, reasonable defenses for Jake. New suspicions and fears were forming in her mind. The hammering in her head intensified as she tried to control her fear.

She covered her face with her hands and slumped back on the pillows. "My God, you're not with them, are you?" Fear and confusion were dancing in her mind. She spoke in a choked whisper. "Why did you bring me down from the mountain if you were just going to kill me?''

Trevor looked at her in dismay. Then his expression changed from bafflement to enlightenment to outright anger. ''Because I care about you, that's why! Don't you know that? Why in the hell do you think I followed you to the cabin? And Julia's so worried about you that she's in her room crying her eyes out. If you weren't so damn self-centered—'' He broke off as if remembering Cassie's vulnerable condition.

''How could you believe that I would want to kill you?'' He spoke flatly and the coolness of his tone chilled Cassie's heart.

''But the phone call?'' Cassie responded weakly.

''I don't know what you're talking about.''

''Don't you want to know?''

''Not right now. Believe me, Cassie, you're in no danger here.'' He stood up and turned toward the door. ''I'll tell Julia you're awake. She'll want to see you.'' He didn't look back as he talked but simply opened the door and stepped outside. ''Although I don't know why.'' Then he closed the door behind him.

Cassie stared at the closed door for a moment, then buried herself under her blankets. Things were slowly becoming clear. If there had been a plot to kill her, she wouldn't be alive right now. Julia could easily have hidden Cassie's absence. And if Trevor had intended to harm her, he would have left her on the mountain to die. It all would have been so easy. So neat. Which meant . . . which meant, that she was wrong. Whatever the meaning of that cryptic telephone conversation, it wasn't murder. And that meant that the person who was trying to force her to leave Mesquite was still unknown. Trevor had said he had information, but she'd been too proud—and too frightened—to ask about it.

A tidal wave of self-reproach swept over her. Her paranoia since her father's death had deeply hurt the two people she loved most. So badly that they were probably lost to her, also. She wrapped her arms around her body, truly wanting, for the first time in her life, the cleansing flood of tears. But nothing flowed. Unlike her weeping soul, her eyes were hot, dry, remorseless. She heard the door open, but didn't move.

"Trevor said you were awake." Cassie stuck her chin out from beneath the blankets. Julia stood in the doorway looking as contrite as Cassie felt. Walking hesitantly to the chair beside the bed, Julia perched tentatively on its edge. She held a packet in her hand. Her eyes were red and swollen.

"Did Trevor tell you what I accused you of?" Cassie muffled her voice in her covers, still trying to avoid her guilt.

"Yes." Julia's answer was simple and direct, no explanations or questions added.

"I'm so sorry, Aunt Julia. I don't know how I could believe those things of you."

Julia reached out and took Cassie's hand. "Honey, it is I who needs to beg forgiveness. I have done horrible things. Things beyond forgiveness."

Cassie inched up in the bed causing a fresh stab of pain. She winced and Julia patted her hand sympathetically. "That's quite a lump you've got there."

Cassie touched her head cautiously. "What a goose egg. Reminds me of when I fell off that big roan. You fixed me up that time, too."

She stared silently at the rose wallpaper of her room and allowed her thoughts to settle. Somehow, with

Julia sitting beside her, Cassie's earlier accusations seemed absurd. But Julia's expression was gravely worried, and Cassie couldn't forget those damning words she'd overheard on the phone. "Why do you say you need forgiveness, Aunt Julia?" Just asking the question caused Cassie's heart to race.

Julia ran her hands through her disheveled hair. Her usually tidy chignon sat low at the base of her neck and strands of loose hair hung limply around her face. Deep circles surrounded her eyes. "I don't know where to begin, Cassie, and what I'm going to tell you is so hard to say.

"First off, you need to know that I'm responsible for almost everything that has happened to you since you arrived. The attack at Chez Teton. The fire and for Chauncey's near-poisoning. Even for the broken water line and the fallen tree branch. I hired Luke to scare you into leaving. When his first efforts didn't work, I went away for the weekend so he could try again. He got...well, shall we say, carried away. I never dreamed he would use such tactics and he knew that. And he knew I was afraid you'd find out I'd hired him. So he started blackmailing me."

"Why? Why would you want me to leave? I thought you liked having me here." Cassie could see the tears brimming on the edge of Julia's eyes, but again her own were dry. She'd had so many shocks in the past twenty-four hours that she felt numb.

"Because of the Evergreen trust. I knew once you found out Jake and I were the silent partners, you'd want to know all the reasons behind such a restrictive agreement." Julia heaved a large sigh and leaned her head against the back of the chair. "Oh, Cassie, I know how you are. You get hold of something and you don't let go. I knew you'd dig and dig, and I didn't want you to discover the answers. I thought if I could get you to leave, you'd forget about it. I should have known better." Her aunt's words were very clear, but for some reason they weren't sinking in. Cassie felt something was missing. The reasons weren't compelling enough for Julia to do what she did.

"What about the gun? Why did you take the gun from the case? I thought you were going to use it to shoot me."

"I must have been a little crazy, Cassie. I took the gun, planning to go to Luke and force him to leave Mesquite. I don't know what I would have done if he'd refused. He was threatening the very thing I value most. You." Julia reached out and touched Cassie's hand. "I'd never hurt you intentionally, honey. Never."

"But there's something more I should know, isn't there, Aunt Julia?"

Julia didn't answer at first. Instead, she lifted the tattered envelope she'd been holding and extended it to Cassie. "The rest of the conversation you overheard was about this letter. As he has done so often before, Jake was asking me to give it to you. I was so afraid of what might happen if I did."

Cassie took the envelope and removed the letter. The frayed edges of the envelope and pages revealed frequent handling. The paper had yellowed with age except for one fresh sheet. She recognized the small, careful handwriting. "It's from my father." She laid the letter on her lap.

"Yes."

"Why were you afraid?"

The twitch of Julia's jaw betrayed her apprehension. "It will tell you things you should never have known. He wrote it shortly after he sent you to boarding school. It broke his heart to send you away. But he knew he was slipping. His drinking was becoming uncontrollable. After your grandparents passed away, there was no one but you to keep up appearances for, and he didn't think he could do it. He asked me to give this to you if the need ever arose. It seems the need has, indeed, arisen."

"I never saw Papa drink, Aunt Julia. He was always so good to me. I still miss him."

"I know you do, honey. Just read the letter. Everything is in there." Julia stood up, her face infinitely sad. "I'm going to my room now. I'll be back in awhile and we'll talk."

Cassie watched as Julia slipped quietly out of the room. At the sound of the closing door, she looked down at the letter. She felt as if there were a live snake in her lap. *Tear it up,* a small voice inside her said. *Tear it up before it destroys you.* Part of her wanted to heed the voice, but another part yearned to know what was written there. She picked up the worn pages and clutched them to her breast, reflecting, considering, for a long long time. Finally she started to read.

A few minutes later, Cassie's eyes were no longer dry. A tear fell onto the page in her hand causing the ink to blur. She tried to blot the spot but only succeeded in smearing it more. Damn it, why should she care? These pages shattered everything she believed about her life. She should have obeyed her little voice. Nothing—nothing—would be the same again.

All she had ever wanted was to continue believing in her father. To remember the wonderful man he'd been.

The letter sliced her beliefs wide open, exposed them to the light of day and left them there to decay.

Cassie crumpled the pages in her hand and flung them across the room. Captured by the air, they separated midflight and fluttered individually to the floor. She cursed herself for not wadding them firmly enough and slipped out of bed. Her head spun as she cautiously put her weight on her feet. After leaning against the bedpost to balance herself she walked to the bedroom door. Colored balls danced before her eyes but she continued her questionable mission. Something was missing. There was something more to know. An indefinable pull was compelling her to the balcony.

When she reached the door that separated the balcony from the east bedroom wing, she hesitated. What secret lay behind that door? What good would come of peering into the darkened ballroom?

She took a deep breath, causing a sharp pain to shoot through her head, and opened the door. The passageway light was on and it cast ominous shadows onto the narrow balcony. Without reason, her heartbeat quickened. She walked to the center, approached the mahogany railing and looking down into the ballroom.

Nothing was down there, of course. Just old furniture covered by canvas. What did she expect? Her eyes took in the shapeless lumps below her, then moved to the open door through which she could see the stairway, its steps glistening in the hallway light. Glistening. Cassie felt as if she were floating, and the present became very dim....

THE BALLROOM was filled with the sounds of country music, tinkling laughter and dancing footsteps. Colorful streamers appeared to float around the sparkling chandelier.

She had crawled into the space under the stairs to watch her parents waltz, dipping and twirling in rhythmic steps, gracefully moving around the edge of the floor. The other dancers watched with admiration, and Cassie, filled with childish pleasure in seeing her parents look so beautiful, fell asleep on top of her stuffed bear, Herby.

Footsteps clicking in the hallway disturbed her slumber, and afraid of being found, she dragged Herby behind her and crawled deeper into the hiding space. She wasn't supposed to be here. Mama and Papa had told her to stay in bed.

Sneaking an occasional peek, she saw the band and household help leave. Guests begin to trickle out until only Mama, Papa and that nice gray-eyed man and his pretty red-haired wife remained. Aunt Julia was busy tidying up the ballroom as Papa walked the tall man and his wife to the door, talking about the evening. From where she sat, Cassie could see their feet. They stopped as a loud crash came from the ballroom, their shoes just inches from where Cassie hid.

"Stupid bitch." Tears formed in Cassie's eyes. Why was Mama talking to her beloved aunt like that? Cassie saw Julia stoop to pick up the pieces of a shattered crystal punch bowl.

"Are you going to let her talk to Julia like that?" the pretty woman asked Papa. Her husband told her to be quiet. But Papa didn't answer, and then Cassie heard another crash and saw Mama slap Julia.

Cassie wanted to run from her hiding place and tell Mama not to hurt Aunt Julia, but she was too afraid. She was supposed to be asleep and Mama might spank her. Tears began streaming down her face when she heard Mama say, "I don't know why we let you stay around here, Julia. I have half a mind to send you packing."

Cassie couldn't see Mama's face, but Aunt Julia wore that mad expression that used to scare Cassie. She didn't look like that often but when she did, her auntie meant business. With squared shoulders, Julia said, "Don't talk to me that way."

"Don't talk to you that way? Who do you think you are? You're nothing but a hanger-on. George and I have done everything for you. You should be grateful you have a home here. Being my sister doesn't give you the right to a free ride at my expense."

Cassie heard Papa gasp and start to walk into the ballroom. By the way he hurried, she could tell he was upset.

"I'm not the one who should be grateful. You should be grateful to me." Julia spoke in an icy, even tone as Papa rushed into the ballroom. "Believe me, I know who I am."

"Don't, Julia," Papa said, but Julia wasn't listening.

"Oh?" Mama's voice sounded very snooty. "And who might that be?"

"I'm Cassie's mother, that's who I am." Julia wore a proud, defiant expression as she looked at Mama and Papa. The gray-eyed man uttered a bad word.

"No!" Mama screamed. She spun and ran out of the ballroom. Cassie could hear pounding feet on the floor and she shrank farther back into her hiding place.

Something very bad was happening. She was so scared but afraid to cry. What did Julia mean, saying she was Cassie's mother? Julia was her auntie. Cassie tried to work out the contradictions in her mind.

Suddenly Mama came back. She was on the balcony, holding something, one of those things Papa had told Cassie never to touch.

"For God's sake, Sara, put down that gun," Papa shouted. Julia yelled, too, then her feet pounded up the stairs, rattling the tiny space where Cassie sat shriveled into a tiny ball, clutching Herby.

"Adulterer!" Mama shrieked. "I'll kill you for this, George." She aimed the gun at Papa.

As a small, unwitting whimper escaped Cassie's lips, Julia appeared behind Mama. She grabbed the barrel of the shotgun, pushing it toward the ceiling. As they struggled for control of the weapon, they slammed, again and again, into the balcony rail. Suddenly the shotgun discharged. Crack! Fragments of the chandelier plummeted to the floor as buckshot peppered the ceiling. A lone purple streamer floated slowly after the clattering glass.

Cassie buried her head in Herby's soft body and covered her ears. This couldn't be happening! Mama would never shoot Papa. Then she heard another cracking sound. But different. Cassie lifted her tear-streaked face and watched with a soundless wail as the handrail gave way, splitting with an ear-wrenching squawk. The two women's terrified screams mingled in the air, tearing at Cassie's ears. She squashed her hands more tightly against her ears wanting to cover her eyes also, but was frozen with horror. She shrieked hysterically, her voice lost in the resounding crash as Mama disappeared over the edge. Then, only Julia remained on the balcony, clinging to fragments of the railing.

Cassie watched in stunned horror as Julia climbed shakily to her feet to stare through the chasm in the railing. Mama lay on the polished floor below, head cocked at a crazy angle. The purple streamer was beneath her, one tattered end resting on her shoulder.

Papa and the couple bent over her broken form, and Cassie saw Julia run from the balcony. Grabbing Herby, Cassie scurried from her hiding place. She tripped at the bottom of the stairs and began crawling up, whimpering silently through blinding tears.

She heard Julia's running footsteps on the stairs and her aunt's stunned voice penetrated the wall of fear surrounding her. "Cassie! Oh, God, no!"

"Auntie Julia!" Cassie plunged her shaking body into Julia's arms as her silent cries broke into heaving sobs. While Cassie wept piteously, Julia sat on the broad steps and crushed the tiny, trembling form against her breasts. Julia held her, rocked her, soothed her. "It's just a nightmare. Cassie. A bad dream. Forget it, forget it." She crooned the words over and over. . . .

CHAPTER FIFTEEN

"CASSIE?" For a moment she wasn't sure if she was hearing a voice or an echo from her memories. Julia stood in the open doorway between her bedroom and the balcony. "You remember, don't you?"

Cassie, dazed by her overpowering memories, nodded mechanically, staring at the ballroom floor. She still clung to the railing, illogically afraid that the past might sweep her away.

"It's the one thing George omitted. That you'd witnessed the entire thing. I thought you would probably remember once you read the letter. I'm so sorry, Cassie. I thought if you forgot what you saw that night, it could never hurt you. Obviously, I was wrong." Julia's face was drawn and white, her words spoken simply and quietly.

"You and Papa told me she was killed horseback riding. That's what Gran and Gramps said, too. But it was all a lie. How...?" The rest of the question drifted off.

"The guests and household help had all left and your grandparents were out of town. George took your mother's body to a place several miles from the house and Jake followed on Sara's favorite horse. George forced that poor animal to jump over an icy gully, again and again, until she finally fell. Then he let it go. It ran back to the ranch for the staff to see. That's all it took. Nobody questioned the cause of death. Sara had a reputation for being reckless. She could easily have gone riding on a dark, icy night, just for a lark.''

"Why did you have to hide it? It was an accident.''

"Yes, but the social climate was different in those days. Your father's parents were away that night. They were quite old and very proud of their position in the community. A scandal would have destroyed them, and if there had been an investigation, scandal would surely have followed. The buckshot holes in the ceiling would have seen to that.''

Julia's eyes held naked anguish as she recalled events long buried. Cassie supposed she should feel some emotion viewing Julia's unveiled pain. Compassion? Pity? Sympathy, perhaps? But her feelings were encased in ice. Cold, hard ice, which Cassie doubted would ever melt.

She lifted her head and looked at Julia, then moved her gaze to the portrait of her mother hanging on the wall. Blond, aristocratic, probably tall, while Cassie was short, dark, gypsylike. Why had she never suspected before? How many times had she lamented not inheriting her mother's cool, fragile beauty? Looking at Julia was like standing in front of a mirror, and yet not once had Cassie experienced even a small glimmer of the truth. Now truth was standing before her, and looking at her own true mother aroused no responsive chord. Just emptiness and the distasteful acid of bile in her mouth.

"Everything I've believed about my life is a lie, isn't it? How did you get away with it? Everyone thought I was a natural Cambridge child. How did you hide the truth all this time?''

"Sara was subject to spells of depression, Cassie. She either immersed herself in constant activity or became so blue she couldn't leave her bed. She told George her unhappiness was because she couldn't have a child. She wanted a baby. George wanted a baby, too. Then I became pregnant.

"George sent her away to rest and, as he had done before, told everyone that she was in Europe. While she was gone, George arranged for adoption proceedings. I stayed at a home for unwed mothers until you were born. Then you were taken to Sara and she came back. People believed she'd delivered in Europe."

"So Papa kept you here as his mistress. Right in my mother's home?" Cassie's horror at her father's behavior was becoming a monster, a fanged, snarling monster. "How could he do that? How could you both sneak around right under Mama's nose? How, Aunt Julia? She was your sister."

"I had nowhere to go at first. After I came here I started taking care of you. Sara wasn't good at that kind of thing. And I couldn't stay away. I ached to hold you in my arms, Cassie, and you can't imagine how much I loved your father. We were both young. His hair was black, black as coal, like yours." She reached down and touched Cassie's tangled hair. "He was so...so splendid." Her eyes gazed dreamily into a gloomy corner as if remembering something special.

Cassie suppressed an involuntary flinch at Julia's touch. Until that moment she hadn't realized the extent of her revulsion.

"Sara didn't know I was your mother and had no reason to think that George was your real father. He stayed away from me for a long time. But Sara was wrong about the reason for her depression. It came back. When George sent her away again for a rest, I saw my chance and took it." Julia's tone contained a mixture of remorse and pride.

"He should have been mine, Cassie. Just as you were meant to be mine. I know it was wrong but I'm not sure I would have done things differently even if I'd known the consequences. I was too young to think of consequences. When your mother returned she became suspicious but your father and I hid our relationship well. Until that night... when I spoke in anger. He never touched me again... after that night."

Cassie tried to understand but didn't think she'd ever been that young. Since early childhood she had tried to please Papa and to make him proud. Consequences were a way of life with her, at least when it came to her father. But then, she'd never been a young, unwed mother in love with her sister's handsome, powerful husband. Cassie thought of the deep love she felt for Trevor. Would she have done the same for him? She didn't know because she'd never been tested. The first test of her love had been followed by so many events and now an internal glacier had frozen all emotion, even love.

"And I loved you, too. I couldn't stand the thought of..." Julia hesitated.

"Losing me?" The words were spoken through the iceberg in Cassie's heart. She felt nothing. Not dismay. Not anger. Not grief. Her entire heritage had been shattered this day. Nothing she'd ever believed about herself was true. Her mother was not her mother. Her aunt was not her aunt. Only her papa was her papa. She didn't know who she was anymore.

Except now Julia seemed to be a stranger, totally different from the woman who had loved and nurtured her. The woman she had loved wholeheartedly in return.

Julia stared, eyes glistening with unshed tears, seeming to sense how dead Cassie felt. She stopped talking, walked over to the railing where Cassie still huddled, and gently loosened her grip on the post. Bending over, she lifted Cassie to her feet and placed an arm about her waist. Cassie didn't resist. "Come," Julia said, "I'll put you into bed."

Cassie rested her weight against Julia and submitted to her care. But she no longer felt safe. Julia might be her mother but she wasn't the woman Cassie had grown up with. She allowed herself to be silently guided to her room, helped into bed and gently covered, and didn't protest when Julia placed a kiss on her forehead. All Cassie wanted was sleep. Julia sat down in the chair and murmured something, but Cassie was already drifting away. As she slipped into a deep sleep, she wondered what Julia had said. The word *daughter* darted through her mind.

"WAKE UP, CASSIE." Someone was softly shaking her, and light hurt her eyes. She brushed the disturbing hands away, but they continued jostling her. Finally she opened her eyes and saw Trevor standing above her. His face was gray and drawn, as though he hadn't slept well.

"You have to get up, Cassie. The storm is over and we're going to take you to the hospital."

"Mmm." Cassie rubbed her eyes, noting that movements no longer caused shooting pain in her head.

"Can you stand up?"

Cautiously, Cassie pushed herself into a standing position. Her legs felt strong and only a mild headache remained. "Seems like I can."

"Good. I'll go get Julia to help you get dressed." For the first time Cassie noticed Trevor's attitude. Reserved. Polite and cool.

She knew he had a right to be angry. But on the other hand, her suspicions had not been totally groundless. He should be able to understand. "I'm sorry about the things I said last night, Trevor," she finally said, with only partial sincerity.

"Forget it. You had reason to be frightened. But how could you think that I might..." As his voice trailed off, Cassie knew he wouldn't forget. She didn't know what else to say. Words seemed inadequate to excuse such a breech of trust. She only wished she could truly care. Sleep had not melted her heart.

"You don't need to get Aunt Julia. I can get dressed by myself."

"Always the independent Cambridge, aren't you?" His bitter tone revealed a crack in his polite armor.

"All right." Cassie shook her head. "Send her up, if it will make you feel better."

"I was planning to." He walked to the door and opened it.

"How did you sleep?" Cassie didn't want him to leave. Maybe the warmth of his arms would make her feel something again.

"Fine," he responded curtly and stepped through the door. Just then a thought flashed through Cassie's mind.

"Trevor, where's Chauncey?" She was certain he was fine. Probably safely standing in his stall. But it was a loose end, a worry, and Cassie wanted to know.

"Chauncey?" Trevor looked at her as if just re-membering. He rubbed his hand over his face and sighed. "I don't know, Cassie. With everything else, I'd forgotten all about him."

A beam of alarm shot through the ice surrounding Cassie's emotions. "Forgotten? Oh, Lord, then he's been out there all this time."

"I'm sure he's all right, Cassie. Horses survive snowstorms all the time. After we get you to the hospital, I'll go out and look for him."

"No!" Cassie said. "That could take hours. I'm going after him now." She walked to her dresser and opened a drawer.

Annoyance flashed across Trevor's face. "Damn you, Cassie. You are in no condition to go riding after him. You were unconscious for a while and I know you have a concussion."

"As long as I can stand and walk, I can ride. I'm going after him Trevor. Don't try to stop me."

Trevor threw up his hands in exasperation. "I'm going to get Julia."

"She won't be able to stop me, either." She turned away from him and pulled a pair of jeans from the dresser. "Now if you don't mind, I'm going to get dressed."

She heard Trevor swear under his breath, and then the door slammed. She pulled her nightgown over her head and began quickly slipping into her clothes. A knock came at the door.

"You can't talk me out of it, Aunt Julia." The door opened and, as Cassie expected, Julia walked through. "Do you mind closing the door? I'm dressing."

"Cass, you can't do this."

"I can and I am. I told Trevor that you couldn't stop me, either. I meant it." At this moment, nothing was more important than finding Chauncey.

"But you're so weak. What if you fall again?" Julia's voice quavered as it rose in pitch. "You have a concussion, Cassie."

"I must find Chauncey. Why can you never understand what's important to me?"

"What I understand is that last night you thought we were trying to kill you. This morning it looks as if you're trying to kill yourself." Julia's voice contained an anger that Cassie had seldom heard. She wasn't sure if she was the target of that anger or if Julia was angry at herself. But the words caused her to reflect a moment. And then she knew the answer.

"No, Aunt Julia. I'm trying to save myself. I'm trying to save all of us." Without Chauncey there would be no Cambridge Stables and without Cambridge Stables there would be no future for any of them. Not for Julia. Not for Trevor. And not for herself.

Strangely, Julia seemed to understand. She nodded. "Yes, I guess you have to do this. But be careful. You're all I have left. I couldn't stand it if I lost you."

A barren sadness overcame Cassie as she listened. It might be too late; she might already be lost to Julia. The chill in her heart said she was.

There was nothing more to say, and after a long pause, she simply asked Julia to have Trevor saddle one of the mares.

Julia left and after Cassie dressed she headed downstairs. She pulled on her warmest gear then walked out of the house to the stables. Snow blanketed the ground, brilliantly reflecting the naked sun, sending spears of pain through her eyes. She moved her eyes upward and saw Jake and Trevor standing by the corral.

"Why are three horses saddled?" This was her quest, and she didn't welcome company.

"We're going with you, Cassie." Jake spoke first and the firm set of his jaw left no doubt about his determination.

"I'd rather go alone."

Trevor uttered an exasperated expletive. "I'd ask you to listen to reason, Cassie, but it would be a waste of time." He planted himself, feet apart, in front of her. "We're going with you. No argument. Otherwise, we'll physically restrain you and take you to the hospital."

"You wouldn't dare," Cassie sputtered.

"Try me." Trevor took a menacing step forward, blue eyes turning to flint.

Cassie shifted nervously from foot to foot. She could play Annie Oakley, jump on a mare and gallop onto the range. But she didn't think her head could take it. Besides, if they caught her, she knew Trevor wouldn't hesitate in carrying out his threat. She studied the toe of one of her boots intently. "I suppose you're right. If I got dizzy, or something happened, I'd be in trouble if I were alone."

"Right." Cassie felt herself melt a little bit under the rays of Trevor's sunny smile. It was the first one she'd seen in two days. "Besides that, I've got these." He lifted a pair of binoculars. Cassie wondered why she hadn't thought of that.

"I guess two heads, or three—" she motioned toward Jake "—are better than one."

Jake's face formed into a broad grin and an immense kindness flowed from him. "As long as they don't go knocking together." Cassie relaxed and smiled at his quip.

She and Jake each mounted one of the mares and Trevor mounted Beau. Cassie asked Trevor which way they should go.

"Last time I saw Chauncey, he was barreling down the mountain trail. Best we ride in that direction. He would probably head for home."

They moved at a snail's pace, painstakingly examining every foot of the trail. Their horses sloshed through snow that was deep enough at times to reach their boots. Taking turns with the binoculars, they searched the landscape on either side of them.

Occasionally spotting something black in the snowy expanse of land, they veered off the trail. Each side trip turned out to be a wild goose chase, usually the sighting was just an exposed rock. On one occasion they found a dead moose, already decomposing, and their approach scattered the carrion feeders feasting on the remains. Cassie shuddered, thinking of Chauncey and the fate awaiting injured animals in the wild.

Her head ached and the sunlight hurt her eyes as they rode. From time to time she felt dizzy but hid her weakness, afraid that Jake and Trevor would force her to turn back. The day was moving along too quickly and the sun was starting its westward descent when they entered the clearing to the cabin. "Didn't even know this was here," Jake commented, and Trevor gave Cassie a knowing glance, reviving memories inside her of the wonderful days they'd spent here.

They dismounted and looked around. It was possible that Chauncey might have returned to the cabin, to the certain source of food. But Cassie didn't hold much hope that he had, and she was right. He wasn't there.

They returned to the forest tunnel. Only a smattering of snow had managed to sift through the thick foliage, but icy patches covered the ground, and they carefully guided their horses around them. About halfway down, Beau neighed. The sound startled Cassie from her concentration and she looked up to see broken underbrush on the left side of the trail.

"Jake! Trevor!" She pointed to a massive hole in the foliage.

"Looks like a freight train went through there." Jake said. "Seems we've found a trail for our missing stallion."

"I'm going after him." Cassie kicked her horse into a trot and before Trevor or Jake could object, moved through the hole into the thick forest beyond.

"Damn! What a fool she is!" she heard Trevor say, and crackling branches told her he wasn't far behind. Chauncey had left a wide swath through the dense growth, and she followed it, urging the mare into tight twists and turns to avoid crashing into the bushes and trees. The animal quivered beneath her legs, breaking into a nervous lather. Slowly, the light grew brighter, indicating a nearby clearing.

The western sun blasted Cassie's face as they burst into the clearing and pain seared her eyes. She pulled the mare to a sudden halt. Even through sun blindness she could see the sharp drop-off ahead. Her heart lurched. Chauncey had been running in the pitch-black of night. Would he have seen or sensed the danger?

She tried to extinguish all thought of what lay beyond the ridge and inched her horse forward at a tortoiselike pace. She was no longer in a hurry. Her temples throbbed mercilessly, and over and over she told herself to stop being silly. Chauncey was probably ambling around a meadow just on the other side of the ridge. Finally she reached the edge. An involuntary cry escaped her lips. A large black shape contrasted sharply with the pristine snow. A coyote skulked close by and a crow cawed in the distance.

She hesitated, hands trembling, heart beating wildly. Hoofbeats pounded and underbrush rustled reminding her that Trevor and Jake would stop her if she didn't move quickly. She pushed forward to the edge of the ridge.

CHAPTER SIXTEEN

TREVOR ENTERED the clearing just in time to see Cassie go over the ridge. He uttered curses he hadn't known were in his vocabulary, galloped Beau forward to the edge of the drop-off, then pulled to a skidding stop. What was she doing? She was riding headlong down the rock and snow-covered slope to the meadow below. Riding where even a fool would get off and lead a horse. He caught his breath as her horse skidded sideways on loose rock. Cassie deftly lifted her leg free while the animal struggled for footing, then swung back into the saddle after the horse regained its balance.

Pell-mell, slipping and sliding, the horse continued down the steep mountainside. Trevor looked beyond the edge of the slope into the open meadow and the reason behind her mad dash became clear. Cassie couldn't face that alone. It was time to be a fool himself. He kicked Beau into motion and followed Cassie down the slope.

He allowed the surefooted Beau to choose his own pace and concentrated on maintaining his seat as they swerved and side-slipped down the treacherous slope, gritting his teeth as his tired muscles protested. He lost sight of Cassie somewhere along the way, and when he reached the bottom safely, a stand of trees blocked his view of the meadow. As he rounded the trees, a crow took flight and lighted on the branches above him, angrily protesting his presence. Cassie was standing knee-deep in snow beside the mare, her arm raised in front of her face. Trevor pushed Beau into a high-stepping trot and quickly covered the ground between them. Cassie had taken a tentative step forward.

"Don't," Trevor said. "Don't do this to yourself."

She looked up at him with dry eyes. Trevor had expected tears, not this heartbreaking agony that dulled her ebony eyes, killing all the light. "I have to, Trevor." Her voice was as flat as her eyes.

He moved his horse toward the dead animal that had once been Chauncey. Beau snorted in protest and Trevor gave him a kick, forcing him to within a few feet of the body. The distant coyote eyed them suspiciously, then turned tail and ran.

It was Chauncey, all right. One leg was twisted in an obscene position, obviously broken, his once glossy coat torn, hair matted with dried blood. Scavengers, already beginning to feed, had knocked the snow from the horse's body. Memories of Chauncey's high vitality, his superb performance at the futurity, flashed past Trevor's eyes. His stomach lurched. He turned to Cassie and raised his hand, trying to stop her. But she shook her head and continued her trudge through the deep snow. When she reached him, he lunged forward and pulled her against his leg, covering her eyes with his hand.

"Let go, damn it. I've got to know." She twisted her head toward the carcass. An agonized moan tore from her lips, and she fell to her knees beside her mutilated champion. She leaned forward and retched, staining the snow with bile. She heaved, again and again. Trevor dismounted and knelt beside her, holding her until the convulsions finally left her body, then took out his handkerchief, dipped it in the snow and washed her face. She shivered from the cold, but passively submitted to his care, kneeling, unmoving, where she had fallen. Trevor stood and removed his jacket, placing it over her shoulders. She looked up at him then, and he saw into her soul through her aching eyes. The depth of the pain she revealed shocked him.

"It's over. Cambridge Stables is dead." Her motionless body, her lifeless tone, alarmed Trevor. "It died with Chauncey."

Trevor searched for words of comfort. Something, anything that might ease Cassie's sorrow. But words eluded him.

"I have to bury him." She struggled to her feet. Her chaps were water-stained and she was shivering. Trevor helped her into his jacket, trying to reason with her.

"We don't have any tools, Cassie, and the ground is probably frozen solid."

She nodded. Trevor took that as agreement but he followed her eyes, which roamed around as though searching for something. Then they stopped moving and fixed on a spot near the stand of trees. Trevor looked in that direction and saw a pile of rocks jutting above the snowbank in front of the frost-trimmed trees. "I'll build a cairn." She said the words simply as though this were an everyday ordinary idea.

She began kicking at the snow around Chauncey's body, clearing it away down to the grass. Trevor saw then what she meant. She planned to carry the stones, one by one, and pile them on top of the carcass.

"That will take hours and it's already getting late."

"I can't leave him here for the animals to eat." She continued kicking the snow. When she had cleared a circle around the dead stallion, she trudged toward the rock pile through the knee-deep snow.

Trevor followed, taking high leaps through the powder. When he reached Cassie, he was shaking from worry and anger. "Damn it, Cassie, you can't do this. You brain is probably swelling right now inside that thick skull of yours. That kind of exertion in this altitude could kill you." With supreme effort, Trevor regained control of himself and in a more composed tone, added, "Cassie, please let me take you back."

She stopped and ran her hand across her forehead. Beads of perspiration already dotted her skin. "You can go back if you like." She spoke without inflection, the passionate determination gone from her voice, but Trevor knew that this time she was more immovable than ever before.

"Right." The sarcasm was lost on her. He wouldn't, couldn't, leave her and he thought she probably knew that. He thought, also, that she probably didn't care. She resumed her methodical plodding, moving like a zombie. It was as if something inside her had died along with Chauncey, and he didn't know how to reach her.

A horse whinnied and he turned. Jake was approaching from behind the trees, leading his horse. Trevor wiped the tear that had escaped his burning eyes and turned in his father's direction.

By the time Jake reached them, Cassie had already carried one rock to the circle and had started for the second. "What is she doing?" Jake inclined his head toward Cassie.

"She wants to bury him. She's building a cairn."

"Won't do any good." Jake pointed in the distance. "The scavengers will just dig under it."

"I know. But try to tell her that. Jake—Dad, I don't know what's wrong with her. She—"

"She's in shock," Jake finished for him. He put a hand on Trevor's shoulder. "Let's help her. It'll be getting dark soon."

Jake gathered the horses. They were uncomfortable near a dead member of their species, nervously snorting and pawing at the snow, and moved eagerly to the stand of trees where Jake tied them securely.

He and Trevor joined Cassie. They hauled rock after rock to the burial site, piling them, one on top of the other, until finally, as the sky turned crimson, Cassie climbed to the top of the unstable structure, causing Trevor's heart to race with apprehension, and reverently placed the last rock. "There," she said.

She eased her way to the bottom, replacing dislodged stones as she descended. Trevor could see an easing of the agony in her eyes, a sign of possible peace.

"My dream is buried. Let's go home now." Desolation wrapped her words like a shroud, and Trevor's heart ached for her pain. The peace he thought he saw in her eyes was just an illusion. He wondered if it would ever return.

He held her in his arms. She didn't respond or resist, so he released her and walked to the horses. He brought Beau to Cassie. She would be safer on his gentle back. "Climb up."

She mounted without complaint or comment. She didn't speak at all. Concern gnawed at Trevor's gut.

They climbed the steep slippery slope, with Trevor leading both Beau, with Cassie astride, and the mare she'd ridden earlier. Trevor worried. Cassie was too calm, too placid.

"I think we'd be better off going to the cabin instead of back to the ranch." Jake scowled under the brim of his hat. "It will be dark soon. Our clothes are wet and if we don't get shelter soon, frostbite will be our next visitor."

Trevor could see the logic in Jake's statement. He looked toward Cassie, who sat quietly in the saddle. She offered no comment. Just sat, eyes vacant, holding the saddlehorn. "Julia will be fit to be tied if we don't show up tonight," he responded. "But I'm worried about Cassie."

"Julia will manage somehow. I'm worried about Cassie, too."

Trevor suddenly appreciated his father's presence. He was beginning to realize that Jake didn't miss much and had excellent judgment. He nodded. "Let's go, then." He mounted and moved his mare into an easy walk, leading Beau behind. Jake followed behind Cassie.

They reached the cabin just as the sun disappeared in an exuberant blaze. Trevor lifted Cassie down from Beau and led her inside. She followed compliantly and didn't ask why they were there.

Jake began building a fire while Trevor removed Cassie's jacket. He untied her chaps and pulled off her boots and jeans, then sat her on the sleeping bag in front of the fireplace. Her easy acquiescence to being undressed in front of two men caused his concern to move to full-scale alarm. He pulled the sleeping bag over her shivering shoulders, while she stared into the fireplace, watching Jake strike the match. When the logs ignited she continued to gaze at the flickering red-gold flames, seldom blinking. Jake gave Trevor a worried frown as Trevor gently pushed Cassie into a reclining position, a push she didn't resist.

"You'd better take care of yourself, too." Jake tossed a few sleeping bags on the floor and began shedding his damp clothing. Trevor followed suit. As he picked up one of the sleeping bags, he remembered happier times at the cabin, especially the trip when he and Cassie had brought the bags. They had laid them all on the floor and "christened" them, as Cassie had termed it, by making love all afternoon. The thought made him sad.

Cassie had rolled onto her side and, eyes now closed, appeared asleep. Trevor wasn't certain she was.

"We'd better take turns sitting up with her." Jake's voice interrupted Trevor's thoughts.

Trevor shook his head. "There's no need for you to stay up, Dad. I won't be able to sleep, anyway."

"I suppose you're right." Jake walked to the cooking area, dragging the sleeping bag that he'd pulled around his shoulders. Trevor thought he looked like Henry VIII, and if the situation hadn't been so grim the sight would have amused him. "Let's see what we can find to eat," Jake said.

"There must be food here. Cassie appeared to be planning to stay for a while." Trevor spied a saddlebag next to the sink counter. "There."

Jake rummaged through the bag and retrieved several cans of chicken soup. As he dug for a can opener, Trevor tried the pump. Miraculously, water began to flow. The pipes hadn't frozen. Trevor sat on the floor, wrapped in his sleeping bag and watched his father competently prepare the soup. As he watched, he reviewed what he'd learned about the life-shattering night when Sara Cambridge had died.

"Dad," he asked tentatively. He knew memories of that night were painful to everyone concerned, but an unanswered question bothered him. "Why did you help George cover up Sara's death?"

Jake stopped stirring the soup and looked thoughtfully at the ceiling. After a long pause, he spoke. "I told myself it was to protect Julia...and Cassie."

"But it was an accident. Surely Julia would have been cleared. She didn't do anything."

Jake nodded. "The Cambridge family was famous in quarter-horse circles, Trevor, and things were different then. While the rest of the world was letting it all hang out and practicing free love, quarter-horse people were still leading 'Father Knows Best' lives. If there'd been an investigation, everything would have come out in the open. Julia might possibly have stood trial. Even if she had been acquitted, the scandal would have ruined her. We couldn't take that chance. Cassie needed Julia. At least, that's what I told myself."

"Told yourself? That's the second time you've said that. What do you mean?"

"Somewhere along the line I've learned to stop kidding myself." Jake punctuated his remark with a self-deprecating laugh. "After Sara died, I hated George. Never had I experienced such hate. At first, I blamed everything on him. From my point of view, it was all his fault—Sara's death, Julia's unhappiness, my loss of you and your mother. I vowed to make him pay. I wasted years hating that poor, haunted man, never dreaming his guilt would cost him a higher price than my hatred cost me.

"Then one day I realized that I let it all happen. Let you and your mother leave because looking at the two of you reminded me of my own guilt." Jake stopped.

His thick voice betrayed heavy emotion. He walked over to his pile of wet clothing, rummaged through them until he retrieved a handkerchief, then blew his nose.

"Truth wasn't kind, Trevor. Because then I had to face other secret thoughts. Even before Sara's death, I pretended to be a friend to George but inwardly I despised him. He had everything I wanted. Money, position, heritage . . . and Sara, too. I was so twisted with envy, plotting nightly on how to lure Sara away. And when I learned the truth about Julia, about Sara's darling Cassie, God as my witness, I could have killed him. He was sleeping with both women under the same roof.

"And when Sara died as a result of his selfishness, I had murder in my eye. I loved her with my soul, or thought I did, and she would have nothing to do with me. She was enraptured with George, and he didn't deserve her."

"You still haven't told me why you helped with the cover-up."

"One day, in a regrettable burst of self-honesty, I had to admit I wanted Sara only because she belonged to George. For the same reason I also wanted Cambridge Stables and thought it could be mine one day. The rumors that would have followed in the wake of a trial would have ruined the Cambridge name for years. I couldn't let that happen and that's the real reason I helped George that night." Jake blew his nose again and tossed the soiled rag on top of his heaped clothing. "I've done despicable things, Trevor. Now do you see why I sympathize with Marvin?"

Trevor nodded mechanically, then stood and padded, barefoot, to Jake—his father—and enclosed him in his arms.

"But you're a good man, anyway, Dad," Trevor said over the lump in his throat.

He wasn't sure if he'd imagined it, but he thought he saw Jake wipe away a tear. "The soup's boiling," Jake said gruffly and gave Trevor a squeeze before returning to the butane stove.

Trevor followed him and prepared a bowl for Cassie. She awoke groggily and Trevor hand-fed her. She took each spoonful listlessly, leaning against his shoulder. She was so helpless, so vulnerable right now, and while he missed the fiery Cassie, her defenselessness filled him with an overwhelming sense of tenderness.

Suddenly he realized he truly loved her. Loved her deeply. Deeply enough to want to care for her, be cared for by her, for the rest of his life. Despair followed his realization. After everything that had happened, he knew she would no longer want him. An empty cavern opened inside him as he visualized a life without her. Then he knew what Cassie meant when she'd said "My dream is buried." Knew, because now he felt the same. With a flash of unwanted intuition, he realized that Cassie had not only buried Chauncey and Cambridge Stables that day, she'd also buried any life they could have had together.

He sat in a chair most of the night so he wouldn't fall asleep. As dawn approached, Cassie began whimpering and tossing. Daylight must be chasing her peace away, Trevor thought. He left the chair and lay down beside her, pulling her body against his. Her soft skin, her sweet scent, were nectar to Trevor's aching heart, and he drank it in, never wanting the sun to rise. He held her close until Jake woke them.

CHAPTER SEVENTEEN

"LUKE WILL BE going up the river for a long, long time," J. T. Haggarty commented as he leaned back in his rickety chair and placed his hand on the worn wooden arms.

"What I can't figure out is why Luke loosened Cassie's tire when he knew Julia was trying to come up with the blackmail money," Trevor said.

"He told me he thought she wasn't trying hard enough. He only meant to scare Cassie, thinking that she'd tell Julia what happened and force that poor woman to find the money faster."

"That guy is one dyed-in-the-wool SOB." Trevor's temper still burned hot when he thought of what Luke had done to Cassie, but it no longer reached murderous proportions. Something inside him had mellowed, softened. "Well, it's a relief to know Cassie's safe now." Trevor coughed. Two days in the freezing wilderness had left him with a cold. "What about Marvin?"

"He could be charged with being an accessory, but the only thing he knew about was the fire and the attempted poisoning. We need his testimony to put Luke away. I think we'll probably do some plea-bargaining."

With surprise, Trevor realized he was glad. He would never be fond of his stepbrother, but now he could feel some empathy for him. He could see the boy Marvin had been, resentful at his imagined second-class status. Trevor recognized that when he'd reentered Jake's life, Marvin had felt pushed out.

"So you proved he wasn't responsible for George's accident."

"Yep," said J.T. "Marvin hit George's car, all right. They were both drinking at the same bar that night, and Marvin slammed into it in the parking lot. When Luke realized that Marvin couldn't remember what had happened he concocted that story about Marvin killing George to keep the boy under his thumb. I found three witnesses who saw the accident. Luke had paid them to keep quiet, but they opened up real quick when I explained the penalties for being an accessory."

Trevor knew Jake had been relieved at the news. Wanting his father to be happy, Trevor found that he also no longer resented Jake's affection for Marvin. He seemed to be letting go of a lot of resentment lately. He stood up.

"I'm going to the hospital to see Cassie," he told Haggarty as he picked up his hat.

"How is Miss Cassie?"

"Physically, she's fine. Only a mild concussion and fatigue. But . . . mentally, I just don't know, J.T. She's lost her energy. She doesn't seem to care anymore."

"She's had some major jolts, Trevor. Give her time."

"I'll give her all the time she needs, J.T. All the time in the world." Realizing the utter truth in his words, Trevor placed his hat on his head and walked out the door.

He thought about how hurt he'd been when he realized Cassie thought him capable of murdering her. Her lack of trust had pierced the last of his armor and forced him to hastily rebuild it. But when he'd witnessed her agony after Chauncey died and thought he might lose her, his own ensuing pain had forced him to understand. Pain and shock made people do crazy things.

Then he thought of his departing words to Haggarty. They were true. He had all the time in the world for Cassie. The rest of his life. He hurried. Cassie was waiting.

"YOU'RE LOOKING BETTER today," Trevor said as he stepped into the hospital room, carrying a huge flower arrangement and a large brown envelope.

Cassie had been staring out the window, trying to block out her thoughts, but her heart gave a glad little jump at the sound of his voice. The unexpected reaction surprised her. It was the first real emotion she'd felt in days. "I guess I am better. They're releasing me tomorrow."

"Your head is too hard to let a little bump keep you down. Right?" Trevor gave an awkward grin, and Cassie forced a pleasant smile in response. Her mood wasn't his fault. Even the Keystone Cops couldn't make her laugh right now.

"The concussion wasn't all that serious. The doctor says I'm going to be fine." But they were empty words to Cassie. She wasn't sure she would ever be fine again. Something had died inside her. She didn't know if it would ever come back to life. She gestured to the flowers Trevor had placed on the bedside table, trying to be polite. "Thank you," she said. "They're beautiful."

Trevor rearranged a few buds, then sat in a chair. "Not as beautiful as you, milady."

A cumbersome silence sat between them, heavy as a steel straitjacket. Cassie didn't understand why she was so uneasy. At one time his companionship had been so comfortable.

"I brought you this, too," Trevor announced. He lifted the brown envelope he'd been holding and put it on the table. "It's my manuscript. You might want to read it while you're recuperating. But I didn't come to talk about flowers or my book." He leaned across the bed and picked up Cassie's hand. The warmth emanating from his fingers felt good against her cold fingers. "Cassie . . ." He hesitated, a question hanging on the sound of her name. "Out there when everything was happening, I realized something."

Cassie wasn't really listening to his words. She heard the faltering tone of his voice, let the soothing, husky tone bathe her ears, but the words drifted off somewhere, away from her comprehension.

"God, you aren't going to make this easy for me, are you?" He placed his other hand on top of hers, encasing it in a warm cocoon. "I love you, Cassie. I have never loved a woman—never thought I could love a woman—the way I love you."

"I know." Her answer surprised her. Yes, she did know. At some subliminal level she'd always known. Since the day they'd met, she'd known he loved her. And that she loved him. But it was too late now. She was an empty shell with nothing to offer him. Her heritage was gone. Her future was gone. Her life was a shambles. An agonized yearning filled the empty spot inside her. She turned her head away.

Trevor released her hand. "Don't you love me, Cassie?" A barely discernable crack in his voice revealed how painful he found the question.

"Oh, yes, Trevor. I do love you." She spoke in an aching whisper.

Trevor moved forward excitedly and grasped her hand again. With the other hand he gently cupped her face and turned it toward him. His touch shot a burst of longing through her. Didn't he understand? She had nothing left to give him.

"Marry me, Cassie. Be my wife. I promise I'll work day and night to make you happy." He spoke urgently as if afraid she'd interrupt. Her heart begged her to say yes. But her mind looked toward the hollow spot in her soul and told her otherwise. No, it said, love does not last, and love is pain.

Right then she felt as though her heart were in a vise, but she knew this was minor compared to the pain that love could bring.

Trevor's expression changed from anticipation to concealed defeat. "I'd get down on my knee but it's against all my macho principles," he quipped.

Cassie stroked his hair, those marvelous copper waves. She felt immensely sad. "I can't, Trevor," she said softly. She didn't want to hurt him, this man she loved. "I do love you. But love will destroy us. The way it did—"

"We aren't them, Cassie," Trevor interrupted. "We're us. We can make it work."

"Maybe we can, Trevor." Even as she spoke, she knew she didn't believe her words. "But I'm afraid to take the chance."

"You? You're the original risk-taker. I'm the one who's always avoided risk."

Cassie sat up in the bed and rubbed her hand across her face. "Yes, but something happened to me when Chauncey died. I don't understand exactly what, but I have to deal with it. I'm going back to Denver, Trevor. Back to work. I might be able to sort things out there."

"And us?"

"A week ago, if you had asked the question you asked this morning, I would have said yes, yes, a thousand times yes. But, now...things have changed. There is no *us*, Trevor."

She saw his face change before her eyes. His delightful laugh lines drew downward, his blue eyes dimmed to a cold and lifeless gray. He shook his head, sighed, then slowly stood and moved to the door. Once there, he turned and gazed at her steadily for a moment, his face reflecting the emptiness Cassie felt inside herself.

He disappeared into the hallway and she heard the tap of his footsteps on the linoleum hospital floor. A shiver ran down her spine.

She was alone again. Staring out the window as she'd been doing when Trevor arrived, she wondered what she found so interesting about the view. Nothing was out there. Just dirty snow, a leafless tree and a gray sky. She brought her gaze back to the room and noticed Trevor's envelope on the bedside table. She picked it up listlessly and opened the flap. As promised, inside was his manuscript.

The title, *"Final Triumph: The Last Day of the Whitney-Ortega Wars"* was emblazoned across the cover page. Under that was "by Trevor Austin." Cassie looked at it in wonder. He'd actually done it, and she felt very proud of him. She removed the cover page. The next sheet contained a hand-written dedication: "To Cassie. Our love will endure beyond time." A lump formed in Cassie's throat, and she swallowed hard to fight back tears. She flipped through the pages then began reading.

The story of Betsy Ortega and Tom Whitney.

She didn't stop reading until the nurse brought around her nighttime medicine. "You should sleep now," the nurse chided gently as she watched Cassie dutifully swallow the pills.

But once the girl left the room, Cassie again picked up the manuscript and read to the last page.

Tears of joy streamed down her face when Peter Ortega allowed his finger to be held by the little baby, his infant grandson, who was also the grandson of the man who, until then, had been his bitter enemy.

His novel haunted her. During these past few days, she'd reached her conclusions about love, but his novel told a different story. A story of love healing rather than mutilating, of love's glory rather than love's defeat. It was a view she yearned to embrace, but her wounds were still open, not even scarred over yet, and her fear was too great.

Yet after reading his novel, Cassie loved Trevor even more. She felt as if she'd had a glimpse into Trevor's soul, and she realized, with a deep sense of loss, how truly beautiful he was. She knew it was unlikely she would ever find such a man again.

Besides, it was too late. She'd rejected him with such finality and, she had to admit, with such cruelty, that he would never forgive her.

"THERE'S NOTHING I can do to change your mind?" Julia stood in the doorway watching Cassie finish packing.

"We've been over this a dozen times, at least, Aunt Julia." Cassie replied as she shoved a roll of panties into a pocket of the suitcase. Julia had been hounding her continually over the past week to stay in Mesquite.

"But, Cassie, we need time to work things out. I love you, Cassie, and I've been a mother to you in everything but name all these years. I hope one day you can learn to love me again—the way you did before you learned the truth, though I know I don't deserve it," she added sadly.

Julia's naked pleading was something new, and it embarrassed Cassie. It also evoked a twinge of guilt. She knew her rejection of her mother was cruel. But her knowledge of all the lies, the cheating, the betrayal, that went behind their relationship had encased Cassie in stone... or it had until now.

As Cassie looked up at Julia, seeing her clearly for the first time since that fateful night, she noticed the lines of grief and remorse that had appeared on Julia's face. From her own confrontations with the mirror, Cassie knew her face also showed undeniable traces of the same emotions.

Still, Julia had robbed her. Robbed her of a normal home life. Robbed her of the heritage that was her birthright. Robbed her of Cambridge Stables. Together, Julia and her father had done that. Their unpardonable sin had brought this moment down upon them all.

Despite these justifications, guilt continued to prick at Cassie. Julia had cared for her all of her life. She owed her something for that. "We'll see, Aunt Julia. Give me some time." But the words were mechanical. Cassie didn't believe them herself.

"Cassie, it was hate that brought the Cambridges down. Hate. That's what your father was trying to tell you in his letter. He wanted to release you from the hate, not perpetuate it. Don't let his dying gesture go to waste. Take it with you, honey.'' Julia urged, pulling the letter out of her pocket. ''Read it again when the time seems right.''

Cassie looked at the folded pages in Julia's hand. They were smoothed out, but still bore the wrinkles created when Cassie had crushed them in her hand. Cassie stared at them in horrified fascination. She wasn't sure she'd ever want to read those words again. But they were part of her father, something left behind even though he was gone. Someday, in the distant future, she might be able to face them.

She took the letter from Julia's hand. ''Maybe I will...someday.'' She picked up her purse and slipped the letter inside. ''Let's go. It's over an hour to Jackson, and I don't want to miss my plane.''

Julia drove Cassie to Jackson in the little yellow Volkswagen. They arrived a little early, and as Julia was pulling in to a parking place a curious thought entered Cassie's mind. ''Aunt Julia, knowing how Papa felt about him, why did you become involved with Jake?''

Julia turned off the ignition and leaned back against the seat. ''I suppose it does seem terribly disloyal, doesn't it? But it didn't start out that way. I first got to know Jake again when Marvin was in my seventh-grade class. He wasn't doing well and Jake and I had many conferences about his performance.

''Later, after Marvin had been tossed out of several prep schools, Jake put him back into the Mesquite public school system. Marvin still had problems, and after his mother died they got worse. So Jake turned to me for advice. One thing led to another. Something good did come out of it, Cassie. Your father and Jake were able to resolve their differences before your father's death."

"They what?" Cassie asked in astonishment. "What do you mean, they resolved their differences?"

"Why do you think Jake bought the land? He didn't need any more. But George needed the money to pay for your education." Julia paused and added wryly, "Among other things."

"Why didn't you tell me this before?"

"Would you have believed me?"

Cassie sighed and opened the car door. "I suppose not." She stepped outside. "I'd better check in my luggage."

Julia helped Cassie carry her luggage into the terminal and did not repeat her earlier entreaties when Cassie boarded. She gave Cassie a warm goodbye kiss on the cheek, saying, again, that she loved her. Once seated aboard the plane, Cassie gazed out the window and saw her aunt—no, her mother Cassie corrected— standing alone on the tarmac, the wind whipping her coat, waiting for Cassie's plane to take off.

She looked desolate.

Soon, they were airborne. Cassie reached below the seat for her purse, planning to get the paperback book she'd brought to read on the flight. As she reached inside, her fingers contacted the letter Julia had given her.

She stared at it in dismay. Opening it again would just be like scraping over old wounds, but for some reason she felt there were answers inside. A solution to this awful numbness that had overcome her since learning the truth about her mother's death. She pulled it out and clutched it against her chest, looking out the window at the patchwork quilt of the ground below her. Finally she returned to the letter, slipped the pages from the envelope and began reading the cover sheet. Unlike the others it was white and new. And the handwriting was different. Although still recognizable as her father's, it was cramped and wavering, as if written under a tremendous strain. "My darling Cassie," it began.

If you are reading this letter, my worst fears have come to pass. Now that I am facing the end of my life, I recognize that I sowed the seeds of my own destruction, seeds so fertile that they will reach beyond the grave. I must kill the weeds before they grow.

The enclosed tome seems to me to be a monument to my self-pity. It was written shortly after I sent you to boarding school and was a way of relieving my pain. But now I feel you must know the truth. I have denied you your own true mother and I must set this straight.

Jake and I have made our peace. He is a good man. He was confused during his youth—but weren't we all?

Please do not carry on a vendetta against him, thinking to vindicate my name. He has been my friend these last few years.

What you will read in the attached pages will shatter all your most cherished beliefs. About me, your poor dead mother and your aunt Julia. For that, I beg your forgiveness.

All this horror I bequeathed you, my darling Cassie. Please forgive me for the bitter legacy I've left. I pray from the depth of my heart that you don't and won't carry it on.

                                        Your Loving Papa

So it was true. Jake and her father had resolved their differences. Why hadn't she remembered this from the first time she'd read the letter? This was what Julia had meant when she'd said the letter was meant to release hate, not perpetuate it.

Cassie tucked the cover letter behind the other pages and began reading the words her father had written so long ago:

> I knew Julia had always loved me. She was so young and so extraordinarily beautiful, like a blossom from an alien land. I felt I had to possess her, never realizing the depth of her love. Then she presented a gift I thought would never be mine. Your impending birth.

With a pang of remorse, Cassie realized that her aunt had always demonstrated the depth of her love. Her devotion to Cassie was unquestionable. She'd stayed at Cambridge Stables after the accident, sacrificing any chance of a life of her own. She had done this despite the risk that the truth about Sara's death could come out at any time, possibly to destroy her. How painful it must have been for her—giving the letter to Cassie. After all these years when she'd thought the truth was safely buried, she'd still turned over the letter, hoping to prevent Cassie from repeating the same mistakes of pride and hate. What greater love could someone show? With unshed tears burning her eyes, Cassie continued to read:

> In many ways, Sara was a lovely woman. But not strong either physically or emotionally. Always needing. Always wanting. She vacillated be-

tween elation and deep depression, went in and out of hospitals. It was during one of these times that Julia and I succumbed to our mutual attraction.

Sara had always blamed her moods on her barren condition and felt a baby would make everything right. I also wanted an heir and Julia's conception seemed a gift from heaven. And you *were* a gift, Cassie. I worshipped you. Far more, in fact, than Sara did. Once she'd held you and showed you off to her friends, she was content to turn you over to her sister's care, never realizing she was placing you in the arms of your true mother. I divided my love among the three of you—Julia, Sara and yourself, Cassie—believing in my youthful arrogance that everything I desired could be mine.

Slowly, as she read, Cassie's image of her father changed. Until his death and even far after, she had worshipped him, placing him on a pedestal so high that a fall would be fatal.

The first time she'd read this shattering letter, he'd become a monster in her mind—avaricious, deceptive, devouring, with no remnant of human decency.

Now, her image of him shifted, changing from saint to sinner, back to saint, again to sinner. Finally a different image began to form, a hazy image of someone who was altogether different. A flesh and blood man. A human being.

When Sara died, I couldn't face the truth. I blamed everyone but myself. I blamed Julia, Sara, and Jake. Most of all Jake. Jake because he slept with my wife. Jake because he wouldn't let me forget. And even more, Jake because he was succeeding in life while I was slipping daily. I drowned my guilt and anger in women, liquor and wild spending. Quickly I discovered that my money and reputation wouldn't last forever. That's when I sent you away. So you wouldn't see how fast I was sinking. In doing so I divested myself of the last thing I truly loved. You. I was a man out of control.

A man who was simply human. Silent tears streamed down Cassie's face. Her father had been human enough to make mistakes and human enough to admit those mistakes. Cassie knew it had taken a tremendous effort for her father to write this letter, and her tears were for his torment as much as her own loss. Suddenly she was grateful he'd written this shocking letter, grateful the truth had come out. And suddenly she knew that her new understanding had somehow relieved a burden on her father's soul and that now he could finally rest in peace.

Just as suddenly, she realized that if she were ever to have a happy life, she had to change. Had to accept the bad with the good. Accept the loss of her father, Chauncey and her hopes for Cambridge Stables. She could no longer continue denying anything that didn't fit in with her preconceived notions. Life could only be lived as it was, not as she wished it to be. Trevor and Julia were still very much alive and very much desired her love and her presence in their lives. And because they cared, happiness could still be hers.

Suddenly she recognized the similarity between the story Trevor had told in *Final Triumph* and the passionate hatred between Jake and her father. The first war had ended because two young people loved each other enough to leave behind a hatred not their own. Could she and Trevor do the same? Or was it too late for them?

Remorse overwhelmed her. For once Cassie didn't care who heard or saw her cry. She barely heard the seat-belt light come on as she let all her grief pour out, and the tears cleansed her soul and cleared her mind so that she saw clearly what she would do and the happiness the future would hold.

"Are you all right, miss?" A young stewardess bent over her, her forehead wrinkled with worry.

Cassie looked up and smiled through her tears. "I've never been better."

CHAPTER EIGHTEEN

TREVOR SNEEZED and pulled the down comforter more closely around his chest. Propped up against the pillows, knees bent, he held his manuscript on his lap. The exposed page had several notations marked in red ink but Trevor's attention had long since drifted off.

A full moon was visible through the French doors to the garden off his bedroom. A lovers' moon. The thought depressed him.

He couldn't concentrate, couldn't breathe and couldn't keep his mind off Cassie. He remembered reading once about the ghost sensations that amputees experienced. A missing limb would sometimes itch or ache. That's how Cassie's absence felt, his heart itched as though she were still there and throbbed painfully from loneliness.

How had she wormed her way into his life like that? Somehow she'd become a part of him, an extension. And when she'd left, it was as much an amputation as if he'd lost an arm or leg. Would life without her leave him forever crippled?

He reached over, plucked a tissue from the nightstand and blew his nose. The fireplace glowed at him glumly. He really should add another log. Reluctantly he set the manuscript aside and climbed out from beneath the warm covers. The heating system in this crazy cottage was inadequate, and without a decent fire he'd soon be shivering from cold.

It was already cold. Goose bumps erupted on his arms as his feet hit the floor, and he searched for his slippers. Maybe he should wear something else to bed besides his underwear. He padded over to the hearth, opened the firebox door and began placing fresh logs on top of the dimly glowing coals.

The dying fire reminded him of his relationship with Cassie. Once burning hot, now quiet coals losing their heat. As the new wood ignited, he suddenly realized it didn't have to be that way.

He had to get her back, reignite their love. It could be done. He knew it. She loved him as much as he loved her. Hadn't she said so? She was just hurt, that's all. So much had happened to her in such a short period. She needed more time to get over it. He sneezed again and suddenly his head felt clearer. Not just his sinuses but his brain, also. Ideas clicked through his mind at ever increasing speed.

He would woo her. Send flowers. Write romantic letters. Then, after a few weeks, he'd fly to Denver. Take her to a posh restaurant, ply her with good food and plenty of wine. Trevor smiled as he recalled the night Cassie had become tipsy on blackberry brandy. She'd been so playful—and passionate. He'd serve a better quality liquor in Denver and this time wouldn't let his scruples get in the way.

The headlights of a car flickered against the panes of the bedroom window. It was awfully late for someone to be out in Mesquite. Probably a high-spirited cowboy or a carload of skiers returning from a night on the town. But the light became steadier, finally shining brightly through the window and then went out.

Someone had pulled into his driveway. Who would be visiting him at nearly midnight?

He plucked his bathrobe off the pants rack near his dresser and had just slipped it on when the doorbell rang. It had to be either Julia or Jake, but he wondered why they hadn't simply telephoned. He walked quickly to the door and opened it, turning on the porch light.

"It took me forever to get here. I had to wait for a return flight in Denver and the rental car place took hours to find me a car. But here I am." Cassie stood in front of him, babbling on and on. Her hair was tousled, the unruly curls bouncing above her eyes. A faint streak of mascara ran down one cheek. Her nose was red from the cold. "Al was furious at first when I phoned to say I was coming back to Mesquite, but when I told him why, he said, 'Go for it!'"

Trevor felt his heart stop. He wanted to laugh. He wanted to cry. And he wanted to shout. How dared she leave him and then come running back as if nothing had happened? How dared she stand there looking such a mess and at the same time so beautiful? He stared at her dumbly for a few moments, the icy chill from the outside stinging his naked legs.

"Well, aren't you going to invite me in?" Her earlier smile was replaced by a tentative expression.

Suddenly Trevor's emotions exploded and became a giant ball of delight. He felt a wide smile emerge, so wide that he feared his face would break. He stepped forward and gathered Cassie in his arms. Her coat felt cold against his body but he could feel her heat emanating from beneath.

"Are you real?" His question sounded hoarse even to his own ears.

"Oh, yes, Trevor. I'm real." She ran a hand behind his neck and pulled his mouth to hers. As his warm lips touched her cool ones, Trevor no longer felt as if part of his heart had been amputated.

TREVOR'S LIPS were the sweetest thing Cassie had ever tasted. She melted beneath his mouth, ignoring the bitting wind whipping around her legs. She was finally home where she belonged, safe and loved in Trevor's arms.

She had been so frightened when she'd walked up the sidewalk and rung the bell. What if he no longer wanted her? What if he sent her away? Now his hungry kiss told her he did indeed want her and her heart almost burst with happiness.

"I've been so stupid and pigheaded," she said when Trevor finally released her lips.

Trevor smiled and stroked her cheek so lightly that it felt as if a butterfly had brushed her. "I'm not sure I want to argue with that statement," he said gently, "but I love you anyway. Now come inside, my love." With a soothing hand on her back, he guided her into the bedroom.

"It's not just about you and me." Cassie reached into her purse and mutely gave Trevor the letter.

"Is this the letter George wrote?" Trevor looked at it with an expression resembling awe.

Cassie nodded. "I'm going to wash my face. Read it while I'm gone." She got up, removed her coat and placed it over the pants rack, then went to the bathroom and began running water in the sink. The sight of herself in the mirror made her cringe. Her eyes were red rimmed and mascara ran down her cheeks. Her nose looked like a clown's nose. She grinned ruefully. Trevor must really love her if he could stand to look at her like this. She did her best to repair the damage, lingering overlong to allow Trevor time to finish the letter.

Trevor looked up as she came back into the bedroom, his eyes glistening. "This letter is quite an eye-opener, Cassie," he said in a thick voice. "For both of us."

"What do you mean—for both of us?" She was somewhat taken aback by Trevor's comment.

"My parents got divorced because of that night. Remember?"

"Oh, Trevor, I'm sorry. I did forget. Your life was torn apart, too." She ran her hand across his forehead. "My self-centeredness never ceases to amaze me."

Trevor smiled wanly. "Come here, my self-centered baby." He patted a spot next to him on the bed. Cassie walked over and sat down. Trevor pulled her against his shoulder. "You weren't alone in harboring bitterness. We all did. Your father wanted to protect you and to salvage your life. He loved you very much, Cassie. Now it's time for all of us to let go, to love instead of hate."

She snuggled into Trevor's embrace. He smelled faintly of musk cologne, and she thought she'd never smelled a fragrance more sensuous. "I do love you, Trevor," she whispered softly.

Holding Cassie's face in his hands, he placed a light kiss on her lips. "How I've waited to hear you say those words in the way you did just now. I love you, too, Cassie."

He reached over her shoulder and turned out the light. Moonlight streamed through French doors and bathed the bed in shimmering silver light, broken only by the checkerboard pattern cast by the windowpanes. Wordlessly, Trevor stood and bent before her, removing her shoes and placing feathery kisses on her toes. Cassie shivered in delightful anticipation.

Lifting her to her feet, he pulled her deliciously close and unzipped her slacks. They dropped to the floor, and she stepped out of them gracefully. Slowly, Trevor unbuttoned each button of her silky blouse. Her body felt light and ethereal, as though composed of liquid longing as he slid the blouse over her shoulders, allowing it, too, to fall to the floor. She breathed a deep sigh. Trevor's contained passion, his almost reverent disrobing of her receptive body, was more erotic than all the heated lust she'd ever experienced.

They didn't speak. And in the endless silence, broken only by their breathing and the crackling of the fire, he explored her body with his hands, slipping one hand inside her bra and brushing the firm outline of her breast. Moving his other hand to her back, he dispensed with her bra in one quick gesture, then gently teased her nipple, tearing an agonized moan of desire from her lips.

She closed her eyes and dropped back her head to accept the tantalizing kisses he showered on her neck, shoulders and breasts. Still in his robe, he pushed her into a reclining position and slipped her panties over her hips, stroking her legs as he pulled them over her feet.

Cassie felt as though she had melted, unable to move, as his hands followed the contours of her body. His lingering caresses held exquisite tenderness, and an aching need began to howl within her. She heard his deep, uneven breath and opened her eyes as he lowered his head toward hers, and devoured her lips with a kiss that contained all the sweetness of forbidden fruit.

She responded with such primeval passion that a part of her was shocked. Shocked and then absorbed. Absorbed in the volcanic eruption of their desire—a desire born not so much from physical urging as from a desire to become one, to fuse their spirits.

Abruptly he tore away from her. The pain of separation wrenched a cry from her throat and she turned on her side in frustration. Trevor stood in the moonlight gazing at her as he took off his robe and underwear. The moonlight glistened behind him, casting reflections off his shoulders, his arms, his fiery hair. He appeared as a god, bathed in light. Cassie was suddenly filled with a rapturous love, a love so consuming that she knew it would bind her forever to this man in front of her.

She reached her arms out toward him in an imploring gesture and, with wanton satisfaction, saw his carefully controlled passion explode. In two strides he returned to the bed and pulled her savagely to him, burying his hands in her ebony hair. Glorying in his rough touch and in the power such desire brought, she opened herself to him with total submission and total domination. He entered her quickly, speaking her name repeatedly in a throaty whisper. His very breath made Cassie quiver from desire, and she clung to him violently as together they rose through warring emotions to a place high above, where their spirits joined as one and their bodies exploded in exquisite ecstasy. For a long time afterward, they lay together quietly. Trevor rested his weight on his elbows, raining soft kisses on her face while she stroked the firm smooth muscles of his broad back.

His skin felt like silk, and touching him made her fingers tingle. She wished they could stay like this until the end of time and knew that happiness would be hers if she could be with him forever. But in spite of his earlier words, she couldn't believe he still wanted her. A lone tear escaped her eye and as Trevor's roaming kisses reached its path he arched his back and looked at her.

"Tears? What's wrong, my darling Cassie?"

"Oh, Trevor. I'm just so happy. I love you so much."

"Then why the tears? I love you, too." His radiant smile sent waves of happiness through Cassie's body. By contrast, the thought of losing him was even more acutely painful. She turned her head aside.

She spoke in a halting whisper. "Do you...can you...still want me after all the stupid things I've done?"

His throaty laugh answered her question. Her pain vanished, leaving only the wondrous happiness that his closeness promised. "Want you? More than anyone, anytime, anywhere." He rolled off her, and she uttered a small protesting sigh as he cuddled her against his lean body. "So what do you say we plan a wedding?"

"A wedding?" A new tear emerged. A tear of joy. She hugged Trevor tightly, pouring kisses over his face and shoulders. "Oh, Trevor, I love you so much." She was laughing, she was crying, burying him in kisses and hugs, and Trevor hugged her in return, laughing also, touching the tears streaming down her cheeks.

"I've never known a woman who cried so much."

"Not until I met you."

"Well, I'll have to see if I can fix that." He smothered her tears with a deep kiss, and when at last he released her lips, they talked about the wedding, planning all the details.

Suddenly, Cassie sat upright. "Trevor. There's something I have to do."

His face become solemn and he curved his hands over her cheeks. "Call your aunt Julia?"

"Yes." Cassie felt instantly afraid. "What if she doesn't want to talk to me, Trevor? I've hurt her so badly and thinking about it makes me feel terrible."

"She'll talk to you, honey. Believe me, she knows what you've been through and that she and your father violated all the values they taught you. Besides, Cassie, now that you've decided to forgive those who trespassed against you, it's time to forgive yourself, too. Call her."

"Now? It's nearly three o'clock in the morning."

"She won't mind."

With a trembling hand Cassie reached across the bed, picked up the phone and punched the numbers. Her heart was beating wildly. There was so much to say. So much to undo. What if Julia didn't forgive her?

Then Cassie realized that such a thing was impossible. Julia was her mother. Mothers and daughters were bound by a tie that could never be broken. Bitterness and deception had obscured that tie, but it had never been severed.

When Julia picked up the phone at the other end and gave a puzzled, sleep-drenched "Hello?" Cassie looked at Trevor and smiled. He reached over and squeezed her hand.

"Mama." Her voice was thick with strong emotion. "This is your daughter, Cassie."

ARE YOU A ROMANCE READER WITH OPINIONS?

Openings are currently available for participation in the 1990-1991 Romance Reader Panel. We are looking for new participants from all regions of the country and from all age ranges.

If selected, you will be polled once a month by mail to comment on new books you have recently purchased, and may occasionally be asked for more in-depth comments. Individual responses will remain confidential and all postage will be prepaid.

Regular purchasers of one favorite series, as well as those who sample a variety of lines each month, are needed, so fill out and return this application today for more detailed information.

1. Please indicate the romance series you purchase from regularly at retail outlets.

Harlequin	Silhouette	
1. ☐ Romance	6. ☐ Romance	10. ☐ Bantam Loveswept
2. ☐ Presents	7. ☐ Special Edition	11. ☐ Other _____
3. ☐ American Romance	8. ☐ Intimate Moments	
4. ☐ Temptation	9. ☐ Desire	
5. ☐ Superromance		

2. Number of romance paperbacks you purchase new in an average month:

12.1 ☐ 1 to 4   .2 ☐ 5 to 10   .3 ☐ 11 to 15   .4 ☐ 16+

3. Do you currently buy romance series through direct mail?   13.1 ☐ yes   .2 ☐ no

If yes, please indicate series: _____

                                                    (14,15)   (16,17)

4. Date of birth: _____ / _____ / _____

             (Month)   (Day)   (Year)
             18,19   20,21   22,23

5. Please print:

Name: _____

Address: _____

City: _____ State: _____ Zip: _____

Telephone No. (optional): (_____) _____

MAIL TO: Attention: Romance Reader Panel
                Consumer Opinion Center
                P.O. Box 1395
                Buffalo, NY 14240-9961

Office Use Only   HSRDK

Take 4 bestselling love stories FREE

Plus get a FREE surprise gift!

PASSPORT TO ROMANCE
SWEEPSTAKES RULES

1. **HOW TO ENTER:** To enter, you must be the age of majority and complete the official entry form, or print your name, address, telephone number and age on a plain piece of paper and mail to: Passport to Romance, P.O. Box 9056, Buffalo, NY 14269-9056. No mechanically reproduced entries accepted.

2. All entries must be received by the CONTEST CLOSING DATE, DECEMBER 31, 1990 TO BE ELIGIBLE.

3. **THE PRIZES:** There will be ten (10) Grand Prizes awarded, each consisting of a choice of a trip for two people from the following list:
   i) London, England (approximate retail value $5,050 U.S.)
   ii) England, Wales and Scotland (approximate retail value $6,400 U.S.)
   iii) Carribean Cruise (approximate retail value $7,300 U.S.)
   iv) Hawaii (approximate retail value $9,550 U.S.)
   v) Greek Island Cruise in the Mediterranean (approximate retail value $12,250 U.S.)
   vi) France (approximate retail value $7,300 U.S.)

4. Any winner may choose to receive any trip or a cash alternative prize of $5,000.00 U.S. in lieu of the trip.

5. **GENERAL RULES:** Odds of winning depend on number of entries received.

6. A random draw will be made by Nielsen Promotion Services, an independent judging organization, on January 29, 1991, in Buffalo, NY, at 11:30 a.m. from all eligible entries received on or before the Contest Closing Date.

7. Any Canadian entrants who are selected must correctly answer a time-limited, mathematical skill-testing question in order to win.

8. Full contest rules may be obtained by sending a stamped, self-addressed envelope to: "Passport to Romance Rules Request", P.O. Box 9998, Saint John, New Brunswick, Canada E2L 4N4.

9. Quebec residents may submit any litigation respecting the conduct and awarding of a prize in this contest to the Régie des loteries et courses du Québec.

10. Payment of taxes other than air and hotel taxes is the sole responsibility of the winner.

11. Void where prohibited by law.

COUPON BOOKLET OFFER TERMS

To receive your Free travel-savings coupon booklets, complete the mail-in Offer Certificate on the preceeding page, including the necessary number of proofs-of-purchase, and mail to: Passport to Romance, P.O. Box 9057, Buffalo, NY 14269-9057. The coupon booklets include savings on travel-related products such as car rentals, hotels, cruises, flowers and restaurants. Some restrictions apply. The offer is available in the United States and Canada. Requests must be postmarked by January 25, 1991. Only proofs-of-purchase from specially marked "Passport to Romance" Harlequin® or Silhouette® books will be accepted. The offer certificate must accompany your request and may not be reproduced in any manner. Offer void where prohibited or restricted by law. LIMIT FOUR COUPON BOOKLETS PER NAME, FAMILY, GROUP, ORGANIZATION OR ADDRESS. Please allow up to 8 weeks after receipt of order for shipment. Enter quickly as quantities are limited. Unfulfilled mail-in offer requests will receive free Harlequin® or Silhouette® books (not previously available in retail stores), in quantities equal to the number of proofs-of-purchase required for Levels One to Four, as applicable.

PR-SWPS

OFFICIAL SWEEPSTAKES
ENTRY FORM

Complete and return this Entry Form immediately—the more Entry Forms you submit, the better
your chances of winning!
• Entry Forms must be received by **December 31, 1990**   3-HS-3-SW
• A random draw will take place on **January 29, 1991**
• Trip must be taken by **December 31, 1991**

YES, I want to win a PASSPORT TO ROMANCE vacation for two! I understand the prize includes
round-trip air fare, accommodation and a daily spending allowance.

Name_____

Address_____

City_____ State_____ Zip_____

Telephone Number_____ Age_____

Return entries to: **PASSPORT TO ROMANCE**, P.O. Box 9056, Buffalo, NY 14269-9056

COUPON BOOKLET/OFFER CERTIFICATE

	LEVEL ONE Booklet 1	LEVEL TWO Booklet 1 & 2	LEVEL THREE Booklet 1, 2 & 3	LEVEL FOUR Booklet 1, 2, 3 & 4
Item				
Booklet 1 = $100+	$100+	$100+	$100+	$100+
Booklet 2 = $200+		$200+	$200+	$200+
Booklet 3 = $300+			$300+	$300+
Booklet 4 = $400+	____	____	____	$400+
Approximate Total Value of Savings	$100+	$300+	$600+	$1,000+
# of Proofs of Purchase Required	4	6	12	18
Check One	____	____	____	____

Name_____

Address_____

City_____ State_____ Zip_____

Return Offer Certificates to: **PASSPORT TO ROMANCE**, P.O. Box 9057, Buffalo, NY 14269-9057

Requests must be postmarked by **January 25, 1991**

- ✂ - - - - - - - - - - - - - - - -

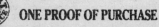

ONE PROOF OF PURCHASE   3-HS-3

To collect your free coupon booklet you must include the necessary number of proofs-of-purchase
with a properly completed Offer Certificate

See previous page for details